a novel

Alex Abella

Simon & Schuster

SIMON & SCHUSTER
Rockefeller Center
1230 Avenue of the Americas
New York, NY 10020

SIMON & SCHUSTER and colophon are registered trademarks
of Simon & Schuster Inc.

Designed by Karolina Harris

Manufactured in the United States of America

1   3   5   7   9   10   8   6   4   2

Library of Congress Cataloging-in-Publication Data

Abella, Alex.
Dead of night: a novel / Alex Abella.
p.   cm.
I. Title.
PS3551.B3394D4   1998
813'.54—dc21   98-21316
                                                  CIP

ISBN 0-684-81426-9

ACKNOWLEDGMENTS

I am not a lawyer, so I'm deeply indebted to all those friends in the legal profession whose advice proved invaluable in the writing of this book. Above all, my most sincere thanks to Scott Gordon for his guidance, pointing out and correcting more than a few technical pitfalls in the early versions of the manuscript. My thanks as well to Joseph Esposito for his enthusiastic comments. I'm also extremely grateful to Los Angeles Superior Court Judge Gregory Alarcon for his pithy observations and, more than anything else, for providing me a safe haven all these years.

Finally, I owe an enormous debt of gratitude to my wife, Armeen, who has stood by me in the dark nights of the soul. This book would not have been possible without her.

Sempre diritto!

To Veronica and Nicolas,

Let the past be your teacher
Not your master.

PROLOGUE

THE stalker slithered through the dry brush behind the wall of the gray stucco house in Highland Park, five miles and many worlds away from the spires of downtown Los Angeles. He crouched behind a boxwood hedge, nauseated by the smell of fried tortillas wafting from a nearby kitchen. The odor of cheap, burnt oil reminded him of his childhood, when his mother earned a miserable living selling codfish fritters at a roadside stand in South Florida and he promised himself he'd do whatever it took to avoid her stinking, sorry life.

Through a window he could see the ramshackle dining room of the house next to his hiding place. At the head of the table a potbellied Mexican in a T-shirt alternately sipped a beer and pecked at his enchiladas, surrounded by a brood of hyperactive children in diapers and soiled pajamas who would take turns to come sit in his lap.

Damn snotty kids should be in bed by now.

The stalker looked up at the sliver of yellow moon floating above the downtown skyscrapers. He stared hard, praying to almighty Oyá, to the great Shangó, and above all, to Ochosí, the magnificent hunter who was the saint of his devotion, to grant him the cover of darkness. His prayers were answered as a shimmer of low clouds drifted out of the Pacific and put out the moon. Then, with feline grace, the stalker vaulted over the six-foot-tall masonry wall of the gray stucco house and landed silently in the yard of his intended victim.

Inside the house, Armando Ponce rose from his recliner and turned off the *telenovela* he'd been watching. Although never a fan of the lachrymose sentimentality of Spanish soaps, Armando had been glued to the set every night for weeks, transfixed by the story of a wayward *santero* in Miami's Cuban community. Based on a real case, the show had been written with just enough truth to tantalize viewers—even real *santeros* like Armando—with tales of improbable supernatural powers.

Now, mindful of the fact that he still had his evening prayers to officiate, Armando shuffled in his terry cloth slippers down to the pristine basement he had turned into his shrine.

Stooped from injuries, arthritis and an aging swayback, Armando treaded carefully, holding on to the rail to prevent a fall. His eyes at his feet, he did not notice the stalker crouching by the waist-high weeds next to the house.

Stupid old fool.

Do you feel so protected you won't even look up to see the enemy at your door?

Your time has come, viejo.

Tonight you will be my slave in my circle of souls.

•

The intruder took out his hunting knife, felt the flat, broad blade, its serrated edge. He hefted it, kissed the blade, pressed it to his heart.

Do my sacred bidding.
Open the gate to the kingdom of Oyá.
Be my lover, my faithful companion.

Down in the basement shrine, Armando bowed before the bone white china tureen containing the sacred stones of Obatalá, the greatest of the saints. The wise spirit had claimed him as his own when Armando was only a boy of six, making Armando speak fluent Yoruba, to the dismay of his plantation-owning parents back in Cuba.

It's those damned niggers with their *brujería,* his father shouted at his mother. Get rid of them!

All the black help had been dismissed. In their stead, the whitest girls from all of Spain, *gallegas* from northern Spain with blond hair and Celtic blue eyes, had been the only servants allowed around little Armando, sole heir to his family's hundred-thousand-acre estate on the foothills of the Sierra Maestra. But his parents did not know the ways of the saints or that, once chosen, the soul is the god's forever.

One of the *gallegas,* sixteen-year-old Pilar, although out of Santiago for only two years, was already a believer. While the master and mistress slept, she took little Armando one night to the thatch roof hut where lived the old scar-faced African with the altars and the beads. There, dressed in white, the blood of an alabaster white dove poured on his head, Armando was re-

13

ceived into the house of the gods. Like the child Jesus at the temple, Armando astounded the *santero* with his wisdom until the sun broke, when he returned to the life and things of a child. But in his twentieth year Armando heard the voices of the gods once more. He walked out of his law course at the University of Havana and followed the music in his head all the way to the banks of the Cauto River, where he renounced his previous life and formally devoted himself to the things of the saints, to *santería.*

It was only now, in his eighties—having become a *babalawo*, a cardinal among *santeros*—that Armando was finally beginning to understand the cosmic presence that so often filled him with awe; it was as though his physical body had to degenerate to the image of Obatalá, white-haired and in crutches, before he was granted the gift of true insight.

The law of compensation, he mused distractedly, taking out the divination board and shells of the *ifá*. One thing must die so another can live. It is the eternal law of the saints. He threw down his cockleshells.

Armando was startled by the message of the shells. He took out the two books of wisdom he had inherited from his *padrino* to make sure he remembered the readings right. He had. The shells spoke of the emptiness at the end and a gate that swings swiftly open. He glanced up at the shelves.

The sacred tureen rattled as though an earthquake were shaking the shrine, the stones bouncing off the china like so many roller bearings. Then the tureen flew off and shattered on the white tile floor, spilling its precious dark liquid.

Armando looked up aghast. He knew now what the message was. He heard a loud crash from the service door and turned to see a figure in black rushing toward him with a glinting knife in hand.

Armando put up his arms, and almost simultaneous with the slashing of his fingers to the bone he remembered the final words of Olofi on the cross, Father, into thy hands I commend my spirit, even as the blade veered and flew up, slashing under his jaw, his blood gushing in a crimson flood against the pristine white wall.

CHAPTER

I T was one of those rare days when Los Angeles, cleansed by Santa Ana winds, lay naked in her fearsome beauty.

I stared greedily out the airplane window, picking out the milestones of my California existence. Over there lay the snaking line of the Harbor Freeway pointing to the Rose Bowl near my house; beyond that, the hills of Los Feliz next to the Hollywood studios that had briefly made my fame and fortune; past that, the congested San Fernando Valley, where half of my cases originated. Then came the broad swath of the 405 freeway, already bumper to bumper with cars heading to the magical mystical lands of Brentwood, Beverly Hills and Pacific Palisades and all the other rainbow vales hiding pots of gold for me and all the fools like me in the City of the Angels.

For a moment I recalled my first plane trip. I was a scared

ten-year-old, riding a Pan Am Constellation out of Havana to a new and uncertain future in the land of the Yankee, *los Estados Unidos de América.* Next to me slept my sister, Celia, six years old but having reverted to the comfort of a pacifier from the nightmare of revolutionary Cuba. In front of me sat my father, chain-smoking Pall Malls as he stared out the window, planning his return in triumph as a commando with a Miami exile group. In the aisle seat, my mother fingered the beads of her rosary while she leafed through an issue of *Vogue,* as though debating whether the secular or the saintly road would be the fastest way back to safe harbor.

Now the little family unit my parents fought so hard to preserve in exile was gone, shattered by time and human weakness.

I had just buried my mother in Miami; my father had died ten years before; and my sister was long ago vanished, lost to the fatal embrace of the Colombian drug trade.

I had always thought of my years in California as a temporary stay, a respite to lick the wounds of my failed marriage and to prepare for my eventual return to the land of Daisy Fuentes, South Beach and *libertad.* But that day, on that plane, I knew any kind of Florida homecoming was ruled out forever. I had become a permanent resident of the land of failed dreamers, incorrigible con men and vicious vermin of all stripes. And when the landing carriage of the 747 lowered into position and the plane kissed the ground, barely missing the traffic jam on the freeway overpass, I once again fell into the torrid embrace of the Queen of Angels.

I was, like it or not, home at last. But, as I was to learn, I was not quite so free of the past as I thought.

Lisa was waiting for me at the American Airlines departure desk, carrying herself with the same air of august self-assurance that had swayed many a jury into conviction even when the evidence was as shaky as the San Andreas Fault. She was the dark-haired version of the California girl, chestnut hair, steel blue eyes, strong hands ever ready to turn the key of success. She pressed through the crowd of waiting relatives squealing excitedly in a babel of tongues. Grabbing my arm, she gave me a quick peck.

"Sorry about your mom."

"That's all right. She's in a better place," I answered, not yet willing to admit the truth.

Lisa looked nervously behind her.

"Let's go out the back, I already talked to the supervisor," she said, steering me down the hall. She nodded at a middle-aged black woman in a blue jacket, who whispered into a walkie-talkie.

"What's going on?"

Lisa pushed open a service door leading to a vast corridor of orange Day-Glo dividing panels. Just before the automatic door shut behind us, I heard my name shouted out by a TV reporter, a young man with curly hair and mustache, standing by a pudgy Asian cameraman dressed all in black.

"Lisa, wait up. What's the story?" I asked, struggling with my carry-on.

"The media has been waiting here for you all morning," she replied, deftly guiding me through the maze.

"How come I'm the plat du jour?"

"Your friend Armando was killed while you were gone," she said as we entered a round hall with rows of plastic seats stacked all the way up to the ceiling.

"C'mon, this way!" she urged, holding the door open. I realized I had stopped in my tracks, blankly staring at a billboard for an old art exhibit:

"The future is coming! Visions of the New Millennium."

I stepped out of the terminal onto a walkway underneath the shiny wing of a parked jet, catching up with Lisa as she flagged down a passing baggage cart. The young Mexican driver smiled at Lisa, lifted his Mickey Mouse earplugs.

"Miss Churchill? Eunice said for me to take you back to the main terminal."

I jumped into the motorized cart, sat next to Lisa. The driver adjusted his giant earplugs again, scooted away.

"Who did it?" I shouted in shock over the din of the revving airplanes.

"Cops don't know," she shouted back into my ear, the smell of her CK perfume mixing with jet fuel fumes. "They found him in his basement. The place was a wreck."

I recalled Armando's shrine in his Highland Park home, the antiseptic cleanliness of the place, the carefully arranged altars and votive offerings.

"The killer left a message," shouted Lisa again.

"What was that?" I screamed back.

"You're next!"

The parking valet drove forward Lisa's gleaming black BMW, purring like a big cat after a warm meal. I was sliding into the passenger seat when the obstinate TV reporter from before charged out of the terminal. Lisa stepped on the gas and we hurried out to Century Boulevard, past the rows of airport motels, fast food palaces and massage parlors. Giant billboards hawking Japanese cellular phones, cameras and TVs loomed over us like the eyes and ears of an invisible stalker.

"The murder book's on the floor," she said.

I picked up the three-ring binder holding the photographs, reports and sketches gathered by the investigators on Armando's case. I blanched when I saw the pictures.

"Sorry, I should have warned you," said Lisa, negotiating around a stalled semi on Aviation.

My stomach heaved. I had read how the Aztecs and others followed the grisly practice of skinning a man alive but I had never seen the actual results—much less on someone I had known and loved.

"My God, what kind of monster are we dealing with?" I gasped, knowing there can never be a satisfactory answer for the evil that haunts us.

Lisa shifted into fourth at the 405 overpass, threw a quick glance in my direction, momentarily pressed a caring hand on my knee.

"At least the poor bastard was dead before they did it."

She grabbed the steering wheel with both hands, cutting in front of the line of cars exiting for Santa Monica.

"We think," she added.

I stared dumbly at the pictures, unable to believe that the only person who had given me some measure of comfort and guidance during my harrowing climb up from self-destruction would have fallen prey to this painful, ignominious death.

Where are your gods now, Armando? What good were they?

"What did the killer say about me?"

Lisa glanced quickly in my direction, almost feeling sorry for my pain, then shifted into fifth, cruising at eighty-five down the Mulholland grade.

"Last page."

A handwritten note in black letters, half English, half Spanish, burning with contempt.

> The last of your warriors is dead.
> You have no more defenses, Charlie Morell.

The next time Yemayá wanes I will skin your hide.
I will see you in the tomb of Oyá.

Oyeyemí.

There followed a crude drawing of a bow and arrow and an *nsibidi* hieroglyph of the Abakuá *santería* sect of Cuba. I held the note paper up to the lemony light.

"Is this what I think it is?"

She nodded. "Preliminary DNA tests confirmed it. Son of a bitch filled up his fountain pen with the old man's blood. What do the symbols mean?"

My eyes drifted, focusing somewhere in the vicinity of the Santa Susana range at the far end of the valley. I took a deep breath, my words bitter fruit in my mouth.

"The bow and arrow is the sign of Ochosí, the hunter warrior of *santería*. The other signs mean this body is dead, this whole country belongs to me."

"Why would he write listen to me at the end?"

"Oyeyemí? That's not Spanish. That's Yoruba, from West Africa. It means son of Ochosí."

We drove in silence into the packed lanes of the 134 freeway, heading for Pasadena.

"Let's go to the house," I said.

"That's where I'm taking you."

"No, Armando's house. I have to see it."

Armando's house was his treasure and his shrine, both to the glory of his religion and the memory of his wife, Josefina. Short, overweight, half Mexican and half Puerto Rican, she was working as a clerk in Van Nuys Superior Court one day when she saw me drag myself into her courtroom. I was depressed by the roller coaster of my life after the Ramón Valdéz case, my subsequent fifteen minutes of fame and the inevitable crash to earth. She made a wisecrack or two about her judge, a blathering sourpuss nicknamed Thundering Thurman, then invited me to a barbecue that weekend at her house in Echo Park.

I still don't know why I found my way to their small Spanish home by the lake, whether I was only looking for another beer and a meal I wouldn't have to cook or whether some other force drew me there for my own good. A handful of their friends had gathered around the *carne asada* on the grill, which gave off huge clouds of spicy smoke. I said hello, grabbed a Corona from the ice chest and walked through the open French doors to the enclosed backyard. Even in my alcoholic haze I noticed that some of the trees were beribboned, like flirty girls for a party, and that a flock of piebald chickens pecked eagerly at the corn on the ground behind a wire enclosure. How quaint, I thought, fresh eggs in the city. But, where's the rooster?

"They are not laying hens," said a warm, Cuban-accented voice at my elbow. "They're for sacrifice."

I turned to a man of medium height, with wide green eyes, aquiline Spanish nose and the pale pink complexion of upper-class Cubans. He smiled knowingly, as though he had already heard and answered my question before it was uttered or even imagined. Dressed all in white, from his shoes to the little *santería* skullcap he wore sideways atop his shiny bald pate, he seemed a friendly priest of some arcane religion—which of course, he was.

"I always wanted to know," I said, grabbing a drumstick from a platter offered by a red-haired little girl, "what do you do with the chickens after you kill them?"

"Eat them, of course," said the old man, laughing at the foolishness of the question. "The gods want only the *ashé,* the essence of the spirit. Once the animals are slaughtered, it's time for the feast. What do you think you're having now?"

I stared at the piece of chicken in my hand.

"Funny, it doesn't taste like communion," I said.

He laughed again. "We're not all like Ramón Valdéz, Charlie. He was a devil worshipper. We follow the path of the light. You should come see us sometime."

And with those simple words Armando opened the door to my own forgiveness. No, I did not find salvation at the foot of some ridiculous idol nor did I pledge my soul to an imp from the African forest. I never believed in the literal truth of *santería* and I still don't. Armando, wisely, never tried to convert me, he did something better—he made me understand. He explained the numinous role of the saints, the African divinities, how in their totality they represent the whole of man's aspirations and desires and how each god, from fiery Shangó to warlike Oggún and Ochosí, are all subsumed within the Creator, the wise old spirit who breathes life into all of us, who ordained the universe and sent forth his myriad representations to illustrate the many facets of His unencompassable self.

I came to see that in its theological complexity, hierarchical subtleties and accumulated wisdom, *santería* was as passionate and stirring as the ancient Greco-Roman myths, as enlightening as the unfolding monads of Hinduism. And, in the process of understanding, I also came to find a kind of peace.

My admiration for Armando only grew after I witnessed his reaction to deep tragedy in his own life. One moonlit night returning from a Malibu beach where he and Josefina had gone to leave a *prenda,* an offering to Yemayá, the goddess of the waters, a Dodge Ram driven by a drunk driver plowed into their old Toyota while they were tooling up Kanan Road. Armando flew out of the car from the force of the collision, landing on a pebbly curb inches away from a thousand-foot-deep ravine. It took firefighters two hours to extricate Josefina from the jumbled remains of the jalopy. She died en route to Kaiser Hospital, with Armando holding her hand, crooning *canciones de cuna,* Spanish lullabies. The driver of the truck walked away from the accident with a scratch on his forehead.

True to his beliefs, Armando refused to testify in the ensuing trial. In his view the fact that the driver had escaped uninjured was clear evidence that he, in his inebriation, had been an instrument of the gods, who for their own unfathomable reasons had decided to take Josefina away. Fortunately the DA's office was not as open-minded and filed charges of vehicular man-slaughter. The driver was sent away for ten years to Soledad to contemplate the consequences of being a tool of fortune.

Armando was in and out of the hospital for more than a year after the accident, undergoing innumerable sessions of physical therapy in between dozens of operations to help him regain his mobility. Never once did he complain, never once did he wish that things might have been other than they were. He prayed, waited and guided others on their own perilous path until the doctors finally gave up and sent him home with only sixty per-cent mobility.

I represented Armando in the negotiations with the insurance company of the drunk driver, the son of a studio head with very deep pockets and an allergy to negative publicity. With the settlement money, Armando built his little house in Highland Park, on a lot he and Josefina had bought years before. The house became his Taj Mahal, a blue-gray temple of marble and stucco whose only purpose was to honor the memory of his faithful companion. Her pictures were on every wall and in every room he built a *retablo,* an altarpiece, in her name. Only in the basement, where he received his followers and imparted the teachings of *santería,* was Josefina's image not present. Yet I always felt that it was precisely down there where she could be felt more strongly, in the heart of a religion that had drawn them together and then given Armando the conviction to go on living without her.

A dusty gray Chevy Caprice which once had been blue was parked against the flow of traffic outside Armando's house, blocking the steep alley. We parked in front, our bumpers butting each other like bucks in a forest glade. I glanced inside the Chevy. Its two-way radio and full ashtray screamed *policía* for all the world to hear.

"Looks like Kelsey's back," said Lisa.

We clambered up, holding on to the railing to avoid slipping on the white marble pavers leading up the grade to the house.

The yellow police tape at the front had been pushed aside, the door left ajar as though telling the unexpected guest come on in, have yourself a cold one, we'll be right with you. We walked inside.

The entire house had been turned upside down, the white walls smudged with fingerprint powder in a murderous trail that led all the way to the basement steps. Josefina's collection of ceramic knickknacks were smashed into smithereens; the many bookcases had been thrown to the ground, its volumes scattered throughout; the sofa was upended, its cushions ripped to shreds; the beaded Empire lamps were broken into shards; a carpet of debris covered the floor. Worst of all, the pictures of Josefina had been slashed up, the face cut out to leave a mocking hollow of a headless body.

"I'm sorry, honey," said Lisa, squeezing my hand.

I nodded, not knowing what to say. Just then someone whistled a tune from *Oklahoma!* and I smelled the acrid scent of low-tar cigarettes.

Kelsey plodded up the basement steps, stopped at the landing as though surprised to see us. He smiled, his sparse ginger eyebrows pushing against his creased freckled forehead, where rested a pair of rimless glasses. Large, round and rumpled, he seemed a bear out for a romp in the woods, hoping to get into some tasty garbage.

"If it ain't the voodoo counselor," he said without a trace of sarcasm. "Let me show you what this animal did."

He led the way down to the basement, his lumbering gait oddly reassuring. The trail of fingerprint powder thickened down the stairwell, the floor stained with reddish brown splatterings of dried blood.

"The call came in Sunday morning, they beeped me at St. James's. Some anonymous tip, couldn't trace the call. Patrolman drove by, saw the back door kicked in, took a look and puked outside. Here you go."

I gagged from the overpowering smell of blood, human feces and urine. Just like in the house, everything in the basement that had been on the walls had been taken down with a vengeance—the shelves, the sacred objects, the statues of Saint Francis, Saint Lazarus, Saint Barbara, the sacred stones of the *orishás* kicked out of their tureens and scattered like so many pebbles on a field. Armando's books of divination had been torn up, pieces of hundred-year-old typed paper strewn throughout. In great arching designs on the walls, splatterings of blood, as though a hose of human fluid had been sprayed through the room. In the middle of the floor, the chalk outline of where the body had been found, headless and skinless.

"Jesus Christ," I muttered.

Kelsey stepped around the debris as gingerly as his portly body allowed.

"Whoever did this held one major grudge against the old man," he said. "First he wounded him, then he cut out the old man's tongue. We found it thrown against the wall over there."

Kelsey pointed at an emptied night stand that had contained the *ifá*'s divining boards.

"Then the murderous bastard skinned him, we figure, put the pelt in a bag and cut off the old man's head, also putting it in a bag. The guy was so cold he left behind the box of Hefties. Oh, and he ripped out his heart. And his liver. Something or other must have scared him away. But not before he took a great big dump and spread it all over. Nice dinner guest, huh?"

I heard a sudden gagging sound. Lisa bent over with her hand over her mouth, her face the color of the alabaster floor tile, exerting a superhuman effort not to retch before us.

"Excuse me, I have to go," she muttered in between clenched teeth and dashed up the stairs.

"I know just how she feels," said Kelsey, shaking his head. "That's why I smoke. Although to tell you the truth, death doesn't smell as strong as it used to. Remember the Hanes case, Charlie? This could be like that."

I glanced at the havoc and I knew it would not be so simple. Richard Hanes was a respected San Marino doctor who one day came home to find his wife, his ten-year-old daughter and his mother-in-law hacked to death. On the walls someone had written, "Baby killers die!"

Hanes claimed he had been receiving death threats since he'd opened up an abortion mill in South Central L.A. But when Kelsey found Hanes had not gone fishing the weekend of the murders but instead had shacked up with his Salvadoran mistress at the Ritz-Carlton, plus that he had taken out a million-dollar insurance policy on the family the month before their death, the motive was all too obvious. In the end a little immigration pressure well applied was enough to get the girlfriend to implicate her *médico*.

A friendly Pasadena judge appointed me to the case and I was able to negotiate a fifteen-to-life plea very quickly after Kelsey found the deadly chainsaw buried in the backyard of Hanes's office in Arcadia.

●

"This is not like that," I said, feeling a strange weight pressing down on my chest. "This is not the work of an amateur. This was a professional of death."

"Skip the drama class, Charlie. What you got?"

"This was part of a ritual to capture someone's soul."

"Get off it. You can't capture a soul. Only God can do that."

I looked at him silently until it finally dawned on him.

"Or the devil," he said, almost to himself.

I cast a last look at the room, knowing that I would never again return there for the hard-earned wisdom of an old Cuban man.

"Let's go back upstairs."

We walked up quietly. Lisa was coming out of the bathroom, the sound of flushing following her out. She was still shaking.

"Sorry," she said. "I'll wait for you in the car."

I nodded. Kelsey and I stepped out to the ragged, dusty yard. The steep hillside behind the house made a sort of natural amphitheater around us, making me feel like an actor in some ancient play whose lines I had forgotten.

"I'll have one of those," I said.

Kelsey shook a cigarette out of the pack, lit it with his Zippo, still engraved with the emblem of his Marine Corps regiment. The acrid smoke rose in thin clouds against the clear sky. A neighbor's dog yelped for a few seconds, then grew still.

"This looks to be part of a ritual of *palo mayombé*," I said. "Whoever came here was intent on desecrating the shrine to deprive the *santero* of the source of his powers."

"You lost me. What's this pale-oh stuff?"

"*Palo*, pah-loh. It's black magic, as opposed to *santería*, which is white or good magic. *Palo* was brought to the New World by slaves from the Congo. They worship the devil and all the dark forces. They cast spells, offer protection. A lot of drug dealers are into it to help them with their business. Most Cuban and Puerto Rican hit men too."

"Where you learn all this?"

"Ramón Valdéz. He was a follower of *palo.*"

A black face, filled with rage, the monster created by racial hatred and uncontrollable lust, surged in my mind's eye, then crumbled into dust.

"Ramón is dead, isn't he?" asked Kelsey.

"Rotting in Hollywood Lawn. An anonymous follower paid for the burial."

"So then what's this? Some kind of revenge killing?"

"I don't think so. Whoever did this wanted to get Armando's power."

"You're assuming it's a he."

"Oh, it's a male all right. Although the *palero* worships Oyá, the goddess of death, mayhem like this is reserved for males. The females poison and cast spells. Besides, he calls himself the son of Ochosí, the god of the hunt. It's in his note."

"So what's he going to do with all the stuff he took?"

I picked my words carefully, wanting, in my mind, to keep honoring the memory of Armando, if at all possible, in the face of such ignominy.

"The skin, he'll put it on over his own in a ceremony to commemorate his victory."

"And the head?"

"Most likely he'll put it in his cauldron, to rot with everything else, to make Armando's soul his slave for all of time."

Kelsey dropped his cigarette, ground it out with the worn-down heel of his battered cowboy boot.

"Tell me something. You don't really believe all this, do you?"

"Michael, it's not my faith that counts. It's the murderer's."

"Well, you better watch out, Charlie, 'cause he's coming after you."

●

Lisa had turned on the air conditioner full blast in the Beemer, the radio tuned in to the New Age sounds of The Wave. I slid into the cool leather seat, grateful for her car, her perfume, her still perspiring body. She looked at me and almost instinctively we grabbed at each other, craving each other's warmth to fend off the cold-blooded death we had just witnessed. After a few feverish minutes, we pulled away, panting.

"Your place?" she asked.

"Yours. The media will be out at mine."

Lisa backed the Beemer all the way down the hill, spun around in a three-point turn and raced down El Paso. She turned left on yellow at Eagle Rock doing sixty and in seconds we were flying into the on-ramp and down the Glendale Freeway. In what seemed a flash, we were at her building on Holloway in West Hollywood.

She parked sideways in her stall and we dashed to the elevator, glued to each other all the way to her front door. We landed on the Tabriz runner in the hallway, tearing our clothes off right on the floor, the pressing urgency of our flesh too powerful to overcome, ridding ourselves of the stench of death through ecstasy.

Later, in bed, I stroked her silky hair absentmindedly while she napped. The sun came in through the wide plantation shutters, casting the grid of prison bars against her umber walls. A signed Mapplethorpe photograph of a sensuous cala lily hovered over her dresser, the white petals seeming to buzz with the intensity of unspoken questions.

Waking, Lisa moved her long runner's legs under the Ralph Lauren sheets, opened her eyes as she propped herself on her elbow.

"Why you?" she finally said.

"I'm sure I don't know. I guess I'm just going to have to ask him."

She glared at me, her eyes full of fear and incomprehension.
"When they catch him," I added.
Outside, an ambulance siren howled. I pressed close to her.
She sighed and closed her eyes.

CHAPTER

2

I didn't want Lisa to panic but I knew perfectly well why this deranged killer was after me: I was the new kid in town.

In a way, it was inevitable. Ever since the death of Ramón Valdéz I had unwillingly acquired a reputation as a man of spiritual power, of great *ashé* in the closed incestuous community of Caribbean cult followers—of *voudun, palo, santería, obeah, juju.* The proof of it, in their eyes, was that I had single-handedly defeated Ramón, one of the highest priests of *palo,* a man who had never before been bested in any contest. I was even mentioned in some books as evidence that the forces of good always righted the world into balance and that evil never prevails.

Never mind that I had barely escaped with my life during our confrontation on Mount Hollywood and that if not for the dazzling intervention of an otherworldy shaft of light I would have joined the long list of Ramón's victims. What mattered was that I had done it. I had killed the monster, therefore I was the superior being. Now, as in the Old West, every up-and-coming young blood wanted to make me a notch in his spiritual handle.

There was nothing I could do, either. I had to accept my fate and proceed with my life as usual. What choice did I have? Stay home and be immobilized by fear? Change my name? Move away? That would mean the killer had already won, that I was already his victim. And the only way I'll ever be a victim is when the gun is pressed to my temple and the bullet flies out to seal my fate, not a minute sooner.

No matter how much I loved Armando, how much I felt his loss, I had to let the police do their work. I was no longer a detective, but a lawyer. When I gave up the thrill of the chase and the jolt of detection, I cast my lot with those who rely on beefy cops and expensive alarms as their bulwark against evil. All the same, I made ready to leave town for a few days while the investigation proceeded.

When I drove back to my house in Linda Vista the next morning, a camera crew was camped out on my front lawn, right next to the friendly LAPD cruiser planted there for too obvious protection. I parked a block away, traipsed down to the storm channel and then clambered up to my backyard, jumping over the back fence. I disarmed the alarm and entered through the side door to the attached garage without being noticed.

I showered, shaved, changed and checked my machine for messages—an overdue credit card bill payment, a friend begging off from tennis because of a bad back. Life goes on, I thought with a smile. I packed an overnight bag and exited the same way I'd come in.

I swung by my office on Second Street before heading down

to the Criminal Courts Building. Tina, my new assistant, had stacked a number of messages from the media on my desk. I went through them quickly, my attention diverted only for a few seconds when an RTD Dash bus plowed into a decrepit Datsun right below my window. From the car emerged three old Korean women and one young Korean man who proceeded to argue violently with the black bus driver, who nodded with tired resignation.

Tina grabbed a few of my cards from the desk, her long black hair streaming behind her as she dashed out of the office.

"Where are you going?" I asked.

"Round up some business!" she said brightly.

I stopped her at the elevator and gently, but firmly, steered her back.

"Tina, I appreciate your initiative, but we don't do personal injury in this office."

"Oh, I thought," she said, then blushed violently, aware of her gaffe. "I'm sorry, that's what Mr. Martínez always had me do when I had a chance."

That was Al Martínez, my former neighbor down the hall, an old-line attorney who had hung his shingle before World War Two, when Los Angeles still reeked of orange blossoms and good lawyering consisted of plying your favorite judges with babes, booze and cash. I had inherited Tina after he'd sold his house in Los Feliz to a Taiwanese toy manufacturer and moved to that enclave of Anglo high-mindedness, Lake Havasu. He'd brought her over the day he closed his office, blithely extolling her virtues like a shady defendant on the dock.

"She's a superb typist and filer. Did I mention she speaks Spanish? That might help with some of your cases."

He pulled on his Camel, grinned a yellow-toothed smile on a creased, nut-brown face.

"She's really been pretty helpful to me," he went on. "Everyone assumes I speak the lingo but in my generation that was frowned upon. I can still remember the nuns whacking me on the lips with a ruler for speaking Spanish in class. What do you say, we got a deal?"

I turned to Tina, who stared embarrassed at the grid ceiling.

"Eres mexicana?" I asked.

"No, griega. Me llamo Tina Costas. Estudié en escuela," she replied in passable Spanish.

"You know WordPerfect and Lexis?"

"I do."

"You're hired."

"I don't understand," said Tina as she eased into her desk, pulling back her hair as she did at least twenty times a day, trying helplessly to control something with a life of its own. "Mr. Martínez said you used to do PI."

"No. I used to *be* a P.I., a private investigator. I don't *do* PI, personal injury."

"Oh," she said gravely, nodding slowly, then turned back to her computer momentarily, only to spin back around.

"So why did you quit being a P.I.? The money?"

I sat on the edge of her desk, thought for a moment. It was a question I'd often asked myself but no matter how many times I'd posed it, the answer always came out the same.

"I had to control my own life. I didn't want to be at the mercy of whatever fool came in through the door, wanting to know if his wife was cheating on him or if the secretary he was banging in the storage room was dipping into the petty cash."

She blushed again. Had I mentioned a sore subject?

"I'm kidding. I was never that kind of dick. I was a court-appointed P.I., working with the public defender and pro per custodies. I was small-change and after a while I thought it was time I became a whole dollar."

"Is that why you wrote that book?"

I got on my feet. Time to face the world once more, to try and make sense of Armando's death and all the other horrors of our world.

"I suppose. Besides, I wanted to set the story straight."

"How come you don't have copies in the office then?"

" 'Cause this is a whole different world. Now get to work. We have to get that billing out to Murphy."

"Yes, Mr. Morell. Just one thing. Could you get me a copy? I'd sure like to read it. I tried to buy it but . . ."

"It's out of print, I know. Why do you think I *really* got back into law?"

She nodded gravely, started typing away. She's taking you seriously, I told myself.

"It's okay, I got a couple of boxes in my garage. Bought them cheap at remainder prices, courtesy of my former publisher. I'll bring you an autographed copy."

"That would be wonderful, Mr. Morell."

Killing the Angel was the title of the book and for a while when it came out I was the toast of the town, which in Los Angeles can only mean wine, women and gross points in the movie. Soon enough I was just plain toast, but it was certainly heady while it lasted, even if it was a poor compensation for the Dantesque hell I endured for two years.

It all started with Ramón Valdéz and José Pimienta, a pair of so-called *marielitos* from Florida, who'd drifted out West in the late 1980s and devoted their not inconsiderable talents to the fine arts of blackmailing, robbery and murder. Cuban, black and violently anticommunist, they were a discredit to their country, their race and their political convictions. Worse yet, they were an insult to *santería*.

Tall and charismatic, the handsome Ramón was a decorated

hero of Castro's colonial wars in Angola and had once enjoyed the reputation of a miracle worker among the faithful. A high priest or *babalawo,* he was a godchild of Oggún, the fierce Yoruba god of war. Ramón was said to have been able to restore sight to failed eyes, to clear ailing lungs and even, if the time was right, to bring back the dead. But pride squeezed his heart when he came from Cuba during the Mariel boatlift and he found himself shunned by both white exile Cubans and black Americans. Enraged, he turned to crime, leaving a trail of corpses all the way from Miami to L.A. I ran across him and his sometime lover, José, when an irascible judge strong-armed me into becoming Ramón's private investigator at his last trial.

Ramón and José had been arrested by a multiagency task force after a six-hour standoff at the downtown jewelry mart when their botched heist went awry, somehow leaving six people dead. I say somehow because there were no independent witnesses to any of the deaths, except for the tragic end of a little Vietnamese girl killed by the stray bullet of an LAPD sharpshooter.

Corpses littered the floor of Schnitzer Jewelers, but who killed the victims or why was not so evident at first other than either Ramón did it or José did it or both of them did it. What ordinarily would have been a legal conundrum was compounded by the fact that Ramón chose to go pro per, that is, act as his own attorney. Not only that, he was a pro per with an absolutely novel defense: he was not guilty of whatever murderous mayhem may have occurred at the store because at the time he was possessed by his god, Oggún, and therefore he was not conscious of his actions—sort of like a sleepwalker out for a midnight stroll on the underground RTD line pushing an innocent bystander onto the path of a rushing train. Of course, just what a sleepwalker is doing at midnight on the RTD subway or why Ramón chose to go to the jewelry store before his particular god got the better or the worse of him are the details on which a successful prosecution rests.

The workings of fate not being the forte of California's judicial system, Ramón had to give a compelling performance to prove his point of possession. It was an act in which I played a very important role, as he used my own shortcomings and my guilt over my father's death—not to mention a ghostly apparition or two—to make me his attorney during the defense phase of the trial. We won but the victory destroyed me spiritually and nearly physically, after Ramón almost annihilated me atop Mount Hollywood.

The book I wrote about the affair, a thinly disguised novel, was more therapy than art, but to my surprise it drew quite a bit of attention. This was before the O.J. Simpson trial, you understand. *Killing the Angel* became—all things considered —a burgeoning success. Hardback sales took off nicely, it was published in several foreign languages and the paperback rights sold at auction for a low six figures. Reviewers compared it to Márquez and Chandler; film rights were snapped up by a major studio. Then, just as the rising swell crested, I wiped out on the rocks of literary reality.

My publisher welshed on promotion and sales tanked; the studio head who bought the book was booted out by the New York office and my novel put in the deep freeze; finally, another Cuban writer, a woman out of Hackensack, New Jersey, of all places, came out with an even gorier, sexier tome on the supernatural and overnight I was fishwrap. I couldn't even get an op-ed piece published in the *Times*.

Fortunately I'd taken out my bar card again, so I was able to make a living plying my profession among the very people I'd lambasted. That's when I realized that in this country, if you want to be respected, you have to bite the hand that feeds you. I still get attorneys who chant "author, author!" from the back of the CCB elevator when I elbow my way in heading to Department 100. And more than one judge has called me into chambers to chew the legal fat and to ask me, quite brazenly, "Am I going to be in your next book?" "Only if you rule against me, Your Honor," I tell them.

But by and large my colleagues and fellow sufferers in the legal trenches have gotten used to seeing me trundle down the hallway, briefcase bulging with papers, motions and demurrers, like any other counsel in the crowd, a man who had his fifteen minutes and now is back at the common trough. Or at least, that was the case until this latest pustule of madness.

●

The long line of supplicants at the altar of justice in the Criminal Courts Building snaked all the way up Temple and down the Broadway slope to the fenced-in parking lot in front of City Hall. Hiking up the incline, I saw a balding, barefoot Chinese man in denim jacket and Midnight Mission giveaways standing at the curb, waving a gray cap, begging for change from passing vehicles. No one rolled down a window, but the man held his ground all the same, shoving that cap against the cars like an usher at church trying to shame some bills loose. When I approached, he turned, mumbling in Cantonese. He reeked of urine and beer, his cloudy eyes almost shut by swollen eyelids. I took out a dollar and paid Charon his fee—who am I to judge the living or the dead?

At the CCB steps, four camera crews posted by the doors picked up their equipment the moment they spotted me. I was quickly surrounded, prodded with sponge-covered mikes, as lenses zoomed in and reporters peppered me with questions:

"What do you think of the voodoo cult murder, Mr. Morell?"

"Hey, Charlie, why do you think you're a target?"

"What was your relationship to the victim?"

"Are you a follower of *santería, Señor* Morell?"

This last question was posed by the same curly-haired reporter I'd given the slip to at the airport. Foolishly I turned to him.

"You are?"

"Max Gómez, Prime Nine News," he rattled, elbowing in closer to make sure his cameraman would get the two-shot.

"Is it true you have been initiated in the religion?" he pressed on.

"That's not correct," I answered in as convincing a tone as I could muster. "I was just Armando's friend. Anyway, I hated catechism at St. Michael's, so you can imagine how I feel about the saints now. If you'll excuse me, I have to get inside."

The reporter smiled, I felt the cold grip of Judas in my heart. I waded through the crowd, paying no attention to the other questions, but Gómez would not give up. He hustled alongside, his mike weaving under my lips.

"Well then, Mr. Morell, how do you explain the fact that your name was on the record of contributors to the victim's church?"

I stopped, as surprised as if I'd read my name in a book about the Kennedy murders.

"It was?"

"According to IRS records, you were Mr. Ponce's largest donor. Close to ten thousand dollars over the last two years. If you weren't a member of the church, how come you were giving such large amounts?"

I stood there, dumbfounded, done in by good intentions. Armando, with his lifelong devotion to law and protocol, had put down on his tax returns the money I had floated him to tide him over until he received his insurance settlement. I had never bothered to collect, thinking it a kind of fee for his services. I never imagined he thought it was meant for the upkeep of the temple.

"Where did you get this information?"

"From the papers seized by the investigators," said Gómez, with a hunter's quick smile. "So it's true, Mr. Morell? You are a believer?"

I stopped in my tracks, flustered. Behind me the line of defendants, witnesses, jurors and lawyers continued their slow descent into the bowels of the CCB. Ahead of me, the closed exit doors of the building. On either side of me, camera crews circling like a pack of baying newshounds.

"What did you know about the killer? Is it somebody you worshipped with?"

"Do you believe in the devil?"

"Do you kill chickens?"

"You kill dogs too?"

"Do you kill? Do you kill?"

Just then, salvation. Marcy Denton, dressed in civilian clothes, opened the exit doors.

"Come on in, Charlie. I think you've had enough."

When the Brink's security guard at the card table began to object, she flashed her deputy sheriff's badge.

"Official business!" she barked at the guard, who took a second look, shrugged and sat back down to finish his coffee and cinnamon bun. I put one foot inside, then turned to the snapping media whelps.

"The only chicken I eat is from the supermarket. Preferably at fifty-nine cents a pound," I added, then banged the door shut in their faces.

Marcy chuckled, walked briskly ahead of me, her compact body badly straining a tight green neo-Versace outfit.

"Foster Farms is on sale at Ralphs this week, Charlie. Maybe you can pick up a couple of birds for your altar."

"Thanks for the assist, Marcy, but lay off, would you?"

"See you around, Charlie," she said, waving at me as she took the service elevator to the deputies' weight room in the basement.

The old black crone in sheriff's uniform nodded, her face so gaunt you could make out the death's-head beneath her shiny skin. She lifted a bony hand, pointed a crooked index at the door.

"She's waiting for you."

I punched in the combination to the safety lock and entered the maze of corridors at the heart of the district attorney's office. As I walked past the cubicles I read the names on the doors, each spelled out in plastic plaques easily removed with the twist of a screwdriver in case of promotion or fall from grace: Bernstein, Romero, Chang, Babajian, Yakishama, Wright, all testifying to the area's polyethnic history. Inside the rooms, deputy DAs plied their trade, waiting their chance for the big case that would make them Grade IVs or, at the very minimum, DICs, deputies in charge of a municipal court. In the meantime they worked with the smell of mediocrity in their nostrils, reading files, barking into their phones and interviewing witnesses under the gloomy yellow lights reflecting darkly off the scuffed linoleum floor.

Window offices are one of the perks of Grade IVs. So how Lisa, an up-and-coming but still only Grade II deputy, had secured her cubicle with a sweeping view of Chinatown, the last foundry in L.A. and, in the distance, smog-draped Mount Baldy, was something I never wanted to think much about.

She stood reading an open file spread out on a chrome and glass desk that would not have looked out of place in a Condé Nast magazine, the orange circles and triangles of the Laddie John Dill print she'd bought at a MOCA auction vibrating in the lemony light. She's in the wrong profession, I decided, taking in the slinky navy blue coatdress, the Chanel red suede pumps, gold Cartier watch and tutti-frutti Pucci scarf tied so carelessly-artfully around her shoulders. She should be a high-powered exec in a real estate brokerage or a haute couture outfit, a killer shark dressed in finery waiting for its next bloody meal. On second thought, I decided, she's perfect where she is. The real question is, what am I doing here?

I knocked on the door. She looked up, gave away a smile to wipe my fears. How can you doubt her, I thought.

She kissed me like she was drawing her own life breath from mine.

"Everything went okay?" she asked, standing so close I was intoxicated by the musk and floral of her perfumed skin.

"Fine," I said, sitting in her cowhide Wassily. In the distance, the foundry let off its first plume of morning smoke.

"All set?"

She pointed at a leather overnighter perched on her cherrywood console.

"All packed. The people at Torrey Pines gave us a break. King with a view for the price of a regular room."

"Throwing your prosecutorial weight around, I see."

"No. Auto Club discount. Let's go."

We took the service elevator to the judge's underground parking lot. Some pathetic joker had placed black duct tape on the no-trucking sign, changing it to "No Fucking on Elevator."

"Calderón lets me use his space when he's out of town," she said, clicking off the alarm to her BMW. "Hop in."

We swung by my parking lot on Second, where I took out my bag from the trunk of my Saab and slipped a twenty to Tomás to keep an eye on the car while I was gone. On the road down to San Diego I called Tina over the car phone, reminding her to transfer all pressing business to my partner, Farris, for the next few days.

"No problem, Mr. Morell. Incidentally, a Mrs. de Palma called twice this morning. She wanted to know if you found out anything about her godson."

We sped by the ziggurat of The Citadel, its friezes of Sumerian warriors in Babylonian dress ominously threatening, like the flashback of a bad LSD trip a lifetime ago.

"If she calls again tell her I'll be in his neighborhood. As soon as I find out something I'll get back to her."

I hung up the phone, watched an eighteen-wheeler clocking eighty change lanes and cut in front of us.

"Problem?" asked Lisa, lowering the volume on her Michael Bolton tape.

"Not really. I have to do a little business in San Diego when we get down there. Shouldn't take more than a morning."

Fateful words. But then, who knew? It was all as unexpected as the call I had received the week before, forcing me to face a reality I'd wanted to forget . . .

CHAPTER

THE white flowers fell on my mother's casket in the sad flurry of finality.

The mourners, who had held back until I finished my brief funeral oration, now pressed forward, flinging the white mums, roses and carnations supplied by the funeral home, until mamá's coffin, her glistening *caja de muerta,* was draped with so many alabaster petals of regret. The Catholic priest, short, chubby, middle-aged, with the burnt cork complexion of so many Nicaraguans, hugged me fiercely.

"Fue una santa," she was a saint, he said in the singsong accent of Matagalpa. "Your mother is now in heaven with the Virgin, seated at the right hand of the Father. *Ten valor,"* be brave, he added, noticing my pained silence. "She knows how much you loved her."

I nodded, dumbly glancing around at the tent and chairs pitched on the flat expanse of green rolling down to the Everglade swamps from which the cemetery was reclaimed. The sun burned clouds of vapor off the lawn, which exuded a vague smell of rot, like the stale breath of a dying patient. Overhead a coven of raucous ravens wheeled about, high above a grove of spindly royal palms, the symbol of the Cuban homeland so long and now finally so absent from my mother's life.

It's commonplace to say that time stops at moments of crisis and acute panic—in battle, in surgery, at your ill-intended wedding or your well-appointed death. Yet although I had been gunned down, married and divorced, set upon, maimed and tortured, had fought for my life atop a Hollywood knoll, defended my soul before a heartless jury, faced down Crips, Bloods, *vatos locos*, Colombian drug dealers, Mafia button men and anointed criminals of every stripe, until the moment of my mother's burial I never had the experience of stepping through time, like a prisoner slipping through the broadened bars of his temporal cell, escaping the tyranny of circumstance that binds us to daily living. Everything was unreal, at a remove, as though I were watching the world through a thick liquid, through the glass of a universal aquarium.

A slight breeze rustled the edges of the striped tent, loosening a lilac cloud from the jacaranda tree a few feet away, the flowers draping the final veil of forgiveness over my mother's coffin. I was sweating but I had never felt as cold or as lonely in my life.

For a moment I thought perhaps it would have all seemed more real back in Havana's Cementerio Colón, where the family's pillared marble mausoleum still stands in proud display next to a monumental frieze to a political martyr. There mamá would have lain in her own crypt, surrounded by the remains of all the Morells who have cut a proud swath through Cuban history.

But in the devastation that has become Castroite Cuba, her

death, as a reminder of past glories, would also have been unreal, surreal even, a futile attempt to memorialize a name that took itself out of island life and came instead to land, with sorrow and regret, on the shifting shores of South Florida. Besides, unreality had already set in from the moment I flew in from Los Angeles, alerted by the brief, tearful phone call of my *tía política*, my mother's brother's widow, Magdalena.

By the time I reached the red-tile-roofed pavilions of Baptist Hospital her body had been removed by the mortuary's attendants, a move dictated both by efficiency and the fear of tropical decay. In a fog I sat at the office of the Palacios Funeral Home, writing out a check for the expenses, while the manager apologized for the swarm of ants scurrying in, under and around the papers, the desk, the chair, the pictures on the walls.

"It's too hot outside, even for them," he said in Spanish, brushing a few of the insects off his *panetela*, his Cuban pancake. "Your mother made all the arrangements beforehand. She said you were too busy to take care of all this. She just left you the bill to pay."

Still in a daze I checked into a hotel in South Beach, where I stayed only long enough to shower and change into a black cotton suit. Maciel, a distant cousin, whisked me back to the mortuary. We drove in silence, a medley of instrumental Cuban classics—"Siboney," "The Peanut Vendor," "Green Eyes"—the only sounds heard inside his painfully air-conditioned Lincoln Town Car. I glanced out the window at the surrounding flurry of exposed flesh, at the overweight tourists, the solipsist models and the drooling hangers-on pounding the wide sidewalk next to the swaying palm trees and imported sand dunes, and the bright gaudiness of South Beach morphed before my eyes into a tropical Brueghel tableau vivant where I played the main, morose part.

El Nuevo Herald, the Spanish language daily insert of the *Miami Herald*, had printed the black-bordered announcement of my mother's passing in between ads acknowledging debts of gratitude to Saint Jude and the Holy Spirit. By the time we returned to the funeral parlor, deep in the heart of Little Havana, there were already a dozen mourners. Elderly women belonging to my mother's prayer circle dutifully waited outside the locked hall, Bible in one hand, rosary in the other, a dark-hued chorus of Latin lamentation wanting only to tell me what a great woman my mother was. They hugged me, kissed me, patted me on my back, cried on my shoulder. I had never seen a single one of them before but they all welcomed me like their errant son.

The day manager unlocked the folding plastic door, then stepped aside, granting me the dubious privilege of being first to witness my mother's body in state. I walked into the chapel alone, my mother's friends and relatives discreetly staying behind, signing the guest register with deliberate care to grant me a few moments of solitary grief.

The cold flower shop smell of lilies and gardenias was a slap in the face, a wake-up call to my benumbed sense of loss. My mother's open casket, surrounded by dozens of wreaths and floral arrangements, sat next to a backlit pane of plastic pretending to be a stained glass window. From the chapel next to ours I overheard the screams of mourners too overwrought to control themselves and the muffled voice of a priest leading the crowd into reciting a Hail Mary. I took a few steps, kneeled at the prie-dieu next to the coffin.

My mother, dressed in the black she had worn the past twenty years, lay with her eyes closed, her head resting on a white satin pillow, her gray hair gathered in her usual bun, her hands clutching the glass bead rosary I'd bought her at the Sanctuary of Fátima during my first trip to Europe.

I should have cried, I suppose. I should have wailed, lost total control, but all I could think at that moment was that the woman who lay in that coffin was not my mother. Yes, she might have looked about the same, allowing for the decay of age and neglect—we had not seen each other in five years—but what lay before me in that fancy oak casket was only the mortal coil, sloughed off by the long-suffering soul. I don't know that I believe in heaven or hell or in any kind of afterlife, but at that moment I knew without a doubt that the woman in front of me was only a shadow, a spiritless doll made up for the occasion. The real woman was long gone.

I lowered my head, said a brief prayer, kissed her forehead. My lips burned from the coldness of her flesh, as though they had touched saintly marble or imperishable limestone. I got up, walked to a wide leather armchair at the corner, and collapsed, quietly watching and nodding as the mourners entered to offer their sympathies and last goodbyes.

I hoped for at least one moment of mystical union that night, that, even if only in my dreams, my mother would return and speak to me, show me the field of flowers where she dwelled or told me clearly you feel so good here or whatever other excuse for death one's mind can conceive. I was a failure as a medium. I did not receive a single message or experience one instant of transport. Instead, I fought sleep as best I could, trying to observe with some dignity the painful burdens that culture imposes on survivors.

At a Cuban wake, a *velorio*, there is no alcohol to ease gnawing doubts, only thimblefuls of potent Cuban coffee downed by the swarms of friends and relatives come to spend the final night with the departed. Funeral homes in South Florida, New Jersey and all other places with a heavy influx of Cubans have had to make special accommodations for these mourners, who keep all-night vigils before the day of the burial, sprawled on couches and armchairs, always within viewing distance of the casket, as though to draw the dead back for one last bit of gossip.

Conversation always starts desultorily, the clock ticking away mercilessly into the long night. First there will be the latest rumors of Castro's impending death or departure, news of Cuba's crumbling economy and darkening racial hue, with someone invariably pointing out to the white exile crowd that the place is becoming a Little Haiti. Once the usual political pieties are dispensed with, personal recollections of names and places in the old country will be trotted out. Great feats will be remembered, daring prison escapes, spectacular bombings and political assassinations, all handled and examined time and again by a people that still can't understand the reasons for its own history.

Then, sometime around the dreaded four o'clock hour, while the children sleep embracing each other for warmth in the frigid halls, the old relations, freed from the obligations of care, take off their masks and bring out the sharp knives. Ugly truths about the deceased rise up like the stench of the dead in a swampy night: who he or she screwed, what he stole, whom she denied, all the nasty, little smutty secrets the one in the casket tried so hard to hide. I was expecting all that and more about my mother—her abusive husband, her ungrateful children, her mean-spirited obsession with her confining faith. I slumped in the chair with eyes closed, pretending to doze, the better to overhear.

I did not hear a single disparaging word about my mother, Lita Zayas Baizán de Morell. Or at least, no secrets that I did not already know.

"Fue una santa," repeated the priest.

I nodded again, rubbed my aching eyes. One by one the guests shook my hand, wrapped me in expansive *abrazos,* the women freely dropping the tears I'd been unable to shed.

First were the elders. I barely remembered Gustavo, my mother's great-uncle, wide blue eyes and rosy cheeks like a ninety-year-old baby, or Rosa María, her cousin by marriage, dressed in black but covering her head with the tricolored Cuban flag made into a scarf "so we won't forget the *patria*," the motherland.

Then came my cousins. Maciel, with his gaunt Castilian mien, tried to say a few original words of consolation but could only echo the priestly oration. Then the other cousins bid their teary farewells. Pablo, Rodolfo, Omar, Reneé, Zoraya, Cristina, sundry exiles all, they'd found their share of fortune and even a sense of connection to the swampland with stoplights that they call Miami.

I, instead, had nothing but memories—of a failed marriage, a failed career, a failed family, a legion of failures still chasing me, like some infernal rat, all the way to the West Coast, where once I dreamed of making a new beginning and now barely kept afloat on the swirling, swilling tide.

I am alone, I thought with some perverse satisfaction under the sweltering sun as the guests scattered down the lawn back to their Lincolns, Mercedes and BMWs. I am alone and it's all over.

Ashes to ashes.

"Dust to dust," said a large, heavyset woman with clear hazel eyes framed by ringlets of salt-and-pepper hair.

"Excuse me?"

She was the last mourner. Behind her I could see approaching the two dutiful workers with the shovels, ready to fill the awful void.

"You were talking to yourself," said the woman in Spanish with a slight Havana lilt. She looked at me with an expression of forbearance. Take heart, her square face seemed to say, this too will pass.

"It must be the sun. You are?"

"Graciela de Palma, a friend of your mother's," she said. "We met while saying a novena for the boat people at the Sanctuary of the Virgen de la Caridad del Cobre."

I nodded, remembering the odd conical-shaped chapel built

next to Mercy Hospital, a few feet away from the lapping bay, an exact replica of the original built for the Virgin back in Santiago.

"Thank you for coming," I said, falling back on the comfortable clichés of the bereaved.

"I am here to share your moment of grief," she said, equally adept at triteness. "Your mother spoke of you often. She was always boasting what a great lawyer you are, you can even get the devil off if he's your client."

For a moment I flashed back to Ramón Valdéz, the scowling *santería* priest trying to throw me off a Hollywood hilltop.

"I'll take that as a compliment."

"It's meant to be. She told me you also used to be a detective."

"That was years ago. I don't do that anymore."

"Oh."

The gravediggers arrived, stood patiently, looking curiously at me as they leaned on their shovels as though to say, *ite vita est.*

I nodded at the workers, then stole a last look at the gleaming casket bearing the bones of my old life.

Ay mamá!

"Come," I said, taking de Palma by the arm and heading back to the road. "Maybe there's something I can do."

We walked in silence to the waiting limousine, the thumping sound of death pounding in my ears. The sun singed my face, the crows cawed as they flew from the palm grove to other, cooler places.

At the curb de Palma opened her purse, took out the tiny rectangle of embroidered lace Cuban women call a handkerchief, daubed at my eyes.

"Thank you," I said, taking a deep breath. "I didn't realize . . . will you look at this, I spotted my tie!"

"That will wash away," she said plainly.

Our eyes locked, the unspoken missing half of the familiar Cuban phrase of mourning lurching like the last survivor of a drawn out war: but the tears of the soul cannot be rinsed away.

We looked back at the grave, then at each other again.

"Words fail me," I said.

"Words are meaningless, it's the emotion behind them that gives them their worth."

She rummaged in her purse, pressed her business card on me.

"Give me a call if you think you can help."

I read the card quickly, noticed her name came with the title of professor at the University of Miami.

"What was it that you wanted, *profesora?*"

"It's about my godson. His name is Ricardo Díaz. But don't worry, we can talk some other time. He's been missing so long a little longer won't matter."

"When did you lose track of him?"

"When he went over to the other side."

She paused, making sure I understood her, then gave a slight shrug.

"I'll be on my way now. But you should remember, your mother was very well loved."

"Thank you for saying that. And thank you for coming."

"Nothing on earth could have stopped me from being here. God bless you."

She spun quickly on her sensible shoes and stepped resolutely down the driveway to a red Nissan. I stared at her car until it became a red spot going through the ornate wrought iron gate.

The waiting driver opened the door to my limo. I sat inside, the smell of leather and the driver's lime cologne a scent that will forever mean loss and death to me. He turned, a young man in his twenties, thin, dressed in black, with equally somber mien.

"Where to?" he asked in Spanish with a Puerto Rican accent.

I thought a moment, then opted to see the pain all the way through.

"Little Havana," I said, then leaned back as he steered out the iron gates and down SW 78th Court, heading for the Palmetto Expressway.

My family's apartment.

Standing in the sidewalk next to the coffee stand I looked up at our balcony—next to last floor, southeast corner—facing the flatlands which lead down to the Miami River and the downtown skyscrapers. Every night in high school I'd taken refuge in that four-by-six overhang, staring at the sliver of ocean and the tufted clouds against the violet sky, plotting my freedom even as the din and curses of my troubled family rang inside the apartment.

I was a boy wishing to be normal in a family that spat in the face of their surroundings, dragging the corpse of their past wherever they went. While my body, my heart and soul ached for the future, my family lost themselves in memories of the Havana Yacht Club and the Country Club, our cattle ranch in Camagüey, the mansions and the maids, the poisonous sweetness of life before the revolution. Yet now that boy who thought he was the present's heir apparent, who aped Dylan and the Stones, that boy was now gone as well, leaving in his stead a man who ached from wounds that never healed and ailments too obscure to diagnose. I too was a prisoner of the past and I would not break free of its fetters until I faced up to myself.

I entered the building.

●

A great silence greeted me on opening our steel front door.

The scent of violets filled the air, a lone moth flapped its ghostly gray wings and flew out to life and safety in the hall.

I closed the door behind me.

Everything was exactly as my mother had left it, down to the neatly folded *El Diario de las Américas* on the coffee table, the lace doilies on the flower print sofa, the votive candles and hollow-core plastic statuettes of the Virgin Mary on every available surface. On the counter between the kitchenette and the dining room, a centerpiece of ceramic tropical fruit—guavas, soursops, avocados, bananas, cherimoyas, all shiny and bright, as appealing then as the day twenty-five years before when she'd bought it at our local Sedano market. My father had scolded her for spending the extra money; he had just bought a second gas station and was pinching every penny that fell into his oil-stained hands. My mother retorted she had a right to some beauty in her life, even if it was a knickknack that only a miser would begrudge. He slapped her so hard she fell backward against a pyramidal display of Del Monte tomato sauce, the cans spilling to the floor in an avalanche. Other shoppers moved their carts around the mess, one old lady offered to call the police as she helped my mother to her feet. That's all right, said my mother, the imprint of papá's five fingers raising welts of fury on her cheek.

"El me quiere pero no sabe como," he loves me but he doesn't know how.

I moved down the corridor to the back bedroom, the green and yellow concrete tiles writhing under my gaze. Maybe I was wrong about that slap, I decided. Maybe mamá fell on the cans another time, when she put a bottle of California wine instead of Spanish *rioja* in our shopping cart and he said she was deliberately insulting him and his family.

Funny. Living with them I learned to distinguish between the planned, methodical punishment, parceled out for a transgression, and the spontaneous reflex of the slap, the kick or the punch when confronted with a perceived sign of disrespect. To the outsider both seem the same act of brutality, but to the connoisseur of pain, a world of difference lies between the two. It was a useful gift, the ability to analyze an act of violence and break it down into its major components. I put its guiding principles to great use in my law practice.

The act is always subordinate to the intent.

I swung open the door to my room. Not much had changed there either. My rock posters were still on the walls. Paul was still walking barefoot across Abbey Road, Mick sang obscenely on a stage, Jimi posed in profile with his psychedelic hairdo, and on the ceiling above my bed still hung the goddess of my morning fantasies, Barbarella on a clam shell.

I walked over to the desk, which faced the air shaft. Banners from Harvard, Yale and Brown—the Ivy Trinity of my choice— were pinned to the wall. Copies of *Cultural Anthropology* and *A Farewell to Arms* were stacked next to the gooseneck lamp, waiting only for the hands of the anxious student that I was to open them and extract the secret of my escape. I turned and walked out, my stomach churning at the memories.

I opened the door down the hall to my sister's room.

Mamá had converted it into a sewing room, cleared Celia's pictures and decorations off the walls, given away her dresser. Only a few party dresses remained, shoved against the far end of the wall closet, dangling from wire hangers like forgotten rags of tinsel, spandex and gauze. In a shopping bag from Burdines, a folded mink coat slowly offered its shedding fur as fodder for insects and regret.

Images of my sister jumped out at me like the frame-by-frame display of a VCR. Celia, at fourteen, with chubby cheeks and swollen eyes, makeup smeared by her tears as papá lay writhing on the living room floor and she shouted out for me to do something to help him and all I did was get on my scooter and drive away. Celia, age seventeen, stumbling home on a high, drunk, dropping from her purse the etched leather case with the vials of snowy white powder that would henceforth rule her life, the vials breaking and Celia getting down on all fours to snort with the intensity of a thirsty dog lapping a bowl of water. Celia, age twenty, entering a nightclub wearing shiny red vinyl hot pants and a see-through blouse on the arm of the lantern-jawed lothario from Colombia she'd soon marry. Celia, age twenty-eight, hair in a jailhouse cut, running down the stairwell from the lockup at the Criminal Courts Building in Los Angeles, refusing my help after being arrested house-sitting a ton and a half of cocaine in her garage in Pasadena.

More pain and suffering, more damaged goods.

My poor Celia.

I walked slowly, deliberately, into my mother's room, fearing the nightmare dogs of my childhood.

A double bed, a plastic crucifix on the wall over the carved mahogany headboard, a devotional before a framed color print of the Virgin of El Cobre, a well-thumbed Bible on the nightstand, and everywhere, like the offspring of some exotic waxy creature, candles of all sizes and colors. The *veladoras*, the votive candles of the Catholic Church, were arrayed three deep on the dresser top, their drippings running down the sides of the piece. When lit, the candles and incense transformed my mother's bedroom into a haunting church, making the place where she was raped and abused a temple of, if not love, at least forgiveness.

I sat on the edge of her bed, overcome by the intensity of my emotions. I should leave, I thought. There is nothing left for me here.

I stood, about to go, when my eyes were drawn to a carved mahogany chest tucked away in her closet under the skirts next to the shoe rack. I drew near the chest. I raised the lid.

Letters. I dug in deeper.

Letters, clippings and photographs surfaced, like the hidden shoals of the archipelago that is Cuba. I pulled out a leather-bound chronicle in fading ink of the misadventures of our clan. From the effusive, flowery phrases that my Catalan great-grandfather used to woo the rancher's daughter who would be his wife to the last staccato message I wrote my mother from Brown, it was all lovingly preserved between sheets of fine tissue paper, a carefully wrapped present for some future dis-coverer.

There were photos of my great-grandfather's tobacco ware-house in Old Havana; of my great-grandmother at age sixteen, in nineteenth-century bustle and skirt, leaning expectantly on a wooden veranda, gazing at the miles of rolling hillside that comprised the family ranch. Wrapped in pink ribbons I found formal photos of my grandparents encased in the stiff-necked costumes of the 1920s, and of my mother at her cotillion at the Havana Yacht Club in the 1940s. Then more pictures of stray moments of radiant Cuban happiness: my mother's wedding at the Cathedral in Old Havana, a party at our house in Miramar, swimming at our beach house in Varadero, horseback riding at the ranch in Camagüey.

At the bottom of this hopeless chest, I noticed an envelope

addressed to me, written in Spanish with the careful script and the rounded European r the good sisters of the Sacred Heart taught my mother. I opened it.

"My dearest son,

"I am writing you this because soon I will be in that other world where the light of eternal love draws us eternally to His forgiving bosom. Dr. Parker, the specialist, has given me only a few more months. He says the cancer in my womb has metastasized and that there is no remedy he knows of. For my part, I am glad to be rid of this world, with its scheming and its lies. I hope that in the next one I will find the peace that has so long been denied me here.

"Every person is a world, Carlos, and there are so many things that all of us regret, words said or worst, words left unspoken. I know that I am a sinner, for I have sinned against Our Lord, against your father and especially against you. Your silence all these years is evidence of my neglect, a silent reproach to the failure of my motherhood.

"I always felt for you, Carlos. I was so happy when you triumphed in the law, crestfallen when the abyss of scandal swallowed you up, and unspeakably sad when you left for California. I know I am the only one to blame and I ask for your forgiveness, just like I ask God for His. I pray you realize all I did was out of love and if I failed, it was from all too human failing.

"I commend you to Graciela de Palma, who has been like a sister in the faith to me. She has helped me face the enormity of my deeds and the finality of my life.

"I love you more than life itself. I only wish I could live my life again to do right by you this time.

"I will always be with you, with all my heart and all my soul,

"Your Mamá."

●

I looked inside the envelope. Taped to the bottom was a silver bullet, a Maltese cross etched into its tip. I took it out.

Hollow tip, .32 caliber.

I read and reread my mother's letter, trying to understand what she had meant. All her life she had been a long-suffering creature who only began to approach normalcy after my father's death. Her only fault was her excessive goodness, which made the ethically challenged, like me, uncomfortable around her. So what evil deeds was she talking about? Was it all the breast-beating of the saint, who thinks himself a murderer for killing the stray sparrow?

I searched the chest, going over the items carefully, hoping for some clue to her confession or to the mysterious bullet.

Nothing.

My heart started to race, the confines of my mother's room becoming oppressive, inscrutable.

A dumdum bullet for what?

Vampires? Werewolves?

In this day and age?

CHAPTER

THE campus was a Bauhaus dream set hard by the Everglades, a forest of severe cantilevered glass boxes surrounded by miles of well-trimmed St. Augustine lawn and hundreds of feather duster palm trees as high as the buildings themselves. It must have been a constant struggle to subdue the unruly forces of tropical nature and make it conform to the severe geometrics of the International Style. I had the feeling it would only take a week-long strike by the gardeners for the campus to revert to the sloppy marsh it had been.

Everyone in the classroom wore jackets or sweaters to ward off the air-conditioning's chill. I sat in the last row and watched Graciela de Palma standing behind the podium, gnarled pink and white hands gripping the sides for support, only occasionally lifting an arm to address the young, multiracial class. On the board behind her the TA had written, *El Siglo de Oro*, The Golden Age.

"So you see the whole notion of royal accountability to the people did not start with Cromwell's Roundheads. That idea had already been present in Spain for centuries. In fact, during the sixteenth century—and this is something Lope de Vega was familiar with, when he wrote *Fuenteovejuna*—there had been a number of revolts by the peasants against the Spanish monarchy."

She sneezed, a girl in the front row offered her a Kleenex. She took it, blew her nose loudly, went on.

"But of course, that's part and parcel of the centuries-old war between the Anglo and the Hispanic cultures. In this country's history books Anglos are depicted as altruistic, enlightened and democratic; by contrast the Spanish are despotic, ignorant and greedy.

"It's all propaganda.

"The moment Spanish galleons began arriving laden with the riches of the New World, the English began the cultural hostilities, concocting the black legend of Spanish mistreatment of the Indians in America. Their cultural war was continued by the U.S., which more than doubled in size at the expense of Spanish America, snapping up the Louisiana Territory in an illegal deal with Napoleon after he conquered Spain. The U.S. then pressured Madrid into selling Florida a few years later. Finally, of course, they provoked and carried out the Mexican-American War, which increased the national territory yet again by one third. The culmination of their drive against us was the Spanish-American War, during which the U.S. Senate openly proclaimed that the American defeat of Spain was the triumph of the Anglo-Saxon over the stunted Latin race. Well, I have news for these Anglo arbiters of history—they are losing the war. We will be the ultimate conquerors."

The bell rang, drawing to a close her curious chapter on

cultural aggression. De Palma smiled graciously at me, certain that she had made a new convert to the church of Hispanophilia. She jammed her things into a blue canvas bag from a Miami Book Fair, hawking *Florida: A Tale of Two Nations*.

"Don't forget, papers due next week!" she said to the class, as it departed. I walked up to her.

"Glad to see you," she said. "I'll bet it's been a long time since you heard a lecture."

"You'd be surprised. Back in L.A. I get at least one lecture a week from some judge or another—they all think they hold a monopoly on the truth. I'm curious, how do you figure Hispanics will prevail when throughout the world it's Anglo-American culture that's winning?"

"Sheer force of numbers. Let me give you a trivial example. You know what's the most popular condiment in the U.S. nowadays? Salsa."

She leaned forward, eyes shiny with deep belief.

"We will win from the inside. Just like in Rome, when the Spanish emperors brought about the Silver Age. So will we conquer. Time is on our side. We're the fastest growing minority in the country, we'll be the largest minority by the year 2000."

A ripple of regret crossed her face.

"That's what my godson Ricardo was doing in California, studying to help with this cultural takeover. Until he went wrong."

I shook my head, amazed by the rad-lib talk.

"Excuse me, *señora,* I don't mean any disrespect, but don't you think you're twenty years behind the times? Or is it forty? I know, when I see him, I'll wave the Spanish flag and I'll tell him we won, time to come out and kill a few more Aztecs."

Her smile vanished, replaced by a disapproving frown. She obviously wasn't used to unruly students.

"No. I want you to tell him that the road home is the shortest road to happiness. How much will that be? I'll write you a check right now."

She pulled out a red leather checkbook from her crocheted purse. I stopped her.

"I'm sorry, I shouldn't have made fun of you. No charge. Mamá called you her sister."

Her features softened, she sighed briefly.

"I loved Lita very much. Your mother was a good woman, even if she made some mistakes. But then, who among us is without sin?"

She handed me a linen envelope, the address written in long, sharp script, slashing swords on paper.

"This is Ricardo's last address. I received this a little over a year ago."

2848 Via de la Mar, La Jolla. A nice place to spend your money, if you have it—or steal it if you don't. Not the kind of town where you want to set up a radical cultural beachhead but then, Lenin started his revolution in the villas of Lucerne.

"The letter?"

"I misplaced it," she said, darting her eyes downward in the involuntary gesture of the unseasoned liar. "I've looked for it everywhere but I can't seem to find it. We moved last year."

"I see. By any chance, do you recall what it was that made you think he had gone, like you say, the wrong way?"

She bit her lower lip, flushed. You're much too old to play this game, I thought. What are you trying to hide?

"Only that he hasn't contacted me in more than a year."

"Is that all?"

She hesitated, then stepped forward, as if wanting to unveil her secret at last.

"He also said he admired the free spirit of the *narcos,* the drug traffickers. Not the cocaine importers, mind you, but the marijuana dealers. He thought it was so romantic. No worse

than rum-runnning and why should we care about Anglo authorities when Latins have always smoked it?"

"Well, I'm sure in Mexico they'll give him all the marijuana
he wants in jail."

She snatched the envelope out of my hands.

"I guess there's really no need for this."

She stuffed the envelope back in her purse, picked up her
bags and in a flash headed out the door. I hesitated for a moment, then followed her surprisingly quick footsteps.

"I'm sorry," I said as we hurried down the congested marble-
clad hallway. "I was out of line. I'll be happy to see what I can
do to find your godson."

She stopped, glanced at me to make sure I meant it, embraced me in her wattly arms.

"*Gracias, gracias.* I knew you wouldn't fail us."

That precious little phrase should have started the bells of
alarm ringing but ignorance, like all bliss, is addictive and I
wasn't thinking well.

She thrust a paper at me with Ricardo's last known address,
his telephone and Social Security numbers, then kissed me on
both cheeks. She smelled of medicine and faded gardenias.

"Anything you need, just ask. Will you call me when you
locate him?"

"I will. Do you have a picture of him?"

Again she dug in the seemingly inexhaustible crocheted bag,
sliding a photograph out of her wallet.

"This is all I have. It was taken years ago. That's Ricardo in
the center. His mother, Monica, is on the left. She passed away
last year."

I saw a high-cheekboned, wide-eyed young man with the
slicked-back hair of the mid-1980s, wearing a dark cotton suit
and a skinny leather tie. The scene had been shot in someone's
living room and the arm of a man was draped over Ricardo's
shoulder.

"I don't know who the other person was. A friend, I guess."

A bell rang for class. De Palma looked anxiously at me.

"I have to hurry across campus. Please call me if you need anything else. Thanks again!"

She scooped up her things and scooted down the hall, an elderly purveyor of subversive fantasies who couldn't help worrying about her wayward godchild.

I saw her turn the corner and melt into the crowd, then I took a second look at the snapshot. That's when I noticed the statue of Saint Lazarus, known as Babalú Ayé in *santería*. At the foot of the statue, the customary offering of a mound of pennies laced with cigars.

Godmother? *Santería?*

I looked down the hall but de Palma was long gone. Suddenly the tanned faces of Ricardo and his mother grinned back at me with the chilling certainty of the future foretold.

I spent the next few days sorting out the innumerable details that attend the final arrangements of a loved one: which charity got the couch and which the books and clothing, settling doctor and hospital bills, closing out bank accounts, all nails in the coffin of my youthful life. Someone once said you are not truly a man until you have engendered a child, but in those days in Miami I came to see you are not truly grown until you finally bury your parents and you stand alone, outside their covering shade. As long as one of them is alive you can harbor the hope, however remote, that you can patch the gaping hole and achieve your youthful dreams. Death wakes you from that illusion. Death teaches you that the country of your past is a place without roads, ports or means of delivery, separated from your present by the unpassable gulf of reality.

I made one last attempt to connect before leaving the man-

grove shores of my childhood. The day before my flight to Los
Angeles I drove down Bird Road and headed for the pink palace
I'd once called home.

At the door the smell of jasmine again wrapped itself around
me and for a brief moment I was the Charlie Morell of old, the
up-and-coming young lawyer with a thriving practice, defending
the princelings of South Florida's Cuban community. I had a
mansion in Coral Gables, a cabin in the Keys and a Porsche in
my garage. The future was as limitless as my ambition—but not
as wide as my weaknesses.

Gladys opened the door, still wearing the odd maid's uniform
she had come up with the day after we hired her.

"Well, hang me if it ain't Mr. Charlie!" she said, in her
Tennessee drawl. "You've been gone so long I was sure you was
dead!"

She extended a ropy arm, uncertain whether to hug me or
push me away, then lowered it so I would shake her hand.

"It's been a while," I admitted, glancing inside what used to
be my castle. "May I come in?"

She held on to the doorknob with her left hand, her thin body
a doubtful barrier.

"Now, Mr. Charlie, I have got to tell you. I know divorce is a
mighty sore subject, people get downright nasty when it come
their way. I should know, I've been there a couple times myself.
But I still work here, you understand?"

"I'll only be a couple of minutes. I want to talk to Julian."

Gladys narrowed her deep blue eyes, the lines on her worn
face gathering into a surly mask of indecision. Finally she re-
lented.

"Well, Miss Livvie's not here right now."

I walked into the vestibule. She closed the carved oak door
behind us. I followed her down the hallway, past the living room
with its vaulted ceiling, stenciled beams and massive fireplace.
The plump couches we'd bought in North Carolina had been

replaced by the angled cartoon furniture that has given Italian design a bad name.

"Where is Olivia, by the way?" I asked Gladys as we walked into the family room. A giant projection TV took position against a wall, right next to a display case holding my former wife's dozen or so Emmy trophies.

"She's down in the studio, interviewing Governor Chiles for her program."

"On Saturday?"

"You know Miss Livvie, it's business all the time. Julian's out back. Promise you won't be long?"

"Cross my heart."

I looked around the wide loggia, expecting against all reason to find the same tow-haired little boy hiding behind the chair saying come and get me. I found a strapping young man, stretched out in baggies on a chaise by the pool, listening indolently to a Walkman with his eyes closed as he basked in the sun. His hair was turning brown and his face sported a few blemishes, while his legs had the spindly look of someone who'd shot up six inches in the last six months. He didn't open his eyes until I was next to the chaise, his expression changing from blissful abandonment to wary recognition on seeing me.

Julian took off his earphones, the ripping chords of a Nirvana song bubbling out. He frowned.

"If it isn't my dad."

I grabbed the green-webbed chair next to the chaise.

"Mind if I sit down?"

"Be my guest," he said, blithely looking away at the hedge of giant palm trees surrounding the property. "You paid for it."

"Maybe, but your mother kept it."

"Yeah, well, mom knows how to hold on to her stuff. Except for her men. They don't last."

The sun beat down, the breeze smelled of the nearby canal, Kurt Cobain sang mutely, what else can I say?

"How was Europe?" I asked, after a minute crawled by in surly silence.

"Okay. You know mom, she planned everything down to the last three-star lunch. Monday Berlin, Tuesday Paris, Wednesday Milan and so on. Very informative. If you want to be a travel agent."

"Do you?"

"Please, *papi*. Only women, gays and losers want to do a job that pays you three hundred a week if you're lucky. I'm going to business school."

"What, you don't want to be a lawyer?" I half joked.

He shook his head in disdain.

"I don't want to be a whore, defending drug dealers and murderers. I want to run my own company and tell others what to do. Maybe I'll go into computers, like *abuela* Lita said. She always said that was the wave of the future."

He frowned again, plucked an odd hair off his earlobe. With a chill I recognized myself and my father and my father's father before him in that gesture, all of us Morells displaying the same nervous tic down the ages.

"I'm sorry you missed the funeral. You meant a lot to her."

He turned to me, suddenly vicious. "You think she didn't mean a lot to me? I wanted to come back but mom said no, we had our own life to live." He paused, the bitter memory making his mouth pucker.

"I'll never forgive her for that. She said you were going to be here and she didn't want to see you."

I took Julian's hand. "I'm sorry, son."

He snapped his hand away, hollering: "Don't you dare! You leave us and don't come see me for five years and then you come waltzing back in here like nothing ever happened. Don't be a fucking phony, dad. Don't pretend you feel anything for me."

I stared at him, his face a mask of rage. I didn't know what to say. My sins had become flesh and were hurling insults at my head.

"Falling out of love is never easy, son. When you grow up you'll see what I mean. But I never stopped loving you. I may not have been the perfect father but I always thought of you."

My words were a trite, petty excuse, but I couldn't come up with any others, the weight of guilt tying my tongue in knots.

"Well, I'm not sure I want you back in my life, dad," he said, putting his earphones back on.

I moved my lips silently, making sure he could see me. He whipped off his earphones.

"What was that you said?"

"I asked you if you want to come stay with me in L.A. during your summer vacation."

His face chilled, his expression flying swiftly from hesitant acceptance to indignant denial. He took a deep breath, put his earphones back on.

"I think it's too late for that. See you around."

I looked at him, my only son, fourteen going on forty, my likeness in more ways than one.

"Goodbye, son."

He turned his head, refusing to acknowledge me. I walked back through the loggia, through the empty family room and the silent living room, and let myself out into a blinding day of punishing sunshine.

It's true what people say about good deeds, they never go unpunished. In fact, I am the living proof. I can trace my son's festering resentment to my last heroic act in Miami, down in the dungeons of Family Court, tucked away in the basement of the Superior Court building in Miami, where Livvie, Julian and I met to finalize our custody arrangements.

Livvie's attorney, Carter Allen, a small, bald, black man who was once my co-counsel on a product liability case, had sat me down in one of the marble benches in the hallway, wearing the benign expression of your friendly neighborhood pharmacist. Livvie was out of earshot some distance away with four-year-old Julian on her knee, distractedly jiggling him as she held the bulky Motorola cell phone to her ear.

Carter proceeded to tell me, in so many words, that with my history and character, I didn't stand a chance in hell of gaining custody. I was about to argue the point when a bearded, long-haired hippie farmer went at it with his former wife, a tiny tub of a woman in a flower print dress. Neck tendons swollen and cheeks flushed, the woman hollered in Spanish, while a little dark-skinned boy wrapped himself around her massive thighs.

"Abusador!" she cried, like any good aroused Cuban mother. *"Pervertido! Animal!"* Child abuser, pervert, animal!

In reply the man took out an automatic pistol and smashed it into the woman's face, opening a two-inch gash on her forehead.

"No one's taking my kid from me!" he hollered, backing away.

Julian chose that very moment to break free of his mother's arms and dash across the hallway. The farmer noticed Julian and swept his arm down as though to scoop him up. I ran to him just as the man's gun hand came down.

"What the fuck?" was all the man managed to say as I grabbed his gun hand, turned his wrist inside, then twisted his arm backward, like Sensei Parker taught me at the kenpo dojo.

"Watch out!" I shouted. The gun dropped in front of my stunned son, clattering on the terrazzo floor.

I yanked the man's arm backward, then I kicked the inside of his right knee, tearing the ligaments. I was about to place a stranglehold on his neck when two heavy bailiffs jumped on me, removing me forcibly from the farmer, twisting my arms behind me and snapping the cuffs on.

"Whoa, you got the wrong guy!" I screamed but to no avail.

It took me forty-five minutes of curses, pleas and threats before I was released, and that only after the shift sergeant had the good sense to bring in the ex-wife to confirm my story. In the meantime, the judge in my custody case had assigned sole custody to Livvie in my absence. Later, in her chambers, I pleaded with the magistrate, a parchment-skinned woman with a string of pearls the size of her capped teeth.

"Judge, he was going for my kid!"

"Cut the crap, okay? Look at your track record. You've left town, you're not practicing in California, you don't even have a steady job yet. Not exactly prime pater familias material. In any case, custody is up for review in a year. Let's see what kind of father you are by then. Now if you don't mind, I got to get back to court. I've got a roomful of vipers waiting to kill each other in there."

But by the time of the next custody review, I was so busy and so poor as a private investigator in L.A. that I couldn't take the time off to wage the high-stakes, high-priced legal battle it would have taken to get Julian back. For years after that Livvie would throw every obstacle my way when it came to visits and time away from Miami for Julian. So, sad to say, in the end I gave up, seeing my struggle as futile as a wasp stinging a light pole.

I'd already lost everything. Now my son had joined the legion from my past who wished I would vanish once and for all and become yet another memory of the drug-hazed years of Reagan, Iran-contra and *Miami Vice*.

I was the repudiated past, a ghost in my own hometown, one of the living dead of night.

CHAPTER

THE weekend I was away in San Diego with Lisa, thinking about my past and wondering about our future, I was visited by the same dark figure who had slashed his way into Armando's house.

As police later reconstructed it, the man had walked up the Arroyo, clambered over the chain link fence at the edge of the property, then slithered through the overgrown brush in the back of my house. Stopping behind the bamboo grove, he must have stared at the large waning moon, then, tilting his head back, howled like a wolfman, unleashing a canine chorus from the neighbors' yards, which carried down the darkened canyon.

The shift supervisor at Home Alert Security later told investigators that he could hear the dogs howling when Willie Chase placed his call to headquarters that night. A serious young man in his early twenties, Willie was working as a guard four nights a week while completing his Associate Arts degree in mass communications at Pasadena Community, so when he asked permission to go investigate, it was readily granted. After all, the police had been there for the past three days and it would be just like them to leave right as a break-in was going on.

A lifelong resident of nearby Altadena, Willie knew all the ins and outs of the Arroyo, the cul-de-sacs and odd alleyways created when the city paved over the park. Black, with a shaved head and buffed like a prizefighter, Willie was also not one to back away from trouble, which was what he thought he was hearing that night.

He parked his Chevy Citation in my driveway, turned off the lights and walked onto my property to investigate. He pointed his flashlight at the side of the house, a blue Cape Cod enveloped by the low-lying fog coming out of the Arroyo. Walking practically on tiptoes, as if gliding over the red pavers in the side garden, Willie silently inspected the house, his Powerlite flooding the woodclap sides. The dogs of the neighborhood, smelling an alien presence, took to barking ever louder.

Willie stole silently all the way to the back, around the small kidney-shaped pool in sore need of cleaning, its surface littered with dead bugs and fallen eucalyptus leaves. He was about to turn around and call in a false alarm when he heard a scraping noise from the far side of the house.

He ran across the backyard, his bulky body preparing for battle, heart pounding, blood freely flowing, a welcome film of sweat starting to flow.

There he is! I got him!

Fixed by the flashlight's baleful circle, a white male in his late twenties, long black hair, dressed in white clothing, was crouched before the back bathroom window, attempting to open it with a crowbar.

"Drop that! Right now!" barked Willie, taking out his Smith & Wesson.

The man turned slowly, his chin pointed queryingly at the light, his wide almond eyes barely blinking. Willie was surprised to catch a well-dressed white man, wearing several gold bracelets and rings, trying to bust into a house. Most home burglaries were the work of hungry Mexicans and blacks from Altadena who traveled down to Linda Vista to feed like wolves on unsuspecting homeowners. It certainly didn't look like the guy needed the money, but whatever it was he wanted, Willie was in no mind to let him have it.

"Drop the crowbar!" ordered Willie again.

The man righted himself, let go of the iron. Grinning, as if immensely amused by the proceedings, he put his arms up.

"This how y'all want me?" he drawled in what Willie recognized as a Southern accent—Georgia, Mississippi?

"That's right. Now step away from the house!"

Willie approached the man, gun still in hand.

"Put your hands behind your head!"

The man, still smiling, did as he was told. Willie felt for his handcuffs, took them out, walked up close to the intruder.

Willie was about to snap the cuffs in place when the intruder turned and, under Willie's surprised stare, in a split second that echoed into infinity, brought out from his waistband a long knife that sliced across Willie's neck, cutting the guard's jugular even before his mind registered that his dream of being the next Bryant Gumbel had just died in that backyard in Linda Vista.

Willie let go of his flashlight, dropped to the ground. The intruder took two steps away, grabbed him by the hair, jerked his head back and, in a swift motion, cut Willie's throat all the way to the backbone as the dogs began to howl once more.

CHAPTER

AFTER a few days in San Diego, on a morning when a thick
layer of marine air had turned our view room into a classroom
for cloud formation, I finally called my friend Marvin Clark at
the County Public Defender's office. I dropped Lisa off at one of
the stores near La Valencia and I drove down to O'Grady's in
the Gaslight District.

O'Grady's was a true relic, the last of the fern bars that once
had bloomed throughout California. In an old brick building,
the place seemed more like a forlorn flower shop than a saloon.
Once I cleared my way past the hanging gardens, I spotted
Marvin at a stool nursing a beer and staring at my reflection in
the ornate bar mirror.

"This is not what you think," were his first words when I
walked up to the carved mahogany bar.

"You quit twelve step, is that what you're telling me?"

"No, partner," he resounded in a deep, chesty voice burnished with bronze, "this is a nonalcoholic brew and this is strictly business. Give me some love."

I gave him a hug, gladly.

Marvin was a wiseguy, a wounded veteran of the L.A. wars. A former sheriff's deputy, he'd jumped at the chance to move his family down from North Hollywood to head the investigation division of the San Diego PDs. It didn't bother him that he would be the first and only African-American in that department, or that he had crossed over to the enemy camp. We're all out to do justice, he'd repeat indignantly time and again when questioned about his move. Besides, wouldn't you want to get your wife and kids out of the line of gangland fire?

"So you say you're looking for Ricardo Díaz," he went on, lighting a Marlboro Light as though we were still downing boilermakers at the Third Street Bar.

"I am."

"Well, take a number, brother. There's plenty of people ahead of you in that line."

"Like who?"

"Like the Small Business Administration, the Consumer Affairs Protection Unit, the Chula Vista Police Department and San Diego's DA's office. He was bad news. Why you want to get in touch with him, anyway? I thought you were out of the PI racket."

"It's an old debt. His godmother was a friend of my mother's and she wants me to find him."

"Shit, in that case, partner, I'm glad I brought you to this place because right here is where Díaz first made his mark in San Diego."

I looked around at the sea of massive oak tables, captain's chairs, turn-of-the-century baseball posters.

"He was a 1970s reject? A failed interior decorator?"

"No, partner, this is where he started his con. By the time he was through, practically everybody in this town was after his ass. See that round table by the window? That's where he used to come every night and read Tarot cards and tell your fortune."

"Sacramento wiped out laws against card reading years ago. That's not illegal."

"Maybe not but what he did next was."

"Which was?"

"Ripping off people he was advising on where to invest their money. Sometimes he'd even take it and invest for you. Of course he was just working a nice little pyramid scheme. But once he got his hooks in you, he'd do you hard. Now tell me, why are you really interested in Díaz?"

I ordered a micro brew from the bartender, a thin blond Gen X'er with two nose rings in her left nostril, shaved eyebrows and a Rasta 'do. Her T-shirt read, "Tim Leary's not dead, he's on another plane." I jerked my head at the help.

"I thought they only drank herbal teas."

"Welcome to the 1990s. You are avoiding the question, Charlie. Why you have a hard-on for this guy?"

"Let me ask you this. Why are you so insistent on knowing?"

Marvin glanced around, to make sure no one else could possibly be listening, then leaned his hefty wrestler's body against the counter, whispered low.

"Because I haven't told you who was one of Mr. Díaz's most devoted fans."

"Let me guess. The district attorney?"

"You *must* be psychic. Actually his head deputy, woman named Elaine Qabar. When Díaz got busted by Bunco-Fraud, this little girl got into her head she'd spring him loose."

"Why do I smell romance in the story?"

"Again, it's not what you think. Díaz wasn't screwing her, he was screwing her *boyfriend.* She thought by getting him off, Ricardo would leave her honey alone. So when the case came up for prelim, she did not oppose a defense motion to set bail at ten thousand. He skipped town across that beautiful waterway known as the River Rio Grande and has not been seen since."

"That's redundant," I said, still relishing my beer.

"What's redundant?"

"River Rio Grande, that's like saying the Big River River."

"Whatever. Point is, the shit hit the fan when the press picked up on this. That's when we found out that Mr. Díaz had a lot of friends in high places."

Marvin took a fat yellow folder from his briefcase, dropped it on my lap. The many-colored rubber bands holding the paperwork together almost covered the name on the tab, Díaz Ricardo M.

"You didn't get this from me," he said in a low voice.

"I can always say I copied it at the library," I said.

"You fuck. You know that is a copy of the DA file. It has a narrative by a certain Raúl Alvarez Donosio. Ever heard of him?"

"The former president of Mexico?"

"Exactamondo. He claims Díaz was a priest of something called polo and that he was into human sacrifice to gain his supernatural powers. You knew that, right?"

The room spun around, my legs weakened, a ringing started in my ears. For a brief moment I thought I heard the distant rattle of gourds, the pounding of heavy drums. I sat down, out of breath.

"It's *palo*," I said, *"palo mayombé."*

"Yeah, that's it. Heavy-duty voodoo shit."

My stool became a slow-moving turntable, spinning me around in a diorama of my own past. Here was Ramón Valdéz grinning his death's-head rictus, there my mother in pasty-faced repose in her casket, behind her the hulk of my father silently begging for death while over there on the other side my ex-wife and son, my law practice and my courtroom victories, all a prelude to my encounter with this malignant being.

This was no coincidence. This had all been planned, for me to come full circle and face down the monster I'd unwittingly created. De Palma may or may not have been my mother's good friend or even Díaz's godmother, but she definitely was my Mercury, my Eleguá, my warning.

I don't know how long I remained silent, all I remember is looking back up at Marvin from the well of my anxiety and wondering, is he in with them too? Is there anyone I can trust?

"You all right, partner?"

"Yeah. I was just thinking."

"Me too. You wanna tell me why you're chasing down our man Díaz?"

I got up, picked up the file, left a five on the counter.

"I'm doing a favor for someone, I already told you."

"Who?"

"Me. Now let me do you a favor."

"What's that?"

"You never saw me. You never talked to me. As far as you know, I'm dead."

Marvin looked hard at me, chin out, eyebrows down, the kind of stare gangbangers in Montebello saw only in their darkest nightmares.

"If that's the way you want it, Mr. Morell."

He hugged me with all his might. I hugged him back, whispered in his ear, "Requiescat in pace."

Lisa was somewhat less than enthusiastic upon hearing of my plans.

"I thought we were coming down here to get away from work," she said, chidingly, while she wrapped a celadon green towel around her wet hair.

We were in the bathroom. She had just stepped out of the shower, the fluffy white terry cloth invitingly half open.

"That was the whole purpose of this trip, wasn't it?" she repeated, growing annoyed at my lack of response. "Spend a few days together, try to forget the nightmare in L.A."

She sat down at the vanity, crowded with her instruments of attraction, the perfumes, lotions, creams that added little to her pale-skinned, high-cheeked beauty. She picked up a powder brush, dipped it angrily into the matte foundation, applied it to her face in quick, jerky motions.

"Tell me, am I wrong? Is it too much to ask for you to spend some time with me, instead of doing favors for some old biddy your mother knew?"

I sat on the edge of the bidet, trying not to sound condescending or flip.

"Some people would say five days together is a lifetime, Lisa."

"If you're a fly."

"Okay, it's long enough."

"Long enough for what? Long enough to catch up on your sleep? Long enough to get your rocks off?" she snapped.

"You're not being fair. Of course I wanted to come down with you but I thought once we were here, I might as well."

"Might as well what? Forget about me?"

"It's not like that."

"It's not? Then how is it?"

I was silent. I couldn't risk telling her, not now, when the monster loomed so near. I had to go and strike out at him before he came near me, that much Ramón had taught me.

"Look, I just have to do this, it'll only take a day. What's so hard about my going to Mexico? It's just an hour away. You can relax, have a massage, get a pedicure, a good night's sleep and I'll be back before you know it."

She threw down her brush, picked up a hand towel to daub away the excess powder.

"You got me so upset I did the foundation all wrong. Oh, screw it."

She scrubbed her face with the towel, looking at my forlorn reflection in the mirror.

"I'm sorry," she said. "I don't do rejection very well."

I stood, embraced her. She leaned into me, eyes closed.

"I'm afraid," she whispered.

My heart quickened, pinpricks of anxiety needled my skin, raising welts of apprehension. I forced myself to speak with as much composure as I could, all the while thinking, does she know?

"What are you afraid of?" I asked, gently, evenly.

"Of being left alone."

"I'm still with you, I'm not deserting you."

"You don't understand, Charlie."

She pushed away, her azure eyes bedeviled by a haunting shadow. "I've been seeing him in my dreams ever since we came down here," she said, in hushed tones, terrified by the intensity of her vision.

"Who?" I asked, dreading the answer.

"The man who killed Armando. In my dream I'm in the living room back home when the front door opens and he steps inside. I can't see his face but I know it's him. You're sleeping on the couch but I can't wake you. He walks in with a knife, dripping with blood. I want to run away but it's like my legs are made of lead, I can't move fast enough. Then he comes at me with the knife and he slashes and I wake up."

Lisa looked away, her gaze drifting to the cutout of ocean blue outside the octagonal bathroom window.

"I can sense him, Charlie. I can feel his hate all around us. I can almost touch it. It's like he's out there, just waiting for us to make the wrong move so he can cut us into little pieces."

She hugged me with all her strength, silently imploring for

me to take action, to do something, anything, that would drive this hateful nightmare away.

I bent down, kissed her forehead.

"He doesn't know where we are. You have nothing to worry about. They're just bad dreams, you shouldn't pay attention to them. Anyway, I'll be back tomorrow, I promise."

She nodded, quietly accepting my departure. We both knew there was nothing else I could do.

CHAPTER

THE twin white buildings rose like the guardians of Mexican might on the rippling shores of San Diego Bay. Dubbed the Tortilla Towers by jealous Anglo neighbors, the structures housed the luxury condos bought by south-of-the-border financiers and politicos. Within the towers Spanish was the language of discourse, English spoken only to outside help and pliant local authorities.

Little whitecaps graced the choppy waters of the bay, as a mild breeze coaxed the hedges of oleander, gardenia and jasmine into releasing their sweet scent. Like the ancient Romans, the Latin potentates of the towers were serving out their exile in a sunny fragrant land, our very own American Provence, while back home the country fell apart at the seams. Rebel uprisings, famine and massive unemployment were distant nightmares, kept safely on the far side of the twelve-foot steel fence running along the Otay River. America, land of the rich, home of the runaway.

The lobby guard was a poster boy for a Goebbels propaganda film about the good Aryan soldier, his Spanish melodious with the accent of Guadalajara as he cleared my way inside the doors. He hung up the phone, slapped a visitor sticker on my jacket, pointed with his solid chin at the double safety doors.

"*El señor presidente* is waiting for you," he announced, adjusting the underarm holster beneath his Armani jacket.

"Why all the security?" I asked, noting the banks of closed-circuit cameras, the maze of alarm boxes, the uniformed guards standing like Nubian warriors by the glistening elevator doors.

"What's it to you, dude?" he said, finally sounding like the beach rat he no doubt used to be.

"I like to know what I'm getting into. Is it safe in here?"

"Safety is a myth, dude. You can lower the odds, but you can never eliminate danger altogether. If it makes you feel any better, whenever *el presidente* is around security in this place is tighter than a flea's asshole."

"I take it you're with the Mexican secret service?"

He smiled impishly, tossed his long blond locks back, quickly patted me down for weapons.

"Dude, I *am* the Mexican secret service. *Orale,* time's a wastin'."

He buzzed me in. I nodded and walked to the elevator, which opened in efficient silence.

Tamayo. Rivera. Kahlo. The works and names of famous Mexican painters echoed in the richly appointed living room where I waited. An entire wall was given over to a casually arranged sampling of twentieth-century Mexican art, the canvases coalescing into one shimmering mosaic of color and desire, as though proclaiming their owner to be so wealthy he need not worry about showcasing or identifying any of the pictures, for they were meant for his private pleasure alone.

I sat on a tasseled velvet sofa, overcome by the visual spectacle. To the right of the art wall, French doors opened to a marble-paved balcony. Scattered throughout the hall were delicate painted Venetian side tables bearing little Olmec, Mayan and Aztec figurines, the kind ordinarily shown behind thick layers of Plexiglas at the museum, here strewn as casually as Burger King toys. On the cut-glass coffee table, a reclining man from the Late Classical Mayan period was being used as an ashtray, a stubbed-out fat Cuban Cohiba in its belly. The only thing missing from the picture was the charred remains of the hundred dollar bill used to light the cigar.

I walked over to a hall leading into the apartment. A series of oils illustrating the different degrees of racial mixes marched down the corridor. The first canvas showed a white Spaniard, fair-skinned and blue-eyed, displaying through the ages the dumb pride of the color he was born with. Across the way a second tableau of an Aztec in full blood-spattered regalia with a sign announcing redundantly, I am Indian. The most interesting of all was some distance down the hall, showing the child of a light-skinned mestizo woman and a Spanish man, the boy as typically Iberian as a young Cordobes or Picasso but still a half-breed. How can anyone tell what you are if they don't know your parents? And why should anyone care?

"That is my favorite picture in the entire series," said a high-pitched man's voice at my elbow. "It expresses perfectly the spirit of Mexico. We all carry an Indian inside us, no matter how white we may look."

I turned to a short, balding man with light olive skin, heavy-lidded almond eyes and long Spanish nose. Spare of flesh, with a wide pleasantly crooked smile, he could have been any one of thousands of merchants of Puebla, Zaragoza or Verona, eager to please and make his sale. He pumped my hand like a true politician under the suspicious glare of two bodyguards who would not have looked out of place lifting obsidian daggers in Palenque.

"Raúl Alvarez Donosio," he said. "May I get you something to drink?"

"No, thank you, Mr. President." He guided me back to the living room, but not before I espied a dark-haired teenage girl in white push-up bra and lace panties peek out of a room, then dash down the corridor.

"I just wanted to ask you a few questions, if it's all right with you," I said.

"Yes, I know. That is, I can imagine what you're here for. I read your book, after all. In fact."

He sat me back down on the tasseled couch while he eased into the yellow cut-velvet divan across the way. His two guards took up position at opposite corners of the room, eyeing me disdainfully, daring me to make their *día*.

Donosio clapped his hands. Like in some pasha's tent, a black steward in English livery stepped out of a side room.

"Edward, will you please fetch me my copy of Mr. Morell's book? It's on my desk in the study."

His English was flawless, as befit someone born in Washington, D.C., raised in Princeton, and educated at Choate, Yale and Harvard. A true cosmopolitan *mexicano*—and the most corrupt president his country had known since the 1911 Revolution.

The steward nodded and exited, deadly quiet. The youngest man ever to wear the tricolored sash of the presidency of Mexico turned on his merchant's charm again.

"I must say you certainly have a way with words, Mr. Morell. Your description of the state of mind of the killer during the takeover of the jewelry store was very persuasive. I mean, I do know a thing or two about the criminal mind myself. You are aware I headed the Interior Ministry for a while, aren't you?"

"Yes, Mr. President. Your reforms were widely publicized in the States," I said, remembering the news of people disappearing, demonstrators getting shot down, rebel guerrillas drawn and quartered, all in the name of anticommunism and the free market.

"Humh, they should have, considering how much I spent on that PR outfit in Washington," he said, shaking his head still at the price of acceptance.

The lugubrious steward returned, bearing a book in white-gloved hand.

"If you would be so kind," said Donosio, handing me his Mont Blanc pen.

The book was the Spanish edition of my novel, edited by a Barcelona house which had refused to pay me for my own translation of the work. I scribbled the usual best wishes and then added, "from one student of the dark to another," signing my name with the expected flourish.

Donosio looked quite pleased when he read the dedication.

"This will occupy a place of honor in my collection. You know I have signed first editions of all the works of Stephen King, Dean Koontz and Ed McBain back home in Acapulco," he said, then he scowled briefly, remembering how far he was from his beloved library.

"You know, it has occurred to me that our political system in Mexico is very similar to your *santería* in the book."

"How's that, Mr. President?"

"It's very simple. Like in *santería* we honor the gods that walk among us with sacrifices—money, drugs, blood. We disguise them with the cover of accepted figures of worship: patriotism, law and order, capitalism. The priestly class, the political oligarchy in this case, interprets the signs and tells the people, the followers, what to do. And the greatest priest of all, the *babalawo*, as you would call it, is the president, who remains *tapado* or hidden until the godhead manifests itself. This is nothing new, you understand. We have been doing it for thousands of years, since the Olmecs. The raiments may change but the body remains the same. Let me show you something. *Felipe, ven acá!*"

He snapped his fingers at the massive guard nearest him, who docilely stepped forward.

"Enséñale las marcas al señor!"

Felipe looked at me expressionless and in one swift move, unbuttoned his shirt, turned around.

The man's entire back was etched with the symbols of *palo mayombé*—the seven lightning bolts, the wandering star, the bow and arrows of Ochosí, the grinning mug of Eleguá, all carved deep into the solid brown flesh. I knew the lacerations had been done by the sharpest knife and that the guard must have endured the pain for hours, while whoever wielded the blade slow-etched to crude African perfection.

"This is the reason why you're here, isn't it, Mr. Morell?" said Donosio.

"Fascinating, Mr. President, but that's not why."

"It's not?" said Donosio, snapping his fingers at the guard, who covered himself and resumed his post at the corner.

"No, sir. I'm here to talk about Mr. Ricardo M. Díaz. I believe you had some dealings with him in the past. I'm trying to locate him."

Donosio gave me a wolfish grin. "And since when does a renowned author and high-flying attorney spend his time working as a missing persons detective? You're much too well off for that, Mr. Morell."

I shifted uncomfortably in my seat—he had put his finger squarely on the wound. I smiled back, trying to downplay my ulterior motive.

"I'm doing a favor for a friend of my late mother's."

"Oh. I'm terribly sorry to hear about your *señora madre*. My deepest sympathies. Yet, please excuse me for prodding, Mr.

Morell, however, this person who wants to contact Mr. Díaz, just who might that be?"

"His godmother."

Donosio looked befuddled by what I'd just said, then turned to his guards. All at once the three of them burst into gales of uncontrollable, back-slapping, rib-spliting laughter, as though I'd made the funniest joke. I had the sinking feeling I had, too.

Donosio looked back at me, tears flowing, his face flushed a deep red.

"Why of course I will help you, Mr. Morell. After all we wouldn't want Mr. Díaz to be away from his beloved godmother!"

Again more guffaws, deep sobs of hilarity drawn from that place where comedy touches tragedy and can make us weep as easy as it can make us laugh.

I sat there, embarrassed, until the laughter eased. Donosio took out a fine linen handkerchief, dabbed at his nose, then asked me in total earnestness,

"Would you like to see my room of the dead?"

We walked past the gallery of portraits into the Saltillo-tiled kitchen, where a handful of white-uniformed servants curtsied before our party. Donosio regally lifted a hand, waving at them to go on with their chores. An old Indian woman was bent over a giant lava rock mortar, a *mojalbete,* slowly grinding with an equally giant pestle the mass of many-colored spices she scooped from open paper bindles on the counter. At the commercial stainless steel stove a man stirred the eternal pot of *frijoles* while nearby a third kitchen helper rhythmically patted a bowl of *masa* into growing mounds of fresh tortillas.

"We're expecting company this evening," said Donosio, casually. "Governor Wilson and former Assembly Speaker Pringle, so everybody's very busy. If you would like to, Mr. Morell, perhaps we could find you a spot at our table."

"Thank you, Mr. President, but just seeing the governor would be enough to spoil my appetite."

"I know just how you feel," he sniffed, "but one gets used to these people. You must remember that saying about politics."

"It makes strange bedfellows?"

"I was thinking more along the lines that it forces you to develop a cast iron stomach, but that too," he said, leading the way through the kitchen into the laundry room. "Getting back to Mr. Díaz, this was all his idea."

He opened a series of doors, which led to yet another narrow corridor, which dead-ended in a small, wooden door painted red and black.

"You must realize I was mad with resentment when this was set up. I was out of my senses over what the party leaders had done to me in Mexico after I left office. I would have done anything to regain what I had lost."

Donosio took out a gold key ring, searching for the right key like Bluebeard in his castle.

"Naturally that's how Díaz takes advantage of people; he is diabolical in that respect. He can sense what it is you crave the most and then that is exactly what he offers you."

Donosio inserted the key, turned the tumblers.

"He demanded that some of my people be converted to his cult, that they might become his warriors as well. Felipe volunteered and for that, I will always be grateful."

He slapped the guard on the scarred back. Felipe grunted, the faithful humble servant. Donosio leaned into the door, pushing it open.

The corroding smell of death and putrefaction rushed out, poisoning our senses with the foul breath of hell.

"The funny thing is, at first it seemed to be working," said Donosio, stopping at the stinking threshold, taking out again his perfumed handkerchief and putting it over his nose. "One of my opponents was assassinated at a political rally, another was thrown out of office because of a bribery scandal. Imagine that, a Mexican politician losing his job because of a *mordida!* If that's not a miracle, I don't know what is. But then, like with all spells, it stopped working. In my opinion, I think it was because Ricardo went crazy."

Donosio groped around the wall, threw the switch on. A single incandescent light bulb in the ceiling cast a yellow light on the small, windowless room. At the far end, a three-tier altar had been erected with pictures and statues of Saint Peter, Saint Lazarus, Saint George. A life-size figure of Saint Barbara stood on the top tier, one hand on the long sword, the other outstretched to ward off evil. At her feet, several baskets of decaying food—chickens, bananas, mangoes—were set upon by a dark, slithering swarm of cockroaches. Several of the insects were crawling up the statue, flecked with a rusty brown substance that could only be blood. Several human skulls rested on the altar, somber death's-heads remembering the way of all flesh.

The rankest smell issued from the black iron cauldron in the corner, the dreaded *nganga* of the *palo* priests. I took a few steps inside, stepped on an errant roach, almost gagged from the stench.

"These insects have become a problem," sniffed Donosio, perfumed handkerchief firmly on his nostrils. "We have to spray the outside of the door every day to keep them from coming into the house. Ricardo loved them. He said they were the souls of the dead returning to him, begging for mercy. But mercy or no mercy, I'm afraid we're going to have to get rid of this thing. I'm glad you're here to see it before we do."

I glanced inside the *nganga*. A foul soup of black, brown and yellow with a few *palos* or sticks of sacred cascarilla wood sticking out. I held my breath, stirred one of the sticks. The liquid belched, a fat bubble broke through the bodies of dead scorpions and spiders. Slowly a partially decomposed human hand, grasping a heart, drifted up. I stepped back, afraid I would not be able to control the tide of burning vomit rising in my throat.

"I've seen enough," I said, walking out of the devil's lair. Donosio signaled at one of the guards, who locked the room behind us.

The ocean breeze was the cool kiss of someone who loved you unconditionally, a mother's kiss, a Savior's kiss. I leaned on the balcony and gulped in the air, wanting to cleanse my lungs.

"Why did you say Ricardo went crazy?" I asked Donosio, who lit a cigarette with perfect ease, as though the sight of a torture chamber were the most natural thing in the world to behold.

"I think it was the human sacrifice that convinced me," he answered placidly, staring at a wildly colored spinnaker raking the bay. "He kept harping on finding humans to be sacrificed, that his magic would really be great once he killed them and their souls became our slaves."

Donosio stopped, looked at me urgently. "I may have been resentful, even desperate, but that kind of *brujería* . . . well, there are things I won't do."

"So what happened when you refused to cooperate?"

"He put a spell on me, the little prick. He cast me out. Me, the president of the United States of Mexico, cursed by the son of an exiled garage owner! I still don't know how it got that far. See this?"

He showed me his wrist, where three small dot tattoos were arranged to form the points of an equilateral triangle.

"He wanted me to get tattooed, *rayado,* like Felipe as well. This was all I let him do. Thankfully I came to my senses in time—but not before he stole two hundred thousand dollars of mine."

I examined the markings. "You know that is the Cuban prison mark of the executioner."

"So I've been told. That's why I haven't had it surgically removed. I think it's appropriate, given my history, don't you?"

He smiled ruefully, as though admitting that in some perverted way he too found humor in his well-deserved predicament.

"Find him, Mr. Morell. Find him and destroy him. If he still has the money he took from me, you can keep it. Or if you want to charge me an equivalent fee, please feel free. Money is the one thing I still have plenty of. And I'm willing to spend it. I don't care what your real reason is for finding him. But get rid of him. Be my sword, be my Santiago."

He stopped, smiled again.

"Besides, it'll make a hell of a book."

CHAPTER

THE sun rose slowly over the scrub-covered hills, swiftly burning up the remains of the fog. Ricardo Díaz, formerly of Miami, Denver and San Diego, now an involuntary exile to the hinterlands of Baja California, grinned with outsize pleasure. He enjoyed the velvety dewiness and spicy aroma of the early morning almost as much as the bottles of Wild Horse Pinot Noir he was carrying in his Land Rover. At times like this anything seemed possible, he could overcome all obstacles, Eleguá, Ochosí and Kadiempembé all smiled on him and pointed his way to success.

The road, barely more than a widened dirt trail winding through the chaparral, dipped into a large crater. Díaz switched to four-wheel-drive and carefully wended his way around the huge pothole which could have easily swallowed up his vehicle.

He descended to the arroyo, the Rover bumping and rattling on the smooth boulders of the dry bed. In winter the rain-swollen creek would become a raging river emptying ten miles away in the Sea of Cortés. But now all that remained of the season's wetness were the scattered cattails and scraggly palms opening up their hairy leaves to the pitiless sun.

Success. Yes, success was near, thought Ricardo, propping up the case of wine in the seat. It was only a question of time, a few weeks at most, certainly before the rainy season, and then their mission would be accomplished and the doors to official Mexico would swing open.

New land, new souls, new sacrifices to appease the gods. How wonderful it will all be, he thought.

He felt a welcoming chill on nearing the ruins of the church. How apt, he thought, a mission with a mission, a Cortés in reverse.

Everyone ran out of the building when they heard his Land Rover approach. Through the dust-covered window Díaz could see his loving disciples gathering before the crumbled adobe wall: Rogelio Llanés, short and pouty, bleached blond hair set atop hard Indian features, an interior decorator just one generation away from the ejidos of Guerrero; Bobby Blanco, the wealthy Mexican son of Spanish exiles, lanky with jet black hair and stone green eyes that softened only when the blood of the sacrifice puddled on the floor; Omar Rangel, a tough pug Chicano from Montebello eager to avenge himself on the Anglo world. There were others but they would come later, once they knew the *padrino* had returned. Only his faithful, the vermin of the gods, remained in the mission to carry out his will.

But where was his princess, the majesty of their realm, *la fille du régiment?* He stopped the Rover, got out, kissed Rogelio and embraced the other two men, cupping affectionately their genitals in his hands.

"I brought the wine," said Díaz, taking out a bottle. "A '94. They tell me it was a very good year."

"And I have the host," said Miranda behind him.

Díaz spun around at the sound of her honeyed voice, ringing with the ease of wealth and privilege. She strutted out of the darkened shed where Díaz kept the stinking *nganga* with the old *santero*'s heart. In her arms she carried a little Indian girl, ten years old at most, who buried her frightened face in Miranda's long, curly blond hair. Miranda had gathered her long flowing skirt, tying a knot at her waist to show her long lean legs, tiny feet in lace-up granny boots.

"And what is your name?" asked Díaz in Spanish, gently prying the girl's cheek away from Miranda. He stared at deep black pools of fear.

"Elenita, señor, para servirle," said the child, hesitantly.

"She's the daughter of a peasant family out in Las Flores," said Miranda in English. "They sold her to us."

"Is she a virgin?" asked Díaz, all the while caressing the smooth brown face.

"At her age?"

"You never know with these animals," said Díaz, smiling sweetly at Elenita, who now dared to hope for the first time.

"I'm sure she is," answered Miranda, shaking her head.

"So tell me, Elenita, are you a good girl? Do you want to go to heaven?" he addressed the little girl again in Spanish, taking her from Miranda.

"Sí, señor, I want to go to heaven because I know my *mamacita* is waiting for me there."

"Well then, my child," said Díaz, carrying her to the shack, "you don't have to worry anymore. I think tonight you're going to be in your mommy's arms."

Elenita looked up at Díaz, seemingly puzzled, unable to connect his sweet words with what they implied, until moments later it dawned on her and she opened her mouth and hollered, as though calling her mother to rise from the dead and come rescue her.

"No! No! No! Don't hurt me!"

But Díaz clamped a hand over her mouth, walking quickly to the shed, followed by his band like a pack after fresh kill.

CHAPTER

THE lanes of traffic at the San Ysidro crossing opened up wide and carefree, as though the gates were pay booths on an ordinary toll road and not the busiest international border on the face of the earth. Like in the old Roman colonies along the Mediterranean, a new culture was said to be aborning on this border strip. With millions of brown faces, billions in foreign investment, and the immeasurable raw materials of mighty Mexico, *la frontera* was hailed as the wave of the future, the new melting pot for the long-suffering lands of the Southwest.

I didn't believe it for a minute.

It was all Mexico, painted, gussied and made up for foreign consumption, like a miniskirted harlot on Avenida Revolución. The natives may have been speaking the tongue of the invaders, but their hearts and minds were still the same beneath the surface trappings—slow, suspicious and pessimistic, waiting only for misfortune to prove them right.

On the northbound side of the border crossing the *palapas,* the palm thatch roof huts of the pervasive poor, were jammed with riotous displays of tourist knickknacks—cloth puppets, ceramic statuettes, leatherette bags and belts, all the cheap accoutrements tourists from Chula Vista, Bakersfield and Tulsa believe typically Mexican. Dashing through lanes of traffic, rail-thin vendors bent by the weight of their packs sadly peddled their wares. Behind them, like the proscenium in some gigantic farce, rose huge billboards promoting the Mexican Health Department, Kool cigarettes and Tia Juana tortillas.

I rolled down my window, letting in the oddly scented border air, with its tang of wood fires, leaded fuel and human waste floating above a bottom of desert dust and marine breeze. On the car radio an old record by Los Panchos played out the eternal song of poor Mexico, so far from God, so close to the United States.

When I was growing up, the Mexican *bolero* was all the rage up and down Latin America, which then as now included the southern tip of Florida. From the corner *bodegas* to the school-yard patios, not to mention doctors' waiting rooms, car dealerships and fragrant restaurants, everywhere you turned trios like Los Panchos, Los Aces and Los Tres Caballeros, with their fancy verses and fancier guitars transformed barroom ballads into paeans to unrequited love. Today any Latin, from the blackest stevedore of Cartagena to the fairest blue-eyed *porteño* of Buenos Aires, the Incas of Bolivia, the *mestizos* of Central America, the Chinese and Japanese up and down the continent, even—as I saw with my own two eyes as a child—the revolutionary leadership of Cuba, all Latins, at the drop of a hat, can start singing the famous lyrics, much like American baby boomers crooning "Feelings" with the gang during happy hour:

Dicen que la distancia es el olvido
Pero yo no concibo esa razón
Porque yo seguiré siendo el cautivo
De los caprichos de tu corazón.

So now, as I entered the capital of the border nation, I too began to sing the old songs, unable nor willing at that moment to escape the past.

Hoy mi playa se viste de amargura
Porque tu barca tiene que partir
A cruzar otros mares de locura
Cuida que no naufragie tu vivir.

The sergeant at the lobby put down his magazine when he saw me come in, the glint of self-interest in his eyes. I walked up to the desk, glanced at the lurid headline, "Pervert Insists on His Right to Anal Coitus—Fifteen Killed in Angry Shoot-Out."

"What's the matter, mister," he said unctuously, almost putting out his hand for his *mordida*. I answered in Spanish.

"I'm Señor Morell, sergeant. Lieutenant Miguel Ortega is waiting for me."

The sergeant shook his head, as though my Spanish or his hearing were giving him problems.

"Excuse me, what you say, I no comprehend you," he insisted in English, refusing to believe that such an obvious gringo would speak his beloved tongue. I was in no mood for games. I smiled as brightly as I could, whispered confidentially.

"I said that when Lieutenant Ortega finds out that his friend from the San Diego DA's office has been detained without reason, that he's likely to send you back to Colonia Corrientes to work the midnight shift with the whores, the coyotes and the drug fiends. Are you comprehending me now?"

The sergeant's face hardened, his upper lip peeled back, then he picked up the phone, all the while fixing me with his deadliest glare. He muttered a few words, hung up again.

"Second floor, third door on the right," he replied in Spanish this time.

"*Muchísimas gracias, señor sargento,*" I said, walking through the swinging door. "You are most kind and a great gentleman."

"*Chinga tu madre, cabrón,*" go fuck your mother, you prick, muttered the sergeant under his breath, returning to his crime rag.

Lieutenant Ortega of the Federal Judiciary Police was a short, compact man with the wide-eyed look of the Oaxaca Indians and the sarcastic attitude of the *chilangos,* the quarrelsome denizens of Mexico City. When I reached his door he was on the phone, fending off questions in heavily accented English.

"No, madam, the investigation by the morgue's forensic doctor did not rule out the possibility of murder, it's true, but it did not, how you say, *necessitate* a finding of murder, either."

He waved at me to come in. I sat on a chipped, cigarette-scarred plastic chair, facing a Tecate calendar picture of a curvy brunette in a tight bikini, beer glass in hand, licking the foam off her lips.

"The boy died from internal injuries, that is all the doctor has determined. Maybe he fell off a motorcycle and was run over, maybe he was beaten, it is not clear. As you know, drug-running *is* a dangerous occupation."

The office was small, its one grimy window caked on the outside with years of Tijuana dirt, pollution and bird droppings. Books, magazines and loose-leaf binders were stacked helter-skelter on two plain wooden bookcases. His desk was strewn with papers, reports, three empty Peñafiel water bottles and the discarded remains of a half-eaten breakfast burrito. In the center of the crowded surface, an overspilling ashtray fashioned out of a human skull.

"Yes, you can be assured I will most definitely call you when I find out something else, that's what we're here for, *verdad?* My pleasure."

Ortega hung up, shook his head as though to clear his ear from the litany of complaints he had just endured. I shook his hand—square, hard, with the manual worker's ridge of callus on the outside surface of the palm.

"Morell. I've been expecting you," he said in Spanish. "*Señor* Clark called this morning. You know, he has been a great help to us when we have cases in San Diego so whatever you need. He tells me you're interested in Ricardo M. Díaz."

"That's right, *teniente.* I have a client who wants to locate him."

He looked me up and down, as though committing to memory any *signos de identidad,* any identifying marks that would allow him to distinguish me should my quest end in potter's field. Then he shared a catlike grin.

"Most curious. So do we. By any chance, would your client be in a position to file it as an extraditable offense?"

"I'm afraid not. This is a private party. I'm not here on an official function."

"Oh, I forget. In *el norte* people still believe in the niceties."

"Excuse me, *teniente,* but what do you mean by that?"

"I mean the separation of public and private life. Have you ever spent much time in Mexico, *Señor* Morell?"

"Not much. Just as a tourist, battling the bug in Cabo and Ensenada."

"Queasy stomach, eh? Next time take a spoonful of Pepto-Bismol before you eat, it'll help you immensely. Well, allow me to inform you that the Mexican Constitution does not guarantee privacy, like the California one does. That is because here everything is private. We are a country of factions, you might even say, families. And public life is a reflection of that family aspect. Cigarette?"

He shook a pack of Marlboros. I waved my hand no. He lit a cigarette with a waxy match from a Papas & Beer book. He blew out the match and dropped it in the skull, which I realized was made out of plastic.

"I mean, it would be easy to say we're your mirror image. Too facile. We're really a distorted lens, through which the onlooker sees what he desires like a, what's the thing that turns colors in your eye?"

"A kaleidoscope."

"That is correct. A cultural kaleidoscope. You turn us one way, we're little triangles of brown and yellow, another we're hexagons of blood red. Depends on how you turn it."

I was about to break into my usual version of Jack Webb's just-the-facts-please when Ortega abruptly canceled his flight of fancy.

"Which brings us to Mr. Díaz. You know, when I was handed this case, my first thought was this is like that famous Japanese movie, the one where the crime is witnessed by so many people, all with a different perspective."

"*Rashomon,* Kurosawa's masterpiece."

"Precisely. The only difference being that here it was all different views of evil and not of an innocent victim."

His rotary phone blared to life.

"I don't believe Díaz has had one single day of innocence in his whole life. And I am including the day he was born. Excuse me."

He picked up the phone.

"*Bueno.* He's there?"

He listened intently, tilting his head, then tapped on the edge of the crowded desk, impatience burning his fingertips.

I could see why he had been chosen for the job of cleaning out what had been the most corrupt *prefectura* in the country, a

Mexican Eliot Ness sent to bring down organized crime on the border. I didn't envy him his job. But then, I'm sure he didn't envy me mine either.

"You get him ready," he ordered, slamming down the phone.

Ortega looked at me blankly, collecting his thoughts, then put out the cigarette in the plastic skull, where it joined dozens of other butts.

"You see, my problem is, I'm a prejudiced man."

"In what way, *teniente?*" I said, playing along.

"I firmly believe in the Napoleonic system, Morell. A man should be presumed guilty if and until he can prove his innocence."

He leaned forward, confidentially, elbow on an open Mexican code book.

"It's so Anglo-Saxon, this belief in the intrinsic goodness of man. Because that is the corollary of your belief system, isn't it? Man is moral. Man is perfectible. Man, when born, is a blank slate and is molded by his environment. The fault is not within ourselves but in the stars. Man, in other words, is good."

He glared at me as though holding me responsible for this gringo affront to good sense. I looked at the circles under his eyes and wondered when was the last time he had a good night's sleep and how much longer it would be before he cracked up.

"Garbage," he sneered. "Man is flawed, Morell. Man is guilty. Without the law, life is, like your Mr. Hobbes said," he switched to English, "nasty, brutish and short."

He smiled, revealing a set of tiny yellow jagged teeth.

"You have a good Catholic sensibility, *teniente.*"

"I do but it doesn't really matter. Living in Mexico I would have arrived at the same conclusion eventually. It is impossible to have those ideals in this country. You either open your eyes or you die young. Very young."

He opened a drawer, threw on his desk a schoolboy's composition notebook with the name Ricardo M. Díaz written in gold Gothic letters on its bright cardboard cover. I opened it.

In red ink on the front page was his *firma*, his magical signature—the crude bow and arrow of Ochosí, the hunter of *santería*, pointing at six arrowheads enclosed by a circle inside a triangle. Carefully written in a small script, the first few pages gave the notations and designs of the throws of the cowrie shells during divination with the *ifá*. Afterward, the *ebbó* or sacrifice the believer had to offer to change his fate.

Ortega pointed at the notebook. "We found it hidden inside a book in one of the houses Díaz owns in Mexico City. Take a look at the last entry."

I jumped to the end of the notebook. In the same methodical script of an accountant or corporate attorney, Díaz had written a recipe for a *cambio de cabeza*. A ceremony to radically alter one's fate, it literally involves changing one's head or ruling deity, through the sacrifice of an innocent girl, no older than ten. Once this was accomplished, then the patron—a woman apparently named Dolores—would take over the child's destiny.

I looked up, horrified. "Do you have any idea whether this sacrifice was carried out?"

Ortega nodded. "A little girl's bones were found buried in the yard of his home."

"How come I've never heard about any of this? There's been no mention at all in the media."

"Morell, you forget where we are. In this country, people in high places, if they want to bury an item, they'll plant it so deep it'll be halfway to China."

Ortega stood, pulled his chair out. "However, I am glad to say this is all about to change."

"Why is that?"

"Come. Let me show you why."

●

We walked down a narrow corridor with umber hexagonal floor tiles, the walls still fresh from recent troweling. Steel beams protruded at odd angles from the ceiling, the smell of plaster and lime floating in the air. Ortega hurried, nodding curtly at the undercover officers in civilian clothes along the way.

"Díaz made a big mistake the other day, we think," he said as we flew down a flight of stairs, then exited out a side door to a parking lot behind the main building.

"What did he do?" I asked as we dodged in between the dusty Chevrolets and Ford pickups of the working officers.

"He forgot the unwritten rule of Mexico—gringos are untouchable. When you're dealing with Americans, you have to play different. You cannot treat them like the nationals."

We entered a squat cinder block structure at the far end of the lot, next to the barbed wire fence overlooking the bilious Tijuana River, its shores teeming with plastic bottles, used diapers and pages of newspapers spread out like grimy petals on the denuded banks.

"*Buenos días, teniente,*" said a dwarfish Indian woman cleaning the cement floor, so short her mopstick was twice as long as she.

"*Buenos días, Gervasia.*" He turned to the stocky, perspiring officer at the desk wearing an oversize T-shirt bearing the logo "Surfer Dude."

"*Habló?*" did he talk, asked Ortega. With the pudgy thumb and forefinger of his left hand, the officer picked up like a precious artifact the .357 Beretta he'd set on the desk, wiping its barrel with an oily rag.

"*A chorros,*" it poured out of him. He jerked his head at the far end of the room, where a wooden door was ajar. Before we entered, Ortega whispered in English,

"Do not say a single word inside. This man may have information on a missing American, a college student that we think Díaz has kidnapped. We detained him at a roadblock."

We stepped into a stifling chamber, four barren block walls without windows. The smell of blood and fear curdled the air, a single spotlight threw a circle of theatrical light on the floor. A round Formica table swiped from a restaurant was planted under the light, a few wooden chairs were arrayed all around. Two muscular men bent over the prisoner, a smaller and dark-skinned man, who dabbed a wet compress to a bleeding, broken lip. A roll of kitchen towels lay upon the table, soaking up a small pool of blood. The guards straightened up on seeing us, stepping aside to let Ortega approach. The prisoner looked up with a sad expression momentarily, then cast down his eyes again, resigned to his fate. Half his face was swollen and red, the imprint of an instrument still fresh on his stubby cheeks. His rough hands trembled, playing with a chip of plaster.

"Fumas?" asked Ortega, offering his pack of Marlboros.

"No, gracias, teniente," said the man, trying desperately to please, his mouth full of blood, a gap in his smile. The chip, I realized, was one of his missing front teeth.

"Now do you remember what he looked like?" asked Ortega in Spanish. The man turned his head dolefully.

"Pues sí, teniente, it is all coming back to me."

"Tell us, then, what was he like?"

The man darted a quick apprehensive look at the undercover officers, who smiled grimly back. The prisoner then fixed his blood-rimmed basset hound eyes on me, as rueful as the family Fido beaten for digging up the prize roses in the yard.

"I don't understand how this happened," said the man, shaking his head. "He said none of this would happen if we followed his instructions. I followed them religiously. I cannot comprehend."

"Who is he?"

"Ricardo, nuestro padrino," our godfather.

"Ricardo Díaz?" snapped Ortega.

"The same. He promised us we'd be able to walk by the cops unnoticed, that bullets wouldn't kill us if we wore this."

He touched a small leather pouch dangling from a thin gold chain around his neck. Ortega snapped his fingers. One of the guards tore the pouch off the prisoner's neck, then handed it to the lieutenant. Ortega emptied the pouch on the table. Dust, feathers, bone chips, a jet stone and a jelly bean spilled out.

"You see, your mumbo jumbo is shit, it doesn't mean anything."

Ortega spat on the spilled contents, then yanked the prisoner by the hair.

"We have the strongest magic, Raymundo. We are the chief wizards. Now talk or I'll rip out your tongue!"

He let go of the man's neck, which snapped back like a rubber band. The man shivered, hugged himself, as though he were standing on a snowy steppe and not sweltering in some stinking hellhole.

The prisoner pointed at me. "He was dark-haired but *güero,* like this one," a white-skinned one, he said, taking in the sandy hair, hazel eyes and fair skin I inherited from my Catalan forebears.

"Ricardo said we needed a powerful sacrifice, a soft gringo for his kettle."

Ortega turned to me, spoke in English. "What's this about a kettle?"

"It's an iron cauldron, where the *palero* cooks his magic potion," I replied, also in English. "In *palo* they believe they have to put your soul in the kettle to make their magic work."

"How do they do that?" asked Ortega, now looking down on the prisoner, who eyed woefully his missing tooth in his hands.

"By killing you in the worst way possible, in the greatest

pain, so that your soul will be a willing slave for all eternity to avoid that pain."

"So what are the chances the guy he captured is still alive?"

"When did they kidnap him?"

"He was reported missing a week ago."

I thought back, recalling the giant moon rising over the mangroves of Florida my last night there. I had laid my mother to her final rest just eight days before. It seemed so long ago already.

"There was a waxing moon then. That's when spells work their best."

"That means they killed him."

"In all likelihood."

Ortega dug in his jeans pocket, took out a much folded photocopy of a picture from a high school yearbook. An open-faced Anglo boy, eighteen or nineteen, with blond hair, wide-open eyes and easy California smile looked back at me. Ortega waved the picture in front of the prisoner.

"Was this the boy?"

The prisoner looked at the picture, as though his eyes were not used to seeing things in print, only in the soiled flesh. As he stared, a drop of blood fell on the boy's face.

"*Ese es el chingón,*" that's the fucker.

One of the guards slapped the prisoner so hard his head swung back and forth, a spray of blood falling on us.

"Where did you pick him up?" asked Ortega, not at all displeased by his underling's behavior.

"At the Mexico Bridge," muttered the prisoner. "Julio and Pablo jumped off the van and when his friend walked ahead of him, the boy went behind a piling to urinate. Julio grabbed him after he was done, but he still had his dick in his hand!"

The prisoner couldn't help but smirk. This time Ortega clenched his fist and smacked him in the face with all his might.

The prisoner's eyes opened wide as he gasped for air, tumbling to the floor. He wheezed when the guards helped him back on the chair, then he spat on the table his remaining front tooth.

Ortega shook his hand from the pain, asked in a low growl more terrifying than a thousand hot pokers: "Where did you take him?"

The man gulped, swallowing the blood that filled his mouth.

"To the church in San Vicente. I don't know anything else, *teniente*. I was the driver, I had to return the van to the rental the next day. I swear I don't know what happened to him!"

Ortega put his face an inch away from his captive's.

"Are you telling us the truth?"

The man literally shook, his voice plaintive and low.

"I swear, lieutenant, on my mother, I had nothing else to do with this. I just drove him there!"

The man gave a great cry and began to sob. Ortega stepped back, spat in the man's face, then he wheeled around and stormed out, calling,

"Let's move it, Morell!"

I hurried after him as he bustled out, hollering at the officer at the table in the adjoining room.

"Get the muchachos ready. We need fifteen men, plenty of ammo. The two armored Broncos and the Jeep. Alert headquarters after we're on our way, I don't want anyone leaking this!"

"*Sí, teniente!*" said the officer, slipping the gun into his waistband while picking up the phone.

Ortega marched back to the main building, headed down to a room in the back where he flung open a steel locker jammed with assault weapons. He took out a Kevlar jacket, slipped it on, handed me another.

"You're going to need this," he said.

"Where are we going?" I asked.

"We're taking down the devil! *Andale!*"

CHAPTER

10

"SAN Vicente was abandoned about eighty years ago," said Ortega, staring at the white line snaking down the blacktop.

We were rumbling down the lifeline of Baja California, La Carretera Peninsular Benito Juárez, commonly known to most gringos as Highway 1. Behind us followed three sport utility vehicles crammed full of agents and enough weapons to take down a minor fort.

We hustled at over two hundred kilometers an hour, muscling other southbound vehicles to the side. All the cars gave way, knowing without need of any outward identification that we were the law.

The sky was a limpid blue; dun-colored hills rose to our left while to our right somewhere beyond the line of taco stands and shantytowns broke the indifferent Pacific. On my lap lay an open binder with the copies of the many police reports on the atrocities of Ricardo Díaz. His picture was pasted on the cover, red letters glued over his young smiling face: *"Asesino!"* murderer.

"The mission was a going concern until the First World War, when the water well ran dry. All the inhabitants then moved to town about fifteen kilometers away."

"What about the priests?" I asked.

A bevy of buzzards danced against the hurtful sky. The overhead console monitor in our Jeep read an exterior temperature of 112 degrees Fahrenheit.

"The *padres* left a long time ago, after the government confiscated their holdings back in the nineteenth century. I was talking about the natives who grew crops around the mission. They stayed behind until everything was played out. That's what happens down here. You cut off the head but the body keeps going. Just like a lizard."

"Or a chicken," I said.

"I wouldn't know," replied Ortega, deadpan, callused hands gripping the leather-covered steering wheel. "I'm from Mexico City."

"You think that might happen here?" I insisted.

"Not as long as I'm alive. I'm going to kill this monster. And his brood."

He frowned, seeming to sink into his thoughts, as though the weight of the past were still digging into him.

A moan from the back seat. I turned. The prisoner, Raymundo, his mouth stuffed with a gauze to stanch the blood, turned yellow-green. One of the two *oficiales* alongside him elbowed him hard in the ribs. Raymundo gagged.

"Aguántate!" hold it in, warned the officer. Raymundo nodded, swallowing the swill that had begun to trickle out of his mouth.

I turned around and concentrated on the files on my lap; this was their country, they played by different rules.

The police reports were written in the heartlessly flat style of investigators around the world. They tersely confirmed the information Marvin and Ortega had given me but with the added details that only a Cuban like myself could appreciate.

Díaz's first contact with Mexican authorities had come three years before on May 20, Cuban Independence Day, in a workingman's quarter of Mexico City. Presumably Díaz had recently arrived from Miami, and a minor officer, sensing easy prey, had detained him for practicing card-reading without a permit. Never mind that just a block away a dozen *brujos*, warlocks, and assorted Gypsies plied their trade openly in the plaza. Perhaps the officer had not been pleased with the size of his *mordida* and had decided to haul Díaz off to the *prefectura* for some friendly lessons.

When first questioned Díaz gave his name as Antonio Maceo, the Cuban equivalent of General Sherman, but he changed his story after "a fall on the staircase provoked a hematoma and blood loss on the upper lip of the suspect, at which point he identified himself properly. He declined to press charges of police misconduct."

None of that was surprising, but what amazed the arresting officer was how within an hour came an order from the mayor's office to release *Doctor* Díaz on the double, even though Díaz had not made a single phone call or alerted anyone to his whereabouts. The officer, a corporal named Matías Pérez, reluctantly let Díaz go.

A coroner's report dated two weeks later put Matías Pérez floating face down in the green waters of the garbage-filled Grand Canal. He had been raped, bludgeoned, stabbed and tortured to death; his genitals had been sliced off and stuffed in his mouth, his fingers choppped off at the knuckles and a rolled hundred peso bill stuffed into the cavity where his index finger had been. Pérez's heart had also been torn out, like an ancient Aztec sacrifice washed up in the waning years of the twentieth century. A third police narrative named Díaz as the main suspect but nothing came of it, as Mexico City investigators were unable to locate him. A few months later, the case was closed at the behest of the mayor's office.

From that point on Díaz was a suspect time and again in a number of crimes, from the merely venal, such as passport counterfeiting, drug trafficking and police corruption, to the hideously malignant: raping children, slaughtering enemies, torturing and dismembering victims for the gods of his religion. He attracted a band of adepts, who catered to his every whim and even pled guilty to his crimes, knowing that within months some high functionary or other would commute their sentence or allow them to escape. This complicity on the part of high officials, never explained but always apparent, shielded Díaz from harm until he finally ran into powers even greater than his own.

The downfall began during the last presidential campaign, rocked by the noise of armed leftist rebels in the south and the growing discontent of poor and middle-class Mexicans sick of a slipping peso, a polluted environment and official corruption on such grand scale it dwarfed the excesses of the Ottoman Empire. The great pyramid of power that had controlled the country since the death of Pancho Villa split open, and out of it stepped a former minister of agriculture, José Benítez Sarmiento, who openly ignored the will of the tycoons of the ruling party. He promised a clean sweep of Mexican politics, an end to the endemic corruption that sucked the life of the body politic. He was called the savior of Mexico and, like all redeemers, he died for his troubles.

During a campaign swing in a *colonia* outside Monterrey,

Benítez Sarmiento was assassinated by two gunmen who broke through the security detail and blew out his brains with a hollow point bullet. The harrowing murder was captured by a news camera and the video was replayed constantly for months throughout the Spanish world. What was not reported then nor later was that the hit men were members of Díaz's bloody cult.

For once the Cuban's reach had exceeded his grasp. Within hours, the combined forces of all the Mexican security branches were combing the country, searching for Díaz. It was a secret search, however, for authorities were not particularly eager to expose the blood-stained garments that implicated the ruling class.

Díaz's cult was broken up, most of its members arrested and charged with conspiracy, but Díaz himself was never found. It was widely believed he had fled back to *el norte*, where he lay low until the storm subsided. He had returned only recently, allied to *narcotraficantes*, the credulous drug smugglers for whom Díaz's promise of otherworldy protection from harm and graft was too attractive to ignore.

But this time the protective shield was off. When authorities in Tijuana heard rumors of a devil-worshipping priest blessing bales of marijuana about to be smuggled through Otay Mesa, they moved in. In a quick raid at a former shrimp-packing plant they captured three tons of cannabis and four suspects, all of whom conveniently died during escape attempts. The squad of *federales*, led by Ortega, also found on the premises an altar to the saints, bedecked with flowers, food and ornaments, as well as other instruments of worship.

The local crime lab had taken a series of well-lit glossies of the altar, stacked with soup tureens containing odd stones, iron bows and arrows, small conical heads with eyes and mouths made of cowrie shells and one very special divination board. I told myself it wasn't possible although it was so obvious that I should have guessed it long before then.

I searched through the prints, found a photograph of the board propped up against one of the plant's filthy walls. In the lower corner of the board I could see the initials A & J, Armando and Josefina.

My stomach turned. I felt as queasy as the prisoner behind me. A line of cordón cacti grew by the roadside, like ghastly candelabra lighting the way to the central desert.

I glanced back at the pictures, examined closely the glossies of the altar. A circle of white denoted where an object had been set and then moved, an object with the outline and deadly configuration of the *palero*'s kettle.

"Did you find any human remains at the packing plant?" I asked Ortega.

He shook his head no.

"There was blood. We couldn't tell if it was fish, fowl or human."

I took a deep breath, took a drink from my water bottle to rid myself of the bitter taste. When would this end?

"I believe Díaz may have brought in body parts of one of his victims in Los Angeles."

"You mean your friend Armando?"

I swung around so fast the binder fell to the floorboard.

"How long have you known?"

Ortega relished my surprise, fulfilling the eternal Mexican need to one-up the arrogant gringos.

"Ever since Marvin told me you were coming. I ran you on our computer. We do have them, you know. It's amazing the kind of thing you can find on the Internet nowadays. I can even tell you exactly how many copies of your book sold in Mexico. And the States, for that matter."

"My book?" I replied, dumbfounded.

"Definitely. You had very good sales down here. In fact if I were you I'd ask for an audit. I think they cheated you out of your royalties. Mr. Díaz is a fan, by the way. Look closely at the picture we took of his office in the packing plant. The bookcase by the door."

I searched through the prints, found the medium shot of the dingy cubicle. Behind the wooden desk, next to a tourist poster of Coahuila, a small bookcase. A familiar yellow tome with red letters lay on top, on its side.

"Why didn't you tell me before?"

"I thought you figured it out. Why else do you think you're coming along on this ride, amigo?"

"*Aquí es, aquí es!*" came the hoarse muffled cry of the prisoner.

Raymundo feebly pointed at a dirt road off the highway about five hundred feet away. A marker read forty-one kilometers. Ortega began to slow down the caravan.

"The mission is another twenty kilometers ahead," I said, double-checking the map.

"I know but slimeball in the back says this is where they took the kid first," said Ortega in English. "I want to see how they did it."

Ortega picked up the mike on his two-way radio, spoke quickly in Spanish for the other vehicles to follow him, then trundled carefully off the road, great clouds of dust rising behind us.

Half a mile from the highway the road dipped to a dry creek, boulders looming on either side, seemingly ready to roll down and crush our slow-moving caravan. We rose up an embankment and down a flat stretch of scrub, cacti and the odd cirios, their fingerlike thorny tops splayed against the cloudless sky. We bumped, heaved and swayed through the rough and rocky spots of the single track road. Four miles in we passed a concrete bunker with broken antennas and gauges rusting in the desert sun.

"Weather station," muttered Ortega. "It was left behind after a flash flood a few years ago. The two weathermen stationed out here drowned and nobody else has ever wanted to come back."

We drove on in silence, the air conditioner wheezing from the effort of keeping us halfway comfortable—the outside temperature gauge read 119 degrees F. The road finally ended at a stone gate with a wooden bar across it. Strands of barbed wire stretched for miles on either side of the gate as far as the eye could see.

"Rancho San Martín," snapped Ortega, stopping the vehicle. "Better clear that gate."

Ortega swung open his door, jumped off.

"Traemos al prisionero?" asked one of the officers.

"Sí, que salga," let him come out, said the lieutenant.

I got off as well, my legs tingling from sitting for so long. We had been driving nonstop for well over two hours. By the map we were somewhere east of the small fishing village of Santo Tomás. The jagged edges of the Sierra San Pedro Mártir, twenty miles away, were barely visible through the haze.

I walked over to Ortega, who was attempting to slide the padlocked chain out of the iron loop. He turned to one of the officers, who stood guard while Raymundo retched a stream of blood and vomit.

"Dame tu pistola," ordered Ortega. The man passed him his Beretta. Ortega slid the carriage back, fired three rounds at the padlock, which split open like torn fruit. Ortega kicked the bar open and strutted back to the Jeep.

"We may have some problems," he warned as we returned to the vehicle.

"Here?" I asked, letting Raymundo climb ahead of us. One of the policemen emptied his bladder, spraying a grove of spiny cholla cactus with gleeful abandon.

"Back in T.J.," said Ortega, who stopped and also unzipped his fly. He let out an arc of dark urine fly against the stone gate.

"This cattle ranch belongs to the family of the minister of finance, the Rochas. They're going to get mighty upset when they find out we broke our way in."

"Did you get a search warrant?"

The arc was down to a trickle.

"Couldn't get one even if I wanted it."

He shook himself.

"So?"

"So fuck 'em if they can't take a joke."

As I climbed back into the front seat, I caught a glimpse of something white, shining improbably from the peak of the highest mountain in the distance.

"Snow," said Ortega, turning on the engine. "We had a cold front last week. It'll melt in a few days. It's over ten thousand feet high, that one."

"What's it called?"

Ortega stepped on the accelerator, the Jeep humping over the rise of the road into the Rocha ranch.

"El Picacho del Diablo," he said, flatly, almost bored.

The Devil's Peak.

We drove on for another mile or so, the terrain gradually rising as we neared the foothills, the desert vegetation changing to the familiar chaparral of Southern California. At a narrow dirt road off the main trail we veered left, following Raymundo's instructions.

We halted at a small vale next to a cement pad where a house had stood years ago.

"My God," was all I could say. Ortega instinctively made the sign of the cross, just like the one we were facing.

On the upper beam of the cross hung the charred remains of a man. His hands and feet were nailed into the wood, his skin seared black from flames, his face a ghastly grimace of pain. Perched on the corpse, a vulture stuck its beak into a large cavity where the man's heart had been.

Ortega walked to the back of the Jeep, grabbed a double-ought shotgun and fired at the vulture, which fell to the ground, squawking and hollering like an infernal banshee. Ortega raised his weapon again, blew off the bird's head.

"Take that down, *órale!*" On the double! he shouted at his men.

The officers trooped out of the vehicles, their expressions convulsed with awe and disgust.

"Take it down now!"

The ruins of the mission straddled a narrow valley at the foot of a high brown sierra, the crumbling adobe buildings spreading out in a rough cross shape northward from the church. Although decaying from age and neglect, the stone pillars and Churri-gueresque facade bore witness to the wealth that the Franciscan fathers had once coaxed from an oasis in a barren inferno.

Our caravan had been joined by two other vans from the local police *prefectura*. Sixteen of us, heavily armed with submachine guns and all manner of automatic weapons, waited nervously on a rise about a quarter mile from the ruins. We watched the mission from behind a creosote bush, its fragrant leaves smelling oddly of dock pilings and faraway ports.

Down below we could see a car, a van, a pickup truck and a shiny new Land Rover parked by the only building that seemed to be in inhabitable shape, a mud-daubed hovel with a flat tin roof. Sweating in the heat, I could only imagine what the temperature inside that shed must be.

Ortega looked behind at his men, all out of view, waiting for the order to storm down. He passed me the binoculars.

"See? Over there, by that second *casita* in the back? The prisoner says that is where the ammo is kept."

I glanced down, the door to the hovel seemingly within arm's reach. A short, fat man in grimy jeans and checked shirt sat on a stool in the shade of the porch, slowly drinking a beer. I adjusted the lens, made out the brand—Tecate.

"Aren't you calling in a helicopter?" I asked.

Ortega smiled, took out a cigarette, stuck it in his mouth, chewing on the filter like the stub end of a rank cigar.

"We don't have money for that kind of thing. Even if we did, we'd have to bring it in from Ensenada and maybe someone would alert our boys. You know, people say this guy is the devil himself. They say he fell out of a ten-story window in Mexico City, landed on a car and just walked away, that he was shot at by a machine gun and that he survived."

"You don't really believe that," I said, glancing now at the main house. All of a sudden a window shutter slammed open.

Without warning Ricardo Díaz stuck his neck out, looked almost directly in our direction. Ortega quickly flattened himself against the dirt, his body obscured by the bush. I focused on Díaz—young, slender, angular, with abundant shiny chestnut hair which glistened in the sun, the high unlined forehead of a poet and a long nose that was immediately familiar.

Ortega snatched the binoculars from my hands.

"Give me that, the lens may glint in the sun!"

He tucked the glasses under his chest and resumed observing Díaz with the total concentration of the feline before he pounces on the sparrow—but I had a feeling this particular bird knew what was coming. Had he been tipped off? And if so, by whom? Or did he truly possesss some kind of sixth sense that had allowed him to escape countless ambushes and tell someone's history just by looking in their worried eyes?

Almost as if he'd heard my thoughts Díaz shook his head no, then closed the shutters.

"He's on to us," I said. Ortega nodded in agreement.

"Most likely he is. But he can't get out. We have cars on all the roads leading out. Behind him is the mountain and we are covering the front. We can rush him before he can get anywhere."

"So what are we waiting for?"

"Help," said Ortega, plainly, before sliding down the rise to his men, who double-checked their *cuernos de chivo,* their goat horns, the AK-47s beloved of drug smugglers and drug fighters alike.

My shirt was soaked through with perspiration, my mouth was as parched as the desert that surrounded us, my head buzzed from exhaustion. Just what kind of help were we waiting for? There couldn't have been more than a handful of people down in the mission. We outnumbered them and we outgunned them. What was the holdup?

I had my answer a few minutes later, when a battered Isuzu truck rolled down to our encampment. A uniformed policeman got off, then, from the passenger's side, alighted an old, pony-tailed Indian. Dressed all in white, multicolored beads slung around his neck, the old man grasped firmly a crucifix in one hand and a bottle of what could only be holy water in the other.

Ortega walked up to the old man, called him *Don* Roberto, embraced him and whispered rapidly in his ear. The grizzled old Indian shook his head, looked in the general direction of the mission, then, holding his cross aloft, moved to all four cardinal points, spraying the ground with holy water around us. A few of the men made the sign of the cross, muttering Hail Marys under their breath.

Ortega tapped me on the shoulder.

"Ready? Or would you rather stay back here and keep Raymundo company?"

He jerked his thumb at the prisoner, loosely chained to a cordón cactus.

"I want to come. I have my own devils to slay."

Ortega's wicked smile creased his face into a sweaty mask of malevolent joy.

"I thought as much."

We climbed back in the Jeep. Ortega rolled down his window, raised his hand silently for all the vehicles to ready themselves for the assault. Down the line, the drivers rolled down their windows too, the barrels of their guns sticking out like the quills of angry porcupines.

"Andale!" he shouted, lowering his hand, starting the engine and brutally flooring the accelerator. The Jeep hurled forward and raced down the grade. We were first over the ridge then, like a mechanized version of the cavalry, the other MPVs and vans rolled down, the officers firing a hail of bullets at the building.

The fat man at the porch dropped his beer and ran inside, but a bullet clipped him just as he reached the threshold. Two of our cars raced around the building to cover the rear and secure the weapons depot. The shutters in the adobe were slammed open once more and the barrel of two Uzis poked out, spewing a blizzard of hate out the building. The projectiles bounded off the armored paneling of our Jeep, as though we were the ones with the juju charm protecting us from harm.

Seeing they could not pierce our vehicle, the shooters aimed low at our tires. Ortega kept firing his Tac 11 even as the vehicle spun around when the right front tire exploded. We screeched into a three-quarter turn and halted in the sandy dirt about three hundred feet from the main building.

Now all our firepower aimed at the adobe, dozens of AK-47s, shotguns, handguns, the bullets taking out chunks of the building in great big jagged bites. Implausibly, three of the men inside broke out running, spraying wildly their submachine guns as they tried to make the few hundred feet to the ruins of the church. I recognized Díaz among them, firing his weapon with the abandon of a cornered commando.

"Cabrón, me las vas a pagar!" you'll pay for this, you bastard, shouted Ortega, who had to stop and reload his Tac 11.

The two men with Díaz fell to the ground next to him just a short distance from the mission, but Díaz, as though impervious to the laws of violence, as though his faith really did serve him as a shield, managed to clear the hundred feet distance and ran inside the church.

Ortega raised his hand to halt the fire, ordered four of his men to surround the building. Now, from inside the hut, a woman screamed, in pure American vernacular.

"No! No! Help me! They're going to kill me!"

The front door flew open. A curly-haired blonde, her khaki shorts and white blouse splattered with blood, raced outside toward us.

"Help! Help me!" she implored. "They're out to kill me!"

She hustled to our side, her patent leather boots raising cloudlets of dust around her ankles, then she threw herself on the ground face down, hands and feet outstretched to show she carried no weapons. One of the officers patted her down with more than a little gusto even in the heat of gunfire, slapped handcuffs on her.

We heard four shots from inside the adobe hut, then silence.

Ortega ordered his men to keep an eye on the church and ran to the adobe, flattening himself against the wall. He wheeled inside, the barrel of his machine gun leading the way. He came back out, shaking his head in a gesture that was half surprise and half a strange compassion.

"They're all dead in there. Three guys. Looks like suicide."

I huddled behind the Jeep, a .45 in my hand. I hadn't fired and I was hoping I wouldn't have to.

"Vamos a la iglesia!" shouted Ortega, who ran for the ruins, positioning himself behind a fallen pilaster.

"Come on out with your hands up, Díaz!"

"Never!" shouted Díaz from inside the building. Ortega nodded at two of his men nearest him, then all three rushed the church, guns blazing. They stopped when they reached the ruins, staring wide-eyed as a vulture flapped its wings almost mockingly and flew out the open doors of the church.

I raised my gun, firing for the first time. The shot missed and the ghastly bird soared away, squawking malevolently as though mocking us for our efforts.

Ortega entered the church, then quickly came back out, surprise splattered all over his face.

"He's gone," he said in English, "the son of a bitch is gone!"

CHAPTER

11

THE media had a field day.

The Mexican press harped on the bloodcurdling evil of the *narcosatánicos,* the devil-worshipping drug traffickers, aware that other, more tempting morsels were political forbidden fruit. No mention was made in the Spanish language media of who owned the ranch where the victim was found or what kind of official complicity had allowed a band of homicidal satanists to take up residence at a historical monument. As if on cue, Mexican reporters turned up interviews with frightened peons who invariably said they had suspected there was something foul in the chaparral but never knew where to turn to.

Ultimately a combined task force of local police, Mexico City prosecutors and Ortega's own haunted *federales* would dig up a total of fifteen rotting corpses from the ranch and the mission grounds. All the buried victims—men, women and children—had been tortured to death, some with their genitals, heart and other vital organs ripped out while they were still alive.

Two of Díaz's band survived: a short, pockmarked transvestite named Rogelio and the glamour queen who had thrown herself at our feet. The fact that Rogelio had blown away his jaw in an unsuccessful attempt to commit suicide when we stormed the mission left him slightly out of reach. That put our captured American babe in charge of the official story and she massaged it for all it was worth.

Twenty-five years old, a former Miss Palos Verdes beauty queen and student of comparative religion at UCLA, Miss Miranda Decker was uncommonly photogenic, a gifted conversationalist and, incidentally, the daughter of the head of the Republican Caucus of the California State Senate, the Honorable Tom Decker from Orange County.

Now this was real news any red-blooded American reporter could sink his teeth into. So what if fifteen wetbacks had been slaughtered in grisly fashion, and that the main suspect, a Cuban-American, had conveniently managed to escape a Mexican police dragnet. Everyone knows south of the border different rules apply. As for the crucified college student, when word leaked out that he had come to Tijuana to score a few kilos of pot, nobody felt too sorry for him either. But a fair-haired beauty of political breeding involved in all this, claiming she was brainwashed and held against her will, a postmodern Patty Hearst shacking up with Charlie Manson in tortilla land, now that was real news.

Media reps from around the world converged on the high school auditorium taken over by the Tijuana police for a press conference the day after we returned. On a long table set midstage, Mexican authorities stacked all the implements of war and torture they had found at the mission and the ranch. Full-color pictures of the victims' remains were handed out like mint candy to the pressing reporters, while, sitting behind the table, a collection of overfed officials from different agencies claimed credit for solving a crime they had refused to acknowledge before.

The star was Miss Decker, who had changed into a pristine white Mexican wedding dress for her appearance. Morbid curiosity drew me to the auditorium. Ortega's people waved me inside, clapping me on the back for a job well done. An *L.A. Times* stringer took a picture of me but I managed to elude the bearded, tequila-smelling hack they sent down to cover the story. I stood in the back of the hall and listened incredulously to Ms. Decker's tearful assertions of innocence. She wove a sorry tale of innocence deceived, how as a gullible UCLA student she had been seduced by the deep pools of hazel that were Ricardo Díaz's eyes; how his hypnotic spell was such that when he ordered you to do something you couldn't find it in yourself to say no. I walked out when she started quoting from Revelation about the coming of the Beast.

I ran across Ortega in the parking lot, sullenly smoking, staring at the hills across the border as though challenging Díaz to come back.

"You should be in there. It was your operation."

"The big pigs always push the little ones out of the trough," he said in Spanish. He threw down his cigarette, furiously stepped on it.

"Any idea how Díaz got away?"

"None. We searched the place up and down. Didn't find a tunnel, secret passage, *nada*. If I didn't know any better I'd swear he was that buzzard. But I know better, brother. He just outsmarted us, that's all. This time. Just this time."

"You think you'll ever find him?"

"Oh, I'll find him, all right, I promise you. I'll get him if I have to come back from the grave to do it."

. . .

I was stunned when I came up to the border crossing at San Ysidro and found myself in the middle of a noontime traffic jam. While Ortega and I had been trying to capture Díaz for the past forty-eight hours, the rest of the world had gone on its merry way as always, hustling, scheming, fighting for a bigger slice of the pie. People had died, evil had been foiled, dubious good had triumphed, but the human ant cared not at all for that, thinking only of the bread crumb it would take back to its ant hill, hopefully a bigger, tastier crumb than yesterday's or last week's. Forget the heel that could crush them, or the flood from the hosing down of destiny, that was all speculation; the only thing that mattered was the greasy bread crumb to feast on back home.

That was why people like Díaz were so dangerous, so destabilizing. They offered the easy way out, the crumb without the work, golden futures without toil. Just turn in your soul at the door and leave the rest to your friendly fiend.

Satanism, drugs, orgiastic sex, it was all of a kind, people seeking transcendence from their situation, from this life and this accursed flesh, from the job and the wife and the kids and the mortgage payments and the credit cards and all the panoply of our consumer society. With a flick of the wrist, a line of toot or two, a couple of dead chickens and a bleating goat—even the goat without horns, man—Díaz would make everything all right. You'd be in the driver's seat, achieving your wildest dreams, stepping away from the ceaseless toil that is the fate of the ant and, like a grasshopper, you'd sing a song of freedom.

You'd still be an insect. But at least you'd be free.

Like Miranda Decker. Like my own sister.

All at once Celia's sad countenance sprang to my mind's eye

and I finally understood the mystical connection between *santería* and the tons of powder the lords of Cali peddle our way. They don't just sell ecstasy, they sell talismans, magic carpets secreted in two-kilogram plastic-wrapped bundles.

I couldn't blame Celia for falling for that line.

Not one bit.

Because I too sought magical transport from our impoverished exile. She looked for it in slim-hipped boys and bags of a white powdery substance; I found it in icy blondes and thick tomes of law. Escapees, both of us, refusing to acknowledge our confinement. Displaced and penniless, we were embittered from having to start anew in a sleepy resort town run as a fiefdom by a handful of Southern crackers, from being Spanish-speaking scum pushing broomsticks, mopping floors and wiping dipsticks. That is why *santería* has become so big in Miami, when in Cuba it was the province only of the poor, the black and the dispossessed (all synonymous once upon a time). *Santería* is the magical door to the land of Anglo wealth, to the kingdom of God on this earth and not, like Christianity, to bliss in the hereafter.

My poor sister.

My poor people.

"Anything to declare?" asked the smiling young Customs woman, face full of freckles, California sunshine in her voice.

"A heavy heart," I said, realizing I'd been daydreaming for too long.

"Can't help you there, dude," she said brightly, waving me through. "Don't party so hard next time."

"I'll try and remember that."

I swung down the visor, lifted the mirror flap, looked at my reflection. Haggard, unshaven, unbathed, my tongue covered with a thousand coats. I closed the mirror. There would be time enough for self-inspection later.

After the raid I'd checked into a cheap motel by the Tijuana *prefectura* and tried unsuccessfully to reach Lisa in San Diego. I left a message so I could tell her what had happened but the next thing I knew it was morning. I had fallen asleep in the rawhide chair, my head resting on the rusted iron and glass table in my room. Lisa never called.

Cars honked, weaved and cut in front of me during my drive back. I ignored them, my eyes stabbed by the piercing reflection of the sun on the windshields and chrome strips of the cars trapped by the early rush hour. Traffic finally dropped away once I left downtown behind and by the time I swung off the I-5 to La Jolla Village Drive, I had the road practically to myself.

A black Jaguar followed me north on Torrey Pines Road. I kept my eye on the vehicle, thinking it was tailing me, and for a moment my heart raced wildly, fearing the improbable. But for once in my life the improbable turned out to be just that and at the Salk Institute the sedan slunk off and melted into the driveway greenery.

I can't say I was surprised when I opened the door to our hotel room and found Lisa had checked out. She had packed up all her things, leaving only the fragrance of her perfume floating in the stillness of the empty room. A small handwritten note had been stuck in the frame of the dresser mirror. I stepped outside to the balcony to read it in the cool clean air of a sunny California afternoon, miles away from the dust, blood and madness of Mexico.

"Dear Charlie,

"I'm sorry but I can't wait anymore. Since you are so busy with your cases, I thought I should take care of my own life.

"See you in L.A. Maybe.

"Lisa."

I set down the note on the glass table and stared at the blue Pacific. A handful of surfers bobbed patiently amid the mounds of tinsel that pretended to be waves. I waited for a brace of dolphins to jump up and carouse, just as they had when Lisa and I checked in, but they had moved on. Only masses of dark seaweed drifted in, lapping onto the shore.

Still exhausted, I walked back into the room and collapsed in bed. I meant to call de Palma to find out why she really had me follow Díaz but I fell asleep all at once, as though the weight of tragedy had remained on the other side of the tainted river.

Then I dreamed of Díaz.

As in Lisa's dream, he was a darkness felt before it was witnessed. My room door opened of its own accord and Díaz flew inside, like a vulture or a bat, opening and closing his black cape, showing himself naked under the cloth as he perched on the edge of the dresser and stared at me, still sprawled unconscious on the bed covers.

"No me conoces, mi hermano?" don't you know me, brother, came the honeyed voice, so soothing, so fatal. "You're never going to fuck me, Charlie. You know that. I'm unstoppable."

In the dream I rubbed my eyes open, sat up and looked at him. Streaming rays of sunlight issued from the back of his head and a deep voice from below rumbled a message in a language I couldn't recognize as a cloying smell of boiling molasses and burning fat filled the room. Then Díaz laughed and he spread his arms again opening his cape, and he flew out the window.

I turned and glanced in the mirror.

I was horrified. His face was my face. I had become the monster.

I woke up with a start, sweat pouring out of me. Outside the open balcony door night spread its starry mantle. I heard laughter again, a deep maniacal cackle coming from outside. I ran to the balcony.

Down below, skimming the cliffs, a great black bird spread its wings and flew east into the darkened hills.

Kelsey was waiting by my front door when the taxi I'd taken at Union Station dropped me off.

"Lisa told us you were in Mexico. Was it something I said?"

I ignored his wisecrack, walked around him to my door.

"You heard about Armando's killer?" I asked.

"Hey, these things take time. What the hell, you're still alive."

"Don't put yourself out, Michael."

"You know some animal messed up your backyard?" he added, pointing at the side path to the rear.

"You came all the way to Pasadena to tell me a bear came down from the woods? I didn't know LAPD was working the Park Rangers. I didn't know you were working Pasadena. In fact, I didn't know you were working, period. All you ever do is mouth off."

I had just opened the door when Kelsey grabbed me by the shoulder, spun me violently around. He stuck his face next to mine, the edge of his morning beer still on his breath, little capillaries swelling with rage over his dilated nostrils.

"Listen, asshole, I don't know who popped you but you're smelling like shit right now. You're trying to wiggle out of it but you're not going to wiggle out of it while I'm around, *comprende?*"

I pushed him back outside, stepped inside the supposed sanctuary of my home.

"Get your fucking hands off me, Michael! I don't know what the fuck is wrong with you but I'm tired, I'm dirty, and I want to go to sleep in my own bed. Now stop pushing me around or I'll file a brutality suit with IA so fast it'll make your fat head spin like a cheap Chink top. Now fuck off!"

Kelsey rose, all six foot three, two hundred eighty pounds of Irish bad temper up and atremble, his face as red as a boiled beet.

"I can slap you a warrant in a New York minute," he growled.

"Then I suggest you go get it."

I shoved the door shut but he stuck his foot to stop it from closing.

"Where were you two nights ago at ten forty-five P.M.?" he said, speaking flatly, soberly. That's when I knew he wasn't just trying to goose me.

"I don't know. I was in fucking San Diego, fucking my fucking girlfriend. Or rather, fucking my fucking ex—fucking girlfriend. What is your point, Michael?"

"Come 'round the back," he said, shoving the door open again. I dropped my bag in the foyer and followed him out.

My house sat on an irregular three-quarter-acre lot, its size being one of the reasons I bought in Pasadena instead of Los Angeles. The equivalent house in my former neighborhood of Los Feliz would have set me back well over a million dollars instead of the four hundred thousand I paid, using up every penny I had from selling my book to the movies and then some. The eucalyptus trees, the running trail right next to the Arroyo Seco, it all had seemed like an Arts and Crafts, Greene and Greene home illustration when I bought it. Yet when Kelsey led me to the backyard and I saw the yellow police tape, the place became a lost Eden and I knew I wouldn't be able to live there much longer.

A couple of technicians from SID, the Special Investigations Division, were still going over the grounds, picking up samples, rechecking their measurements. Kelsey didn't have to say much; I knew right away I was staring at a working murder site.

"Call came in yesterday morning from the outfit that keeps an eye on your house," said Kelsey, walking with me down the side path. He lit another of his generic supermarket cigarettes.

"They'd sent a guard out here to check out a report of a noise of a suspicious origin. The guy walked right into it, probably caught him trying to break into your house."

We stopped by the window of the rear storage room. A bed of petunias had been trampled, the white flecks of plaster in the mud showing a mold had been taken already. The pool of blood had caked dry on the flagstones. On the baby blue siding the killer had written, in blood,

"See you soon, Charlie!" and then added, "XXOO"—love and kisses.

The nightmare crawled back inside my skin. Would I ever escape?

"How did he kill him?" I asked.

"Sliced his throat to the backbone, then snapped off the head. Which he took with him. No prints, no sign of forced entry. I guess he gave up after he had his fun and games."

"Meaning?"

"He sodomized the guard after he killed him. We found the patrol car up by JPL."

I nodded, Kelsey's words coming through a filter of wounded consciousness.

"That means he had an accomplice following him?"

"That's our working assumption. Or maybe after he dumped the guard's car he stole another car and drove off. Don't know for sure right now."

"I have them, sergeant!" cried one of the officers, tramping through the bush up the slope from the arroyo.

"Found them in a nest. Good thing I remembered crows eat raw meat, eh, sergeant?"

The fresh-faced officer came near us, holding up in his white latex glove two gristly black pieces of all too human flesh.

"The guard's testicles," added Kelsey, unnecessarily.

NOTHING had changed, yet nothing was the same. During the two weeks I stayed away from the Criminal Courts Building the sky had not fallen, the streets had not buckled and the buildings had not been swallowed by the earth, in spite of some people's fondest wishes. But the gradual deterioration of the city was a cinch to spot when I returned, as though no one—cops, politicians or voters—gave a damn about the aging, arteriosclerotic heart of Los Angeles, every day clogged with more garbage, junkers and loonies.

I saw more beggars downtown than I'd seen in Tijuana. Each and every one was an around-the-bend case, from the dotty white old lady reciting Psalms and panhandling for quarters at the bus stop by the Civil Courthouse, to the wild-eyed Asian woman skulking around the MIA park singing snatches of opera in a clear mezzo, down to the gaunt, half-naked black men, shadows of death ambling down the middle of Broadway holding up their pants with one hand and gesturing at the indifferent sky above, remembering to beg for meals only when the voices in their head stopped their chatter long enough for the rest of humanity to sweep back into view.

The wheezing RTD buses were still jammed full of brown-skinned passengers, the long-suffering Hispanic underclass that keeps the wheels of commerce humming in the Southland; the Mexican hot dog vendors still stirred their grilled onions in their carts, the smell of cooking fat mingling with the diesel exhaust of the buses and the growing stench of human waste from the homeless encampment in the ruins across City Hall.

Something scurried across my foot as I waited for the light at Broadway and Temple. I glanced to my left. In front of the old Hall of Justice building, now boarded up and marred with gang graffiti, on the dried-out front lawn once so carefully tended by County Jail inmates, swarmed a pack of rats. There were rats feasting on the bread crumbs bird lovers scattered for the pigeons; rats gnawing on discarded chicken bones tossed by the homeless sleeping in the bushes; rats munching on a pile of rice and beans vomited by a drunk overnight; an army of well-fed, sleek rats taking their leisurely meal on a sunny morning.

At the bus stop, a little curly-haired Mexican girl, shiny gold studs in each tiny earlobe, waved her pudgy hands at a long-tailed Norway rat a few feet away. The rodent, as big as a small cat, came in close, wrinkling its nose, writhing its tail.

I hollered, banged the fence with my briefcase. At once, the rats took flight, darting for the safety of the bushes and the ever growing layers of garbage—pieces of cardboard, old shoes, empty Styrofoam boxes, crumpled issues of the *Times* and *La Opinión.*

I crossed Temple and raced down the flight of stairs to the Criminal Courts Building. An Asian security guard was barking

orders at a scrawny Hispanic gangbanger, size fifty pants floating on a twenty-four-inch waist, tight white tank top hugging a
pigeon chest. The boy's head was shaved convict clean, the
dread initials of the Mara Salva Trucha gang tattooed on his
neck. On the bridge of his nose the numbers 666 wriggled with
biblical fervor.

"Take off the buckle," said the weary guard.

The boy removed his dirk-shaped buckle, holding his enormous pants with one hand, to the giggles of his two *ruchas*, his
gangland girlfriends, their eyes rimmed in black, hennaed hair
in long jelled ringlets, voluptuous figures barely covered by
flimsy rayon spaghetti strap dresses.

The guard looked dubiously at the buckle.

"This here looks like a weapon, you're going to have to check
it in."

"Hey, man, how am I going to hold up my pants?"

The guard moved in closer, ran a handheld metal detector
over the boy.

"Okay, okay," he said, handing back the buckle, "just go in."

"Pinche chino," muttered the young man as he ambled to the
bank of elevators, proud girlfriends by his side.

I placed my briefcase on the X-ray machine's conveyor belt,
took my metal wristwatch, placed it and my key ring in a blue
plastic bowl and stepped through the standing metal detector. It
buzzed.

"This way, counsel," said a squat female guard, running her
detector over me. "What's that in your pocket?"

I extracted a roll of foil-covered mints.

"That'll do it."

As I pocketed my change a young black man hushed two
friends sneaking in through a side entrance around the corner
from the metal detector.

Behind me, Bob Gordon, the assistant head deputy of the Sex

Crimes Unit, was undergoing his own third degree. He glanced at me, embarrassed.

"I left my badge home," he mumbled, before being waved on.

"It's not fair, you don't see the judges going through this," he bickered as we pressed in together, headed for the erratic elevators. "They cruise in, park in the basement, take their private elevator and bingo, they're in chambers."

"The perks of power, Bob," said Terry Longo, late as always for his latest multidefendant, multikilogram coke bust preliminary hearing. "It's like *Damn Yankees,* remember? Whatever Lola wants, Lola gets."

"Wait a minute, Terry," I replied as he turned away. "Wasn't Lola working for the devil?"

"Hey, if the shoe fits," he said, dashing away.

Bob and I squeezed into the upper-floors elevator moments before the door snapped shut like a guillotine. An unshaven man planted himself inches away from me, reeking of a Russian distillery.

"Charlie, don't you know the rule?"

I turned to Roger Tippitoe, standing behind me. A bald walrus of a man, he had become, by dint of personality and TV advertising, the king of drunk driver defendants.

"What's the rule?"

"The rule is, he who has the power to make rules follows the rules he likes. And now, if you'll excuse me, the one who has the power is waiting for me in Department 100."

He exited at the thirteenth floor, taking the Stoli lover and half of the other passengers in his wake. The remaining half got off on the fifteenth. I ascended to the DA's office on the eighteenth all by myself, admiring the Rolling '60's gang graffiti etched on the brushed steel doors.

●

Lisa sat lightly on her Wassily chair in her office, deep in conversation with a man whose broad back was turned to the open door. She lifted her eyes the moment I walked through, quickly removing her hand from the man's knee.

She stood, pecked me on the cheek, looked at me intently for a beat, her look a commingling of regret, pride and relief.

"Sorry I didn't stay, Charlie. If only I'd known."

"That's all right, I understand. Too hot not to cool down, right?"

Might as well be a good sport about it, I thought. It had been over between us long before this madness infected us, only we didn't know it.

She didn't reply but nodded with more than a twinge of regret, then gestured at the man in her office.

"You remember Phil."

Phil Fuentes stood up. We'd met years before, at the beginning of his precipitous ascent in the office, when I was still a private investigator and he was handling gangbanger cases. I'd lost the trial, a drive-by shooting on a donut shop in Pico Union, but I never held it against Phil. For one thing my client was guilty. For another, Phil's personality was so sugary it was hard to hold a grudge against him for long. It would have been like hating the golden retriever who snatches the partridge out of the bush and lies, panting and eager to be petted, at your feet. Phil was now DA Antonetti's right-hand man, groomed as his possible successor should the big A run for state attorney general as everyone expected him to.

We shook hands, charisma exuding from his every pore like the smell of garlic from a Korean. Tall, with thick wavy black hair, beaming brown eyes and olive skin complexion, he made other men feel that they were his inferiors but that he wasn't going to hold it against them.

"We've gotten reports from the FBI and the DEA on Díaz." He gestured at a stack of files on Lisa's desk. "They would love for us to turn over our evidence so they can make this a federal case."

"Are you going to?" I asked.

He shook his head with the dolorous stock expression hacks trot out for matters of life and death. For the briefest moment I wondered whether Phil ever stopped acting or whether posturing was simply the way he chose to lead his life.

"Antonetti says no way and I concur. If we pass it along they'll just make it another count in the indictment. Besides, Armando Ponce's murder is special circs and with the Polly Klass thing now, this is a slam-dunk fryer."

"That's assuming Díaz is ever captured," I rejoined.

"He'll fall all right. Kind like him has got to strike, that's what he lives for. Our job is to be there when he does it."

"Phil, I hate to remind you but you're no longer with the Sheriff's. And our black and blue are not exactly known for their perspicacity. Nowadays they want a court order for a jaywalking ticket."

"Well, what do you want after King and all that bullshit? Let's skip to brass tacks, okay? We got to capture this *cabrón* or he's going to put a brake on the system," he said with a nice-guy smile.

"Your system," I said, equally smiley.

"Everybody's. And we think you might be the guy who brings him in."

"Funny. That's what Kelsey said. All you guys seem to think I know something you don't."

"C'mon, Charlie, you know all about this hocus-pocus voodoo *brujería santería* bullshit stuff. We need a profile and we figure you gotta know what makes this guy tick."

"Lust for power, an affliction that befalls a lot of people," I replied. He grinned once more.

"Touché. But most of us don't go around slaughtering our fellow human beings to get it."

"But that's the whole point, you see."

"No, I don't see," he said, a touch of anger beginning to steel his voice. "What are you talking about?"

"To Díaz, we're not human. We're animals. If we're not members of his cult, if we are not one of the chosen, killing us is as inconsequential as stepping on a roach. Messy, but nothing to lose sleep over."

"That's so evil," said Lisa.

"No, Lisa, wrong. He's beyond good and evil, he's in another world."

I paused, letting the words sink in. They both stared back, now more convinced than ever that I held the key to the case.

Phil looked almost hungrily at me.

"How much *do* you know about this guy? Can you give us a profile?"

I leaned back, wondering just how much I could safely disclose without revealing my secret suspicions. I had a feeling I was tied to Díaz in more ways than I cared to imagine and I didn't quite have the heart to admit it even to myself. Looking out the window, the columns of white smoke bellowed from the foundry like the evil plumes of Bergen-Belsen. Again I smelled the foul odor of death, in Armando's house, at the mission in Baja, in my own backyard. Destruction was all around me, the end was near. But whose, his or mine?

"You realize I'm not a professional at this," I countered. Phil shook his head; he wasn't going to let me off that easy.

"I know, but what's your take on him all the same? How far will he go, if he thinks we're no better than insects. What's he after?"

"Like I said, power is his goal. And eternal life. I don't know what the FBI has been telling you but I would assume he comes from a poor, powerless background, most likely a single-parent household. He was a loner, always in trouble with other kids, maybe because of his single-parent status, maybe because he was poor or because of his parent's religion. He harbors deep feelings of revenge against society. And he saw *santería* as his ticket out of his powerlessness. He's the kind to whom all these magic rites appeal so much, makes them feel special. When you think you have the cards stacked against you, you change the deck. That's what makes him different from other serial killers."

"If that's the case, then how do you explain Miranda Decker?" asked Lisa. "There's a girl who had everything, her father is a powerhouse in the state GOP, yet she joins up with this guy."

"You always have to allow for personal idiosyncrasies, the rich kid who becomes a drug addict and shoots up his life away, et cetera. But if I'm not mistaken Miranda does fit part of the profile. Wasn't her mother divorced from the senator? Didn't she grow up separated from him?"

"Not exactly," said Fuentes. "Her mother died and the senator remarried when Miranda was in her teens. That's the one he divorced, not her natural mother. You know, I met her dad."

"No kidding. Tell me how."

Phil suddenly blushed, as though he'd let flash the ace in his vest pocket.

"He's an alum. I met him on rush week, he was touring the campus with his son, Miranda's half-brother."

"Whoa, hold on a second. Where was this?"

"Phi Delta Kappa."

"USC?"

"Uh-hum. I got a scholarship, you know."

"Did the kid make it?"

"He was only in for a semester before he transferred to Stanford. Rod's his name. Great tennis player. Killer backhand."

"Gee, that's nice. So, what did the senator tell you about his daughter's troubles? Are you going to pin it all on Díaz, the Jim-Jones-the-devil-made-me-do-it defense? Or maybe it wasn't his idea, maybe you're doing all this on your own and you'll stick him with the bill later on, when you're up for office your-self?"

"What are you two talking about?" asked Lisa, her thin eye-brows clenched together in puzzlement. Phil waved his hands in the air, as though shooing away some pesky fly.

"This has nothing to do with my relationship to the senator," said Phil, defiantly. "Look, okay, so maybe the old man called asking for my advice but that's natural. He wants to know what's going to happen to his daughter if she's extradited back to the States. In any case, it's all speculation, she's not in our custody, she's still in Mexico, remember?"

Phil's protestations just made it more apparent, this was all a song and dance. But for whose benefit? And how much did they know?

"Yes, my friend, but we are both very much aware of how the system works in Mexico. For all we know she's already on her way to Sacramento after the *mordida* and if she still has this little thing pending in L.A. where she could be held as an aider and abettor to Armando's death, then things could be very *caliente* indeed for Goldilocks. Witnesses spotted our little princess driving the getaway car."

He flushed, stammered, cornered. "Who told you that?"

"Educated guess. I didn't think a West Side babe would stoop so low as to actually kill somebody, but I'm sure she wouldn't mind being at the wheel or even handing him the knife."

"You never told me any of that," said Lisa, looking reproach-fully at Phil.

"It hadn't come up," he replied, shrugging.

"When was it going to come up? When you went through your files and you discovered Díaz had actually been in custody and you had refused to press charges? This was about three years ago, a Ponzi setup. You were in Consumer Affairs for a while, weren't you, Phil?"

"I hope you're not implying that I let a known murderer go, because if you are, you should take it up with the State Bar."

"No, it's not that serious. We're not talking murder, at least not that we know of. We're talking about embarrassment. I read the Díaz case file the San Diego DA had. One of his victims was a certain Judge John Kramer. Name ring a bell?"

"The presiding judge?" asked Lisa, looking incredulously at Phil.

"That's right. This was before Kramer rose to such empyrean heights. You were the deputy assigned to the case, Phil. Somehow Judge Kramer's name never came up in any of the news accounts. It would have been interesting to find out how a Superior Court judge thought he could get a hundred percent return on his $10,000 investment in thirty days without thinking he was getting involved in something illegal. I mean, it's true judges come from another planet, but that kind of judicial naïveté would have been hard to swallow, even in Los Angeles. Luckily for Kramer he never had to answer the questions. Shortly thereafter he became presiding judge and you were assigned to his courtroom until Antonetti picked you out. I don't know if Díaz had anything to do with that, after all I'm sure you're a handy guy to know if you're in a political pickle, but I wouldn't want to look too closely at that evidence either."

Phil got to his feet, veins in his neck throbbing from barely controlled anger, then took a deep breath, thought better of it and sat down again. He grabbed a copy of *Vogue* from the desk and leafed it so violently the pages came off in his hands.

"What's the name of that high horse you're riding, Morell?"

"I'm not riding any high horse, Phil. And frankly I don't even know why I bothered. Complaining about sleaziness in L.A. is like bitching about the smog, it comes with the territory. I suppose this is a roundabout way of telling you that I'm not going to get involved in your gyp."

I got up, started to walk out but Phil's voice stopped me.

"So where you gonna go, Charlie?"

He glanced up from the ripped Versace ad. "We're the only game in town."

"I know. God help L.A."

Down at Broadway and Temple a raggedy preacher, dressed in dingy white, held up his Bible like a searchlight, bellowing time and again at the top of his lungs:

"What shall it profit a man to gain the world if he loses his soul?"

The rats were out in full force again at the Hall of Justice. I didn't scare them, I didn't shoo them away, I simply waded through the crowd and headed on down to my car.

Unlike the dubious preacher, I'm not so sure about salvation, at least on this earth. Besides, I wasn't expecting Divine Providence to mount a rescue operation. I knew I had to do that myself. After all, if we are but instruments of His will, then our actions are the vehicles that make Him manifest. Therefore it was my obligation, through my deeds, to render Him present.

God needs us as much as we need Him, for where would God be without His creation, without the universe, the plants and the stars, the hosts of seraphim, cherubim, archangels and other minor angels on His shoulder, even the dark evil spirits that He allows to exist for reasons known only unto Him? Our very existence exalts the Lord and our lives—be we sinners, saints or just ordinary people trying to live ordinary lives in extraordinary times, which is always—confirm that we are but a troubled reflection of our Serene Maker.

That was the message of a Greek theologian from the fourth

century, a time much like our own, troubled by decay, violence and the clash of cultures. But I doubt that even the saintly Bishop Athanasius of Alexandria would have known what to make of the jarring dislocation of Los Angeles. He would have been hard pressed to imagine a place where the fair denizens of the north and the dark-hued people of the south, the straight-haired and curly-haired, the round-eyed and the slant-eyed, the short and the tall and the thin and the fat, all the people of all races from all corners of the world would come and meet and hustle and bustle and shove and shout and claim their own stake of land on the streets of a city that was stolen and passed from hand to hand to hand for centuries until at the end every-one owned it and therefore no one did and everyone opened their stores and sold their goods and offered their services and raised their troublesome children under the same polluted sky in the semiarid corner that once was the closest thing to Para-dise man had ever known. Not only would the Bishop have had to imagine it, he would have had to accept it. That would have been the hardest part, just as it is for so many Angelenos.

Perhaps good Athanasius could have told us where is the face of God in the streets of Los Angeles today. Because I certainly did not see Him anywhere. In fact, I couldn't even find the person I was looking for in the crowded corners of Pico Union, amid the statuettes, potted herbs and cheap charms of Botánica Row, one small *santería* shop after another like so many prayers for love and redemption.

At a T-shirt outlet where once the *botánica* Yemayá Siete Potencias had stood, a walnut-skinned stub of a woman finally told me that the party I was looking for had moved out by Rancho Calamigos. She had bought out the shop from the party, originally intending to keep it as was, but when she found Jesus amid the clapping and the shouting and the speaking of tongues of the Iglesia Manantial de Agua Viva, the Source of Living Water Church, she had given up the cause of the Evil One. Now the only demon she trucked with was the counterfeit Tasmanian Devil printed on the cheap Chinese cotton garments hanging from her racks. She did, however, have the address of the party, and would I like to buy a T-shirt for my wife or my girlfriend or maybe even my child?

That was how I wound up with a bag of folded T-shirts bearing the helmeted visage of Marvin the Martian stashed in the back seat of my car as I trundled up a steep grade off Kanan Road, ten miles uphill from Malibu.

When the dirt road wound around a bend, a sliver of blue Pacific glinted like the last hope of the far horizon. The road then plunged into a private valley, at the far end of which stood a lonely wooden cabin. I drove up to the house, stopped the car, got out.

The noise of a thousand crickets assaulted my ears like the rat-tat-tat of a machine gun. The air was stifling, the sun burning like I was back in Baja and not just forty minutes away from the spires of downtown L.A.

A small creek ran behind the cabin, its coolness a welcome relief from the afternoon's scorching heat. The structure was little more than a lean-to, made of unpainted plywood panels and rolled red roofing. Someone had tried to white out the swastikas painted on the front door without much success. I knocked.

"Anybody home?"

No answer. I knocked again. Silence still.

I tried the door handle. It gave and opened into the shack. I stepped inside.

It took my eyes a few seconds to adjust to the dim interior. In a space roughly twenty by thirty feet, a cot was lodged against one wall, next to a small bookcase and battery-operated camper's lamp. In the far-off wall, a rudimentary kitchen—a sink with a hand well pump, a small propane gas stove, vegetables and fruits in wooden bins. By the nearest wall, an enormous

multitiered altar, as high as the cabin itself, stacked with statuettes of saints and dozens of bowls containing offerings of fruit
and beads.

I was about to step closer to the altar when I heard a cocking
sound. I turned.

A tall, short-haired woman, dressed all in white, covered the
doorway, pointing what looked like a snub-nosed .38 Colt at me.

"What the hell are you doing here?" she asked.

CHAPTER

S HE entered, wheeling around slowly, keeping the gun trained on me. I didn't dare move. Amateurs have twitchy fingers and I was afraid she might not recognize me after all those years.

She moved to the corner nightstand, her white garments vibrating in the darkened hut, as though still reflecting the violent sun outside. Turning on the camper's lamp, she squinted at me, searching her memory, then brought down her gun, ruefully shaking her head.

"*Coño, Charlie, tu mami* didn't teach you not to break into people's houses unannounced?"

"Hey, Shana, I thought, you know, *mi casa es su casa.*"

She came over, hugged me. She smelled of wild sage and Florida water, the universal cologne of those whose life is guided by the worship of the saints. I felt like an old Roman, chastely embraced by a vestal priestess.

"It's been a long time," she said, stepping back for a better look. She sat on the cot, pointed at a Mexican rawhide stool. "Sorry about the gun, some punks have been coming around, painting graffiti on the cabin. Had to drive them off."

"Still your father's daughter," I said, sitting on the stool.

"And Catalina's kid," she added, with the same crystalline laughter that once, almost, bewitched me.

Back then her hair was longer, falling in honey blond tresses around a small, apple-cheeked face, her round blue eyes shining with charm and determination. The only daughter of a U.S. marine and a Cuban schoolteacher, Shana had been instructed in the ways of *santería* as a child. She had turned her back on the religion during the usual display of adolescent rebellion but had come back to the saints after the death of her imperious mother. She must have been in her early twenties when we met, a willowy part-time model heartbroken with grief, following Armando's footsteps and hoping to become one of a handful of female *babalawos.*

I'm not sure if she was ever aware of how taken I was with her melancholy beauty but I never took it beyond the infatuation stage. Making love to her would have been like romancing the bishop's niece or, more to the point, the village priest's. Instead I kept my feelings to myself and merely admired, from afar, a beauty that was never to be mine.

Now the softness in her face was gone, her cheekbones high and sharp, her skin golden brown from the sun, her tall body honed down to muscular slimness. She looked like the kind of woman who could hike thirty miles and still think nothing of playing two sets of tennis—or chop down a tree and haul the firewood back another thirty miles.

"Strange you should be here today, Charlie," she said, walking over to the makeshift kitchen. "I had a dream about you. Tea?"

"No, thanks. It was a good dream, I hope."

She took a kettle, filled it with bottled water, lit the Coleman stove.

"I don't know, Charlie. There's a lot of unresolved tension in our relationship," she said coolly, measuring some loose tea from a can.

"Excuse me?" I said, surprised, her comment as seemingly out of place as a prayer to Shangó in a psychiatrist's office.

"I had a crush on you when we met years ago," she said, matter-of-fact. "It was the hardest thing for me to forget about it while I was being initiated by Armando. Luckily he said you were an honorable man. At times I wished you hadn't been."

She turned, fine features beaming with pixieish pride, if you can call a six-foot-one, hundred-and-sixty-pound Amazon any kind of pixie.

"Don't look so worried, that baby's dead," she added.

I closed my gaping mouth and pondered, briefly, on the bliss that might have been. Shana went on, casually dropping two sugar cubes in her cracked mug.

"You want to hear about the dream?" she asked.

"I'm dying to know," I said. Outside, a bird cawed, almost like laughing.

"All right then. To begin with, you were naked *y, qué te digo*, you were, how can I say this, *muy* excited. Sexually."

Her eyes glowed impishly for a moment, then dimmed.

"But you were also carrying a silver tray. With Armando's head on it. I was seated at the altar, in a place I couldn't recognize, and you came and laid Armando's head at my feet. You kneeled, touching your forehead to the ground like you're supposed to do in our rites, then you left the room.

"I was stunned speechless. Then Armando's head opened its eyes. 'Guide him,' he said. Then a giant vulture came into the room, smelling of shit and blood and he pecked Armando's eyes out and dropped them at my feet, laughing like a man.

"That's when I recognized I had become Oyá, the wife of Oggún, the goddess of the dead, the lover of Shangó. And that's when I woke up."

The tea kettle gave out its piercing urgent cry. Shana poured the water in her mug, turned graciously to me.

"*Chico*, are you sure you don't want some? It's Herbalife."

The trail sneaked up the mountain, under the overhanging branches of spindly elms and massive California oaks. We'd climbed through chaparral, bushes of wild juniper, sage and thyme brushing against our legs. I'd given up shooing away the horseflies buzzing around us like lunch on the shank. Shana pressed on ahead, as blithe in white as Canova's *Diana in Arcadia*.

"I had to get out of the city," she said, leaning over to push a branch of something or other out of the way, helping me hop over a sloshing creek. "When I saw in the paper that the Customs Service was auctioning off this parcel, I just knew I had to get it."

We halted at a fork in the road. To the left, the path ended in a gully; to the right, the trail tilted up in an incredibly steep incline, the seventy-five percent grade a collection of rocks and boulders scattered on dry clay.

"You've got to be kidding," I said, looking at the hill. I was panting, drenched in perspiration. "Where's our mule?"

She took one big step forward, leapt to the next big boulder on the right of the road, then proceeded up the incline in a half-bent, half-crouched position, clambering over rocks with the practiced agility of a mountain goat. I clumsily followed suit, slipping down at one point before she quickly latched on to my wrist and literally hauled me up next to her.

"The hard part is the beginning," she said, toothy smile at my discomfort. "And you just got over it. We're almost over the ridge."

She pressed forward, following a well-trod path that was unseen just a few moments before. We passed a hollow in the bush with the remains of a campfire, scattered beer cans littering the site.

A great buzzing cloud suddenly surged out of the chaparral, headed our way.

"What the hell is that?" I asked, with some trepidation, watching the cloud draw near. Shana glanced over her shoulder, took a quick measure of the thing.

"Bees. They're following the queen to a new home. Don't worry, they're not interested in us."

"I certainly hope not," I said, picking up the pace.

A few yards behind us the great swarm flew by, thousands of stingers ready to do or die for their monarch, intent on starting a new life in some more hospitable corner of the bush.

We pushed on ahead and soon began to smell the tangy salt air, then, after two more sidewinder bends, we clambered over a large granite boulder marred with graffiti. The ground was flat on the other side and we descended quickly, the cool sea breeze welcoming us.

Before us lay the immense blue of the Pacific, a vista that stretched from Palos Verdes to Point Mugu, the foam-laced coastline a thousand feet below. Fingers of fog were rising from the corners of the panorama while to the center, directly ahead of us, the red ball of the sun was beginning its slow descent into the mauve sea.

On the lip of the esplanade stood a tall, gnarled tree with a prickly trunk. A small altar of sorts had been set under one of its high massive branches. Shana sat under the thick tree canopy, facing outward to the glorious sunset. I looked at the tree, immediately recognizing the old tropical giant of the Antilles, so massive that the old slaves called it the dwelling of the gods.

"How did this ceiba tree get here?"

She invited me to sit next to her on a soft bed of grass. The sweet scent of wild sage mingled with the dustiness of the bush and the salt air into a whole that forever shall be Malibu in my mind.

"Armando planted it," she said, staring fixedly out to sea, where a veil of seagulls beelined over the horizon. "He'd brought the seeds from Cuba and planted it in his backyard. When it was about six feet tall, he transplanted it here. We watered it every day, climbing up with gallons of water, the first year it was here. Then when the rains came, the roots took hold."

She paused, her voice quavering from emotion.

"Armando used to say that this tree was like the sentinel of our religion. It is the advance guard of the saints, who came all the way to the edge of the Pacific Ocean. *'Muchachita,* we've come halfway around the world already, from black Africa to white America. The yellow world is waiting for us.' "

"He wanted to carry *santería* to Asia?" I asked, a sweet languor coming over me in the perfumed shade.

"He said it was our last frontier. After we went around the world and returned to Africa, the saints themselves would come down from heaven and the world would live in peace."

A moment of silence, angels passed. Then: "I miss him so much."

Grief finally broke through, tears washed down her face.

"How can I help you find the monster who killed him?"

I showed her a photograph of Díaz I'd swiped from the San Diego DA's file, noticing once more the aquiline nose, the feline eyes, the naked hunger that accompanied his steely gaze.

"That's him," I said, handing over the picture. I took out of my pocket a page from the notebook Ortega had found.

"A man down in Mexico gave me this. It's from his *libreta*," his sacred journal.

Shana stared silently at the picture and the writing, then gathered them and pressed them to her chest.

"Let's sit here for a while," she said, "the sun will be going down soon."

I stared out at the flaming orb sinking slowly into the sea, the surfers on their boards so many acolytes to the daily ceremony of renewal, of death and transfiguration, witnesses to the promise that this sun will die but that it will come again tomorrow to bring the blessings of warmth and clarity to us all once more. The flashing stars and the reluctant moon that glowed pale gray in the umber folds of the far horizon all seemed to say hold fast and do not lose your faith, even in this sepulchral hour, when the last rays spread like rivulets of blood over the dark sea, you must know that the sun will rise again, that his light will warm you in the morning and that evil will not triumph.

I'm not certain if I dreamed, imagined or truly witnessed what happened next, all I can say with conviction is that this is how I remember it.

The sun had set, the violet dusk turning to jet stone night. The rising moon flared up like a lamp in the sky, a shower of meteors from the Perseids raced joyfully across the void and in the emptiness of that aerie, I heard Armando's voice.

"It will be a long fight, Charlie," he said, as if he were still alive, still with the maddening habit of seeming to read my thoughts.

"Your enemy is the prince of darkness. Many a light will be extinguished but the solution lies within you."

I turned to Shana, who sat cross-legged, hands on her knees shaped into circles, eyes closed, sitting perfectly still except for her lips, which mouthed the words I was hearing disjointed and out of time, lagging a fraction of a second behind as in a badly dubbed movie where the lips keep moving long after the concise English rendering has been delivered.

"Don't grieve for me, for this is how I had to die. Look inside yourself, Charlie, and the truth you hate to see will come rushing to your aid. We are family, Carlitos, we are all family. Help your brother, guard your sister, *ayuda a tu hermano, cuida a tu hermana.* The future is in your hands."

I saw Shana rise above the grass, levitating to the lower branches of the tree, where a beam of moonlight bathed her in white as a bevy of fireflies surrounded her and a music like chimes from a faraway place was heard, then she floated down to earth and everything turned dark and I opened my eyes.

"Time to go, Charlie, the stars have come out."

"What happened here?" I said, rubbing my eyes.

The moon floated like a Chinese lamp over the stirring ocean. Shana smiled knowingly.

"It's what you think happened that counts. *Vámonos,* it's dark already."

We descended in silence, unwilling to acknowledge the fleeting touch of eternity at the cliffside; in the moonlight, the sandy trail glowed a ghostly white. The rushing murmur of the creek by her cabin was our first hint of normalcy, then the sight of my Saab, parked patiently like an old nag by the door.

We entered the cabin, bathed by the yellowish glow of the Coleman lamp she'd left on. She bowed to the altar, touched her forehead to the ground, then uttered a few words in Yoruba, in homage to her saint, the goddess of water and life, Yemayá. I watched quietly, still in a daze from what I'd witnessed. She rose, walked to her makeshift kitchen.

"It's late," she said. "I can fix you a salad if you're hungry."

"Thank you. I'll stop at an In-n-Out on the way back. Look, what happened up there?"

"You fell asleep, that's what happened."

"I heard Armando's voice. Coming out of your mouth."

"*Ah sí?* Maybe you just imagined it."

"C'mon, you know perfectly well I heard it. That's why you go there, to, to . . ." I sputtered, "to commune with the spirits!"

She laughed, took an apple from a wire basket, sliced it into perfect quarters on the cutting board.

"After all you've been through you still don't believe in the saints."

"That's right, I don't. I believe you believe these things happen. Me, I'm not so sure."

"Okay, *dime*, what are you sure of, Charlie?" she asked, biting into the apple wedge. In the window behind her the fat moon shined up on the hill.

"I'm sure I'm alive. I'm sure I'm not perfect. I'm sure that the law works sometimes but most times not. I'm sure I love my family and my friends and that I often fail them. And I'm sure I have to find Armando's killer before he finds me."

"If you don't believe I can't—"

The blaring of my car alarm cut through the cricket song of the night. I stepped out of the cabin. Two young guys ran from the Saab, jumped on a motorcycle and raced off down the dirt road, their laughter trailing behind them.

"Punks," said Shana.

I walked to my car. They had spray-painted on my hood, "Aryan Power Rules—Kill Wit" when the alarm had gone off.

I cursed under my breath, slid into the driver's seat to check on any further damage. I turned on the ignition. My phone jumped to life, ringing like a clarion in the dark. I picked it up.

"Hello."

Shana was waiting for me by the cabin door, flashlight in one hand, gun in the other.

"I'm so sorry about your car, I don't know what to do about them."

"Never mind that. You better come with me."

"What is it?"

"LAPD found Armando's head."

CHAPTER

14

THE sound of the waterfall reached our ears even before we heard the nervous whirring of the LAPD chopper, pointing its white beam here and there in the overgrown vegetation of the San Gabriel Mountains. The moon, now waxy and yellow, seemed closer than ever while we walked on the bridle path.

"Good thing the moon's out, otherwise the kids would have never seen it," said Kelsey, ahead of us, wheezing from the climb. For once the cowboy boots he always wore seemed to serve their purpose, letting him walk almost normally in the dirt.

"Tell me, inspector," said Shana, walking swiftly in long loping strides next to him.

"Sergeant," interrupted Kelsey, "inspector is in San Francisco."

"Sorry, that's where I'm from," she said, not sounding apologetic in the least. "How were the corpses found?"

"Humh? You mean the remains. Two Cub Scouts lost in an outing. When their troop went out to look for them, they spotted the remains by the tree. Scared the bejesus out of them."

"But the children are all right?"

"Oh, yeah, the two kids just got lost picking blackberries. They found them a little later. So you're an expert in this voodoo shit too, like Charlie here?"

Shana gave him her best condescending smile, spoke with her patronizingly best Anglo accent. Obviously she'd gotten the official treatment before.

"As I'm sure Charlie has told you many times, sergeant, it's not voodoo, it's *santería*. It originated in the Spanish-speaking Antilles and it is a religion, formally recognized as such by the U.S. Supreme Court with all the privileges appertaining thereto. So shit it certainly is not."

"Well, excuse me but the Supreme Court also says a bunch of Indians wearing eagle feathers doing psychedelic mushrooms is a religion too, so I don't know about this, no offense."

"You have to excuse the sergeant, Shana," I said as we rounded the bend, a half mile from the parking lot where we'd left my Saab. "He's a lapsed Catholic."

"Who isn't?" she said. "Is that where it was?"

She pointed at a clearing where a strand of poplars grew gracefully at the eastern shore of the lagoon. On the north end, an eighty-foot-high waterfall clashed noisily against massive granite boulders, the entire scene illumined like a stage set by the portable reflectors of the Sheriff's Department.

"Yeah, right there. There was another bowl of sorts next to it with a couple of chickens and some fruit. You wanna see?"

"That's not necessary," she said, dashing down the slope to the clearing, "this place has a lot of *ashé.*"

Kelsey turned to me. "What's that achee stuff?"

"*Ashé*. A Yoruba word meaning spiritual power," I said, then hurried after Shana.

"Oh God, here we go again," said Kelsey, noisily following me.

Two SID drones were still conducting their investigation at the site, measuring, collecting samples. Shana ducked under the police tape draped around two piñon bushes. One of the latex-gloved officers was about to shoo Shana off when Kelsey waved at him to let her through.

Shana walked slowly, almost reverentially, to a flat rock covered by a plastic tarp. The greenish waters of the lagoon lapped softly at the edge of the plastic, which writhed under the surface like some anemone of doom.

She kneeled before the rock, touched her forehead to the ground, then ordered, with firm conviction: "Let me see him."

"Hey, sergeant, this is highly unorthodox," said a young, freckle-faced officer. "What's headquarters going to say some bunch of civilians come barging in here messing up the evidence?"

"She's a cult expert. Show it to her," replied Kelsey impatiently.

The SID drone shook his head, still disapproving.

"All right, but I'm going to have to put it in the report. I'm not gonna be no Dennis Fung for you."

"Put it wherever the fuck you want, Jason, just do as I tell you."

"All right, all right, don't have a fucking cow, Kelsey. I'm going by the book like we're supposed to, okay?"

The officer removed the translucent covering. At the bottom of a blood-caked straw basket lay two dark, rounded objects, the two spheres butting one against the other, seeking comfort and support from each other even unto eternity. The officer turned the basket around.

To the left was the sliced-off head of Armando, his eyes

closed, his face devoid of all expression, as though the killer had stolen not just Armando's life but his personality as well. His lips were bruised and swollen and his hair was mussed, but otherwise he seemed as though he had fallen into dreamless sleep, only without the rest of his body.

The head next to his was a macabre contrast, the features of an unfortunate young black man frozen into a mask of unspeakable terror and pain. The ears had been sliced off, the eyes gouged out, the nose sliced off and only the stump of a tongue peeked out from between bloody teeth.

"Jesus Christ," I muttered, as though by invoking the name of my god I could make the slaughter more bearable.

"Guy on the right was the guard got offed at your house, Charlie," said Kelsey. "I suppose the gentleman on the left was your friend."

"Hae eh oh ane kile kile, ahe, oh Oyá!" intoned Shana falling to her knees, her sharp cry startling under the artificial light of night.

"Hey, hey, what's she doing?" asked the SID officer, startled by the intensity of Shana's caterwauling. "She's gonna spook the perp!"

"What perp?" asked Kelsey, wide-eyed, unbelieving of the force he'd just unleashed,

"Añe ho ho ni lo, añe ho milo," continued Shana, as intent in her devotion as a Hasid singing Kaddish.

"The one who did this," replied the officer, throwing his hands in the air. "For all we know he's still out there in the bush. Hey, lady, don't touch the evidence!"

"Don't be ridiculous, Jason, guy's long gone. Charlie, what's your friend doing?"

Shana stretched out, her full body before the severed head, her forehead slapping the dust as though in penance for the punishment inflicted, then she extended her hands to touch the remains of her spiritual master.

She began to convulse, her limbs thrashing in the dust, as though a great current of power were being transmitted to her by some means unseen to the eye, as though Armando's head were the repository of some primal energy that was choosing Shana to be its conduit all the while she intoned her guttural chant of mourning:

Oloddumare ayuba!
Bogwo ihu oluwo embelese!
Oloddumare ayuba!

"No, don't touch her!" I bellowed as Kelsey and the SID officer moved to wrest her fingers from his head. "It's a trance, she'll snap out of it in a minute!"

"Sorry, Charlie, I can't . . . Jesus Mary Joseph!"

Kelsey stopped in mid-motion, beefy arm suspended in the air, attempting to push me away but frozen by the chilling surprise of the moment.

Armando's eyes had opened, as though to take in the terror, pain and confusion, to witness from beyond the grave the ritual of departure by his spiritual daughter, who now lay stiff as a board on the ground.

"Fucking A!" muttered the SID man, snapping a series of photographs, the flash going off like so many cannon shots in the night.

Armando's clouded green eyes stared down, his once expressionless face now moving into a shadow of a smile as though to say this is my beloved and then the eyelids dropped and the smile vanished and eternal rest resumed its quiet slumber.

Now Shana got up, calmly dusted herself off, calmly noticed our stunned faces, then calmly pointed at the lagoon.

"Excuse me, sergeant, but isn't that the source of the Los Angeles River?"

●

We cruised through the streets of Atwater Village, Shana holding the Thomas Bros. Guide on her lap, having charted our way down from the precipitous inclines of the San Gabriel Mountains to the flatlands of the San Fernando Valley. For hours the two of us had followed every nook and cranny, every curve and every fold of the waterway, trailing the serpentine path of the once mighty river, now hemmed in, confined and at times even buried under the concrete banks built by the U.S. Army Corps of Engineers after a series of disastrous floods in the 1930s.

So thorough was the taming of the river that in some spots it amounts to little more than a storm channel, a drain practically, twenty feet across and a few feet deep, coursing behind automobile body shops, tenements, strip malls, shuttered factories and service stations. The river has become a pale intruder stealing away in the night, mute witness to the degradation that has befallen the old fields of wheat, walnut and citrus, plowed under in the name of progress.

After a few hours I'd lost track of how many cul-de-sacs we'd visited, how many streets we'd seen dead-end in rusty chain link fences and garbage-strewn lots. I'd even stopped counting how many times Shana had stepped out of the Saab, poking her sharp nose around the night air, flaring her nostrils as though to smell our ghastly prey, only to come back into the car and say, "Keep going, he's not here either."

There was a method to her seeming madness. She'd explained it the moment we'd pulled out of the parking lot in the mountains.

"Those heads were left there for a purpose," she said.

"No kidding."

"*Coño,* don't you see what he's up to?"

"Sorry, I'm just seeing a homicidal maniac making a disgusting sacrifice to his hideous god, that's all."

I eased down Little Tujunga Canyon Road, the great fat moon shining in my rearview mirror.

"No, no. I mean, you're right, but there's more to it than that. *Mira*, the heads were by the waters of the river, right? That's so that their spirits will control the waters as well."

"I still don't get it."

"Por ahí, Pacoima. Let's go there first."

"Excuse me, did you say Pacoima? In the middle of the night? That's MST gang territory; even the natives don't come out after dark."

"Oyeme, you listen to me, *coño!* Díaz is counting on the *ashé* of the river to pull him through. Whether you believe it or not it doesn't matter. What counts is he does. He's set up headquarters somewhere along the river. All we have to do is follow it and we'll find the suitable spot."

"Are you crazy? This river runs sixty something miles down to Long Beach Harbor. You expect us to follow it all the way down?"

We'd stopped at a light in Lake View Terrace, the dried-out dirt embankment of Hansen Dam stretching before us like a promise left unfulfilled. She turned, fixed her eyes on me.

"What choice do we have?"

It was now six hours later and the moon was gone, covered by a bank of monsoon clouds swept in from the southeast. In Atwater Village the streets were perfectly still, its old-fashioned globe lampposts crowned with a nimbus of amber mist. A blanket of slumber seemed draped over the tiny lawns and carefully tended cottages, the kind where the living room is smaller than the van parked out on the driveway.

We stopped at a hofsbrau next to a miniature golf course. On the slopes of Mount Hollywood, west of us across the ever-pressing flow of traffic on the I-5, thrust the darkened silhouette of Griffith Observatory. Just a few years before I had battled at that summit with another dark, malevolent force. Somehow, with God's help, I had triumphed, but now these years later I was again doing battle with the one who never sleeps. Would I win again this time?

Shana ducked through and under a hole in the chain link fence and clambered up the embankment, standing atop the running trail. I followed, dumbly, my mind reeling from hunger, fatigue and lack of sleep. She squinted at a bend somewhere south of Los Feliz.

"There! It must be there!"

I looked at the dank pool of blue-green water, lit up by the arching yellow lights of the nearby train yard. Tons of rocks eroded from the mountains and swept down to the alluvial plains had formed a small island harboring two palm trees, looking like exclamation points in the middle of the stream.

"What are you talking about?" I asked.

"*Estás ciego?* Don't you see it? I should have known. That's the only part of the river the army didn't pave over."

"They couldn't, it's too deep."

"Exactly. *That's* where Díaz is. He must harness the *ashé* of the river right there. What's that area called?"

"Frogtown."

"Well, Frogtown is where we're going."

We drove down Riverside and entered Frogtown past a gutted service station, silently weaving in and out of the cul-de-sacs, which invariably ended at the river, smelling of creosote and chemicals. All the auto repair shops were dark and shuttered. In some of the modest homes nearby the lights were already on, their occupants preparing for another backbreaking day of dawn-to-dusk labor at minimum wages, the smell of early morning coffee and fried tortillas occasionally wafting through the air.

"What is that?" asked Shana, pointing at a white tower. "I can't read signs without my glasses."

I stopped the car, cut the engine. The chirruping of crickets and frogs rose in an unsettling chorus. Down the street stood a white building, a large For Sale sign stuck in its dying lawn, a cross lying askew on the red-tile roof. Above the large wooden doors, a smaller sign in Arabic script, then, in English, the words, "Coptic Church of the Savior."

"An abandoned church," I said.

"Then that must be it."

"How do you know?"

"Because that would be the ideal place for him. This way he can tap into the spiritual power of the water and the prayers of the people that once used the church. It's the vibrations, you know. Holy places have a patina of spirituality."

"A patina of . . . look, I'm fed up with this wild goose chase. It's four o'clock in the morning and I still have to drive you back to Malibu. I want to forget all about this. I don't know how you managed to open Armando's eyes—"

"Rigor mortis," she said, interrupting my tirade. "The head was cold and when I touched it . . ."

"Whatever. I don't care, I'm taking you back right now. I'm off this case. *Se acabó.* It's over. As somebody once said, let the dead bury their dead."

I turned on the ignition. Shana bent over, killed the engine and whipped out the key, dropping it in her bra.

"Stop playing games."

"What if I'm right? What if he is there? Do you really want to take that chance?"

I thought about that as best I could, then stepped out of the car, slamming the door behind me.

"Five minutes. That's all you get."

"That's all I need."

My head swimming with fatigue, we walked quickly down the cracked, weed-choked sidewalk to the church. The windows were boarded up, the stained glass long ago stolen or broken. But there was a light inside the building and a noise as of someone moving something heavy inside.

"Well?" she asked, cockily.

"Let's go around the back," I whispered.

We were heading to the rear of the building when a Chevrolet Caprice rolled to a halt in front of the church. Shana and I took cover behind a hedge of orange-scented pittosporum. Laughter rolled out even before the car doors opened. A large hulking man stepped onto the sidewalk, followed by a second, thinner, sardonic character.

"Isn't that . . ."

"Yes," I replied, "Kelsey. He must have just come down from the crime scene. The other guy is Eddie O'Haran, Vice."

"What are they doing here?"

"What do you think?"

We heard steps resounding in the church, then a door opened. The cops laughed and O'Haran hugged the tall, slim, dark stranger with the lynx eyes.

"Is that him?" whispered Shana.

"Yes, it is," I said, feeling the weight of a stone on my heart as I saw again the dreaded features of my nightmares.

Díaz turned and looked around, as if the mere whisper of his name were enough to make his antenna vibrate, then he welcomed the cops into the abandoned church, slamming the door shut.

CHAPTER

15

SHANA and I sat in my living room, waiting for the phone to ring, my Arts and Crafts furniture as unforgiving as the benches in a Spanish monastery.

"He must be out of town," I said finally.

"Charlie, it's five o'clock in the morning. I don't think he's wearing his beeper."

Of course she was right. But I felt we had no choice but to call in the feds. Now that Kelsey had surfaced as a possible accomplice, there was no way I could trust anyone within the LAPD. I had called and left a message for a U.S. attorney friend, Dick North, but he was either out of town or not in the habit of returning calls this time of night.

"What are you saying here?" I asked.

"I'm saying we go back and get him ourselves."

"Hello? Are you out of your mind? That's like saying let's take down Charlie Manson ourselves. Whatever you've been smoking, I don't want any."

Shana picked up the avocado, onion and sprouts on whole wheat she'd fixed herself when we came in and took a small, careful bite.

"I have a feeling he's all alone now. It takes time to build a cabal, you know."

"Don't you think coven is more like it?"

"Only if you believe in what he's doing."

"We've been down this road before. I'll tell you what I think. He's armed to the teeth and he's going to go down shooting. Mac 11s don't know from *santería.*"

"The mind, Charlie, is the greatest weapon. We have to make him think his weapons will be no good. Then we can go in."

"Fine. And how do you propose we do that?"

The phone came alive. I grabbed it before the second ring.

"Yes, this is he. Of course I'll accept a collect call. Hello? Where have you been?"

I listened to the voice at the other end, then gave detailed instructions for the cabbie on how to reach my home. I hung up, my arms trembling with waves of prickly gooseflesh.

"Who was that?" asked Shana, finishing her sandwich.

"The answer to your prayers, as it were."

Thirty minutes later the doorbell rang. On my way to the door I caught a glimpse in the hallway mirror of a tired old man with graying temples and huge black circles under his eyes. It took me a second or two to realize I was looking at my own wasted reflection. I opened the door.

Graciela de Palma, in a bright yellow silk dress, smiled at me like some exotic Florida toucan just alighted in my yard. She nodded, entered without being asked.

"Shana," she said knowingly. *"Niña,* I've heard all about you. It's a pleasure."

Shana stood, bowed before de Palma, then kissed her on both cheeks.

"Qué va, aboluya," she said, calling her by the honorific title of grandmother in Yoruba. "The pleasure is all mine."

"I see I don't have to do the honors," I said. "Anything to drink? Beer? Wine? Holy water? Eye of newt liquor?"

The women shook their heads reproachfully, still embraced in sisterly greeting.

"Sorry. Bad joke. I always crack wise under pressure. Please, have a seat. Unless you'd rather levitate."

"Stop it, Charlie," said Shana. "You're being disrespectful."

"Disrespectful? Yes, of course. I'm dissing the woman who sends me off after a serial killer but doesn't have the fucking decency to tell me what kind of man he is. So sorry. It's that when I see my friends getting skinned and decapitated I have a tendency to get a little touchy. I say to myself, Charlie, my boy, really, don't be so gauche, so uncouth, so out of it. It's all part of the game, right? The great mandala, the great cosmic wheel of fortune, all that shit. But don't matter, we're all family here, right? You're Díaz's godmother and she's Armando's goddaughter and my mother was like a sister to you so it's one great big happy *familia* around here, right? Us and the fucking Borgias."

"They were Spanish too, you know," sniffed de Palma, sitting on the leather couch.

"Why am I not surprised. So what are you going to do now, lady? Throw some gris-gris powder in the air, kill a couple of chickens and sing the mambo to the gods? Or did you just come here because I'm a hell of a nice guy, even if my dick is between the crosshairs?"

"No, Charlie, I didn't come here for your company," said de Palma, hands crossed on her ample lap.

"So what did you come here for?"

"I heard your call and I'm here to do my duty. I'm going to turn my godson over to you."

The Saab turned the corner off Los Feliz almost as if it already knew the way, past the many-colored Mulholland Fountain across Griffith Park. Riverside Drive stretched out before us in dreadful stillness, quietly paralleling the ebb and flow of the great river of traffic that is the I-5. On the hood of the Saab I could still read, inverted, "Aryan Power Rules! Kill Wit."

"I became Ricardo's godmother by default," said de Palma, almost apologetically from the back seat. "I became attached to him, before I knew his evil heart. His *ayyó* had died during a cleansing of a particularly malignant spirit, so Ricardo came to me for advice."

"You make it sound like he was some kind of intern and you were the head surgeon."

Shana and de Palma chuckled.

"I fail to see the humor."

"You see, that's exactly what we are. *Cirujanos de cabeza.* Of course you know that your *cabeza* is your destiny, which is determined by your saint," said de Palma, ever the professor.

"So what's mine, doctor?"

Her eyes fixed on mine in the rearview mirror.

"Do you really want to know?"

"I wouldn't be asking otherwise."

"Your saint is Eleguá, the trickster, the god of the many paths and incarnations. You are the searcher, the man who opens doors. That was why I came to you, because of your great gift. You are always looking for answers."

"And never finding them."

"Or finding that your answer is your worst fear."

"Cruel saint."

"Cruel world. It's up to us, who are also saints, to make it better."

"How?"

"Through communion in Christ and belief in the life eternal."

"How can you claim to be a Christian when you're a high priest of *santería?*"

"But don't you know? We believe in Christ too and in the forgiveness of sins. This is just a trial, Charlie, a *calvario.*"

"An ordeal," I said.

I looked back at her and for a moment I panicked when I couldn't locate her in the back seat, shaken by the notion that perhaps I was imagining the whole thing, that there was no car, no Shana, no de Palma, and I was all by myself in some primal nightmare. I glanced back quickly and saw her slumped against the window, staring at the hillside. De Palma repeated softly, "A great ordeal."

Shana stared ahead, strangely quiet. I'm in the grip of madness, I thought, but I can't help myself. It's already too late.

"Tell me one thing," I said. "I don't understand why, if *santería* is the way of light, that you have characters like Díaz running around. Can't you just like, curse him out or cast him out or whatever it is you do and just get rid of him? How can he be allowed to exist?"

"Because that is his path," said de Palma matter-of-factly.

"What, you're saying there's no individual responsibility? We are all predestined to become something or other—doctor, banker, killer—and there's nothing we can do about it?"

De Palma looked out at the hulking outline of an abandoned tenement on Riverside, as though her answer was addressed at the ghosts of people who once lived and hoped in fetid squalor.

"The sacred books of Ofa tell us that in the end good will triumph. But sometimes evil will have the upper hand. Evil serves its purpose in the workings of the Creator, Ollodumare. There are greater designs that we cannot divine."

"So I can just go around and kill whoever because that's my karma?" I shouted, afraid of falling for her insidious doctrine. "I mean, the devil makes me do it so I'm off the hook, right?"

"Remember this," she insisted, her voice drifting forward to me as if in a dream. "What man knows his true path? That is why we make offerings to the gods and we throw the shells. They guide us to what is good and away from evil. Only devil worshippers follow the dark."

"But what if you are born to follow the dark?"

"Then you are the devil's brood. And it is our responsibility to eliminate you."

"Some religion you got here."

"One day you'll see our light, Charlie. Sooner than you expect."

"I doubt it," I barked.

I was so angry, angst-ridden and fatigued that I failed to detect the brown Ford Taurus with Mexican plates a couple of blocks away, stopping when we did, turning at the next street over and then coming back out, to continue discreetly tailing us through the deserted avenues of Silverlake.

We parked some distance from the church in the stillness of the pregnant night. I killed the engine.

A chorus of frog songs greeted our arrival, drowning out the hum of the nearby freeway. The undercover squad car we had seen before was gone, and a low-lying mist had risen from the river, clinging like an otherworldly vine to the dilapidated tower of the old church.

"I say we wait, call in the FBI," I said.

A single fat drop of rain splattered on my windshield.

"And if he slips away again?" asked de Palma, leaning in between the two front seats. "He knows he's been found out, you told me the police can't be trusted. He may just decide to pick up and move again. And kill more victims to sanctify his next power place."

"Am I my brother's keeper?" I asked, querulously.

She moved closer, her skin almost glowing, smelling hauntingly of old violets and faded Joy.

"You could be his next victim, Charlie."

"I could be his next victim the moment I go in as well."

"He won't dare shoot his own *aboluya,* it would be the end of his powers."

A succession of raindrops pattered on the roof, a drum roll to my indecision. Shana shifted in her seat, grabbed the door handle.

"Shall we go now?"

I didn't answer. Instead I turned to de Palma.

"Why me?"

She smiled and in the half light I couldn't tell if the grin was that of the con artist or that of the proud mother. Or both.

"You know why. Because this is close to your heart."

Shana suddenly rushed out of the car, almost as if she didn't want to hear de Palma anymore. You fool, I thought, let de Palma handle it!

Shana ran down the street, drawn irresistibly to the fog-wreathed church tower. As if on cue the clouds opened and a monsoon rain shower fell down on us, a huge blanket of warm moisture draping the area. Through the rain I could see hordes of little animals stepping out of the bushes and off the curbs, hopping to and fro, celebrating the arrival of the rain. In a matter of seconds thousands of tiny frogs covered the street, jumping on us, egging us on, their tiny round eyes

observing us, their throaty croaks an eerie chorus of warning
and joy.

I hurried to the church, unable to avoid stepping on the
squishy creatures, their yellow entrails emptying on the rain-
slick pavement. At the church door I glanced back and noticed
de Palma had remained in the car.

Shana tried the door. I grabbed ahold of her hand.

"Don't go in, de Palma's still not here!" I whispered to
Shana." What is it with you?"

"It's my destiny, Charlie, I have to do this!"

All at once the door swung open, as if on its own accord,
ushering us into the bowels of the sanctuary.

"Don't!" I said, but she broke free and entered the cavernous
hall, losing herself in the darkness.

I slipped my Beretta out of my waistband, stood for a moment
on the threshold, knowing I had to make a decision and fast—
should I follow her into the church or should I wait for de
Palma? I looked back at the car through the noisy blanket of
rain. De Palma gave no indication of coming out; in fact, she
seemed not to be in the car at all. That's when I first noticed the
brown Ford slowly cruising down the street, its lights turned off,
like a stealthy animal waiting to pounce.

I looked back inside the church. I couldn't leave Shana alone
with that monster; I had to protect her. I cursed myself for
having agreed to this cockamamie scheme but it was too late to
go back. I turned on a small flashlight, slipped the safety off my
gun, cocked the barrel.

"God help me," I muttered and stepped into the darkness.

The flashlight carved out a circle of yellowish light from the
gloom before me. I swung the light all around like a weapon,
shining it on the plaster walls and the boarded-up windows of
what must have once been a graceful church.

I walked cautiously down the middle of the nave. All the pews had been removed. High above, exposed cross beams served as pathways for long-tailed rats, which scurried away from the light.

All at once I heard a chanting, as though a chorus of thousands of men, singing softly at first, then gradually louder, in a language I soon recognized as Yoruba, the language of the West African slaves who had brought their sad religion to this hemisphere as their only solace for their misery. The singing seemed to come from somewhere very far, as though the church were a long field that loped over the terrain of history, stretching all the way back to the original fields of shame.

A door slammed shut. I whirled around, shined the light on the front door. There was no one there, yet the door was bolted from the inside.

"Shana!" I shouted, knowing the game was up. I had entered the devil's lair and he was aware of every step I took.

I heard Shana screaming up ahead. I ran further inside the church, fighting what seemed to be a stream of invisible forces pushing me away, like so many unseen hands grabbing at me, as though I alone were fighting the currents of time and guilt. Now the fog that had crept outside gushed inside from some unseen opening and I was surrounded by a dark swirling mass, a solid wind tossing me to and fro, even as the music grew louder and Shana screamed again.

Her cries came from above, up a rickety wooden staircase that snaked up to the roof, past the transept of the church and its tower, rising like a cannon pointing at the swollen sky. I glanced at the stone altar amidst the transept, illumined by an odd moonlight that poured down from the steeple's broken windows. The altar glowed in a greenish light, throbbing almost, as though wanting to say not here but beyond, salvation lies beyond.

Somehow I struggled up the stairs through the rushing stream pushing me back, grabbing on to the banister, even as her cries pierced the gloomy confines. I lurched up to the roof, falling on one knee to a sight I would have never conceived of in my most feverish nightmare.

By a makeshift sacrificial table on the far side of the roof stood Díaz, naked and erect, his sinewy body daubed with odd markings and paint, a tattoo of Jesus Christ covering his entire chest. Shana lay on the altar before him, a bleeding wound on her forehead, a gash at her throat, her gauze clothing ripped off.

I pointed my gun, fired. Díaz cackled, laughing as though knowing mere bullets would not harm him.

"I am invincible!" he hollered as he sank a dark jewel of a knife into Shana's inert body.

The knife sliced through her chest, cutting through ribs and cartilage and precious life, then he stuck a hand inside the cavity and in one brutal move jerked out her bleeding beating heart, which he held up to the moon as he howled.

What sort of sick nightmare is this?

Sweet Jesus, save me!

A kick in the darkness knocked the flashlight out of my hand, then a flurry of blows rained down on me, as though an invisible band had surrounded me, wanting to beat me into submission. My gun fell with a clatter on the floor, then a brick slammed against my skull and everything grew pitch black and I passed out in sheer terror thinking when will this all end, dear Lord, when will I exit this nightmare!

When I came to, I found myself at the makeshift altar. My hands were tied, my shirt ripped open, blood clouding my eyes, spasms of pain from my whole beat-up body jolting my brain as Díaz danced all around me, his body jerking in spasmodic jitters, the dark knife still in his hand, flashing and slicing to ribbons the air around me, outlining the shape of my sacrifice before the execution.

Clouds slipped across the moon in what seemed like an instant and the sky opened in a torrential downpour, a rainstorm to cleanse away the sins of the world, a downpour to bless us and curse us, the spilling of the tears of heaven on a sorry sight.

Díaz stopped and drew himself upward, a ghastly naked figure, every inch of his body intent on destroying me and making sure that I knew it. I tried to move but I was still sluggish from the blows and I helplessly, uselessly, moved my shoulders to protect myself as he raised his knife higher in a swift motion that would end with the blade sinking into my chest so that the last image I would have would be of terror and defeat so he could own my soul for all eternity and then the shot rang out.

Díaz jerked from the impact, the bullet piercing his chest, venting with a stream of blood the evil wraith that possessed him. He looked down at the street below, a puzzled expression on his face, as if asking how could this be, then he collapsed. He fell on the sloping tile roof, his body flapping and flopping as he bumped and slid and rolled to the edge, then dropped three stories to the ground with a ghastly thump.

I passed out again. When I came to I saw Ortega's face next to mine, observing me through the thick rain. He saw me stir, gave me his best wily peasant smirk. I sat up, my hands untied, but my head still swimming in aching, throbbing pain.

"I told you I'd get the *pinche brujo* son of bitch," he said, a police siren howling ever closer to us.

"How did you know?" I mumbled, the sound of my voice oddly distant, so much packed into so few words—my life, my hopes, my failures.

"You're easy to find, Charlie. You never look back. *Ahí te wacho.*"

"Wait, Shana is, I . . ."

But he would not wait. He clambered off the roof and leapt

across to the overhang of the house below, falling with a great clatter, then, scurrying like some night creature on the red tiles, slipped out of sight in the darkness. Moments later a raw-faced officer in a slick yellow raincoat rushed up the stairs, burst onto the roof with the controlled panic of a man in combat, gun in one hand, Magnalite in the other. He shined his light on me, the warm glow of earthly salvation.

"What the hell's going on here?" he asked.

"Shana! Look for Shana!" I managed to say, before once again drifting back to the fog bank of unconsciousness.

CHAPTER

16

AFTER three days of X rays, CAT scans, reflexology exams and a thousand other procedures to make sure I'd have no grounds for a malpractice suit, Queen of Angels Hospital finally released me, depositing me on my own doorstep at the break of dawn courtesy of a Medtrans ambulance.

Doctors said I'd suffered a concussion from what looked like repeated blows to the head but that if I took it easy, I'd probably live to a ripe old age, if my high cholesterol didn't do me in first. I didn't find the humor in their prognosis. First Armando was gone and now Shana. It was up to me to make sure their deaths would be avenged, no matter how I was linked to the murderer.

The media around my house had long departed, searching fatter, easier prey. I pulled down the few remaining tatters of yellow police tape, the spoor of a beast gone by. I stood and stared at my Cape Cod, with its blue siding, white trim and gray shutters sitting prettily on my well-tended lawn, the trim Canary palm still standing guard by the white picket fence, gleaming from the early morning dew.

I'm going to hate losing you, I thought, then walked inside my house.

I headed for the kitchen and brewed some thick Cuban coffee, and over the heady fumes of my familiar shot of caffeine, I saw there had to be a better way.

I picked up the phone, dialed Miami. My son, Julian's, gruff voice answered and for a moment I thought I'd finally made contact but it was only the answering machine. I left a message, showered, changed into a pin-striped suit and headed for my office.

It was eight o'clock by the time I rolled into the parking lot by Saint Veridiana, greeted Manuel the attendant and tossed my car keys into his booth. I won't say that I was uplifted by the dark, smoggy street, littered with the cardboard remains of the night's homeless condos, or that the graffiti and the stench of piss and booze or the clangor of roaring buses and snatches of conversations from office workers heading to the state building and the *L.A. Times* made me feel at home. It was proof of life, though, incontrovertible evidence of a great, lost, dirty and bedraggled metropolis, out on one too many benders, heading for work no matter how throbbing the headache or swollen the joints. She had drunk and she had fallen and she had bled but she was still alive and still doing the thing she knew best, to endure. And I was there with her, living to fight another day.

My partner, Farris Troy Mitchell, was hard at work when I arrived. His gleaming pate as carefully shaved as his plump cheeks, he sat at his Barcelona chair in immaculately white shirtsleeves, dictating a letter to Tina, his crepe wool Zegna jacket hung carefully on the back of my desk chair. Tina turned and jumped up, hugging me.

"That's okay, that's okay, I'm all right," I said, gently prying her away.

"Charlie, do you have any idea how much it took to keep your bootie out of the *Times*?" said Farris. "I had to promise Alan a copy of Marty Adamson's prenuptial agreement! It's the biggest thing since Jacko and Lisa, *Vanity Fair* was wetting its pants to have it and I have to turn it over to cover my partner's behind. I could get disbarred for that!"

"I doubt it. Haven't they heard of the Good Samaritan?"

"Only when that's the hospital they're suing. How the hell are you?"

We shook hands, pumping away as though the motion could wipe out everything that was wrong in the world and we'd be left with a world of brotherhood, peace and solidarity. We had never been particularly close, our partnership being one of convenience rather than attraction, yet I was still sorry for what I was about to tell him. But he jumped the gun on me, proving once again there is nothing slicker than a Century City lawyer.

I ushered Tina out to sort the mail and prepare the checks for signing, then closed the old mahogany and etched glass door to the waiting room—one of the building's many 1930s architectural relics that had prompted me to rent the office.

"You, sir, are in dire need of a vacation," Farris started. "In fact, I believe you need a permanent vacation."

"That sounds ominous."

"Not at all. I didn't mean it that way. God knows you've been through a lot lately. What I mean is, I think we should call it quits."

I was about to argue against it just for the hell of it but I decided it wasn't worth it. I sat on our black leather couch, propped my still aching head on a bolster.

"All right, let's hear it. What's wrong?"

"What's wrong? What's right?" repeated Farris, sounding like a banker calling in a defaulted note. "You've been gone for weeks now, totally neglecting the office. I've had to sub in for you in court, putting over all your cases while you chase this Díaz freak."

"Think of it as prestige."

"We don't need that. I don't need that. I've built up a nice, comfortable entertainment law practice. I got Alanis and Julio and Brad and Julia and they keep me pretty busy. I don't have time to be sucking up to stupid judges for two-bit pretrial motions, kowtowing before petty tyrants at the CCB who think they're God's gift to mankind because they get a chance to wear a robe in public."

"I take it Judge Sinclair got to you."

"It's not just him, it's the whole fucking system these guys have set up. There is no way to get a case handled by an impartial judge because they don't exist down there. Besides which, there's no way anybody can turn a profit billing the county at sixty dollars an hour. They were paying more than that ten years ago when I moved from criminal to entertainment. It's a joke, Charlie. The system is rigged and no one gets anything out of it except for the prison guards, who've greased the governor to keep building prisons until kingdom come."

"Getting philosophical, aren't we?"

"Regardless. Point is, I think we should call it quits, like I said. I go back to my poor benighted Hollywood folk and you can close this office. Which is costing us, I remind you, over ten thousand dollars a month, eighty percent of which I cover with my own money. I mean I'm sorry about your mom and I'm sorry about what's happened to you but business is business. At the risk of sounding trite, I hope you realize this is nothing personal."

I stood up and turned my back on him, looking out the window at the loading dock of the *Times* while trying hard not to burst out laughing.

"So what do you propose I should do?" I said, still not daring to look at him.

He walked up to me, lay a brotherly hand on my shoulder, as sincere as an agent in heat.

"Guy out at Fox wants to option the rights to your manuscript."

"What manuscript?"

"The one you're going to write for the book he's going to option for two hundred thousand dollars, up front, against seven fifty in the back end if this gets made into a movie. Two-year option, renewable for two other sixteen-month periods, two extra payments of seventy-five each, not applicable against the purchase price, that's how sure he is this'll get made. They're already talking Michael Douglas but I said I thought Antonio Banderas would be better. Younger crowd. *And* you get to keep the rights to the underlying character, which is only fair considering it's your own life. So what do you say, Charlie, uh? Is it a deal or what?"

The fingernail lady strutted into the Criminal Courts Building doing a slow burn. She headed straight for Deputy Albright, who pumped five tons of iron at the gym before work and ran seven miles through downtown after work every day, daring anyone to disturb his concentration on his comic book physique. But even Captain America would have had a hard time dealing with an enraged black female with fingernails that grew out three feet from their roots, lacquered and pointed and curled like some science fiction creature or some malignant tumor that could not be arrested.

"Deputy, I am a God-fearing person minding my own business," she wailed, waving her fingernails like knives, "and I don't see why you folks has got to be looking everywhere for things that don't belong to you like I was a criminal or something."

Albright put down his grande nonfat decaf latte from Pasqua's on the empty stage in the lobby, took out a notepad and pencil.

"Well, ma'am, this is the Criminal Courts Building."

"I don't give a damn! I am not a criminal even if that lying son of a bitch patrolman says I hit that hoe in the face, she be a lying fool! 'Sides which, she deserved it!"

"Ma'am, I suggest you tell that to your public defender. If you have any comments about our security measures, you may write to the presiding judge and tell him you disagree with them."

"I might do just that!" said the woman.

Albright wrote down the name and address on the notepad, tore the sheet and gave it to the woman, who turned this way and that, contorting her hand so as to be able to grab the note. She then swung around, huffing, and slunk to the bank of elevators, her nails cutting a swath through the crowd in front of her.

Deputy González walked over from the scanners, snickered.

"I wonder how she wipes her ass," he said.

Both men burst out laughing. I picked up my briefcase from the X-ray machine rollers and headed to the open doors of the cargo elevator.

Phil Fuentes was alone in his office, going over a file while listening to the closing bars of the overture to *Così Fan Tutte.* Unlike Lisa he had forgone the opportunity to revamp his quarters, keeping the standard metal desk, plastic chairs and rickety filing cabinet—but his window faced west, giving him a sweeping panorama from the eighteenth floor that encompassed the entire coastline all the way to the distant humps of Catalina

Island fifty miles away. His walls were lined with signed framed Hockney posters of the L.A. Opera and, most important of all, he was just three doors away from DA Antonetti.

A handful of old-fashioned roses drooped from a Steuben vase in careful disarray, loose fleshy petals of creamy reds and yellows scattered on the desk blotter. When we shook hands I noticed he had actually been reading a libretto, which he had slipped inside the case file. He saw I'd caught on to him.

"Do you like Mozart?" he asked, removing the libretto in acknowledgment of my find.

"He can be dry sometimes."

"Oh, I don't think so. Mozart is perfectly balanced between rationality and emotion. The other night I was driving home late from work and Jim Svejda was playing Mozart's Rondo in A and I decided Mozart must be God's court composer. I mean, if there is a heaven, I'm sure Mozart is up there leading the orchestra."

"The music of the spheres," I replied, waiting to see where he was really heading. But Phil was a true fan.

"So to speak. I was just going over the plot to *Così*. Antonetti gave me a couple of tickets for opening night. He hates opera, imagine that? What kind of Italian is that?"

"Excuse me. I thought I had an appointment with Deputy DA Fuentes but somehow I wound up in the Entertainment Section of the *Times*. I better go now."

I got up, picked up my briefcase. Fuentes glared at me.

"Sit down. Please."

He walked over to the Onkyo on the filing cabinet, turned down the volume, then returned to his chair, still annoyed I should interrupt his communion with the exalted realm of high-brow art.

"You know, Charlie, you can be such a pill."

"That's not true, Phil. I appreciate the finer things of life as much as the next guy. But I'm not closing my eyes to what's around me either. I'm not going to pretend this is the L.A. of everybody's wet dream, where starlets jump in bed with you, the sky is clear, the water's clean and the good white cops keep the bad guys off the street. This place has become a cesspool. For the last ten years Los Angeles has been drifting, like a dead body floating down the river, stinking and drawing flies. And while you and your friends live the high life, go to the opera and fancy restaurants thinking everything is fine and dandy, the whole county is up for grabs. Everybody's on the take or totally helpless to halt the slide."

Phil nodded, his neat hands folded quietly on his desk. He was perfectly prepared to meet my arguments.

" 'Twas ever thus, Charlie. This has always been paradise lost. From the time my family came here with the *pobladores,* everybody's been bitching about how nice things used to be before. Selective memory, my friend. Sure, the streets were cleaner but at what price? Have you asked the African-Americans in South Central how things were back in the good old 1950s, when nigger was an official term of endearment? Or the Mexicans, when they were deported in the 1930s, hunted down in the 1940s and segregated in the 1950s, forbidden by law from owning land outside the barrio or even from marrying a white woman? And let's not talk about the Chinese. Or the Jews.

"What's happened here, Charlie, is a failure of nerve. A failure of the Anglos to engage. They don't like the way things are going so they withdraw to their gated communities, take their kids out of public school, pack their jobs out of town and shit on the place of their birth. Let me tell you something. *Inter faeces et urinem.* Between urine and feces, that's how new creatures are born. It's messy and it's painful but what you're seeing here is a new world."

"And Mr. Díaz is a welcome part of that world too, I take it?"

Phil ran his fingers through his luxurious head of hair.

"Ah well, no. He is the exception. A repulsive exception."

He leveled his perfectly tended bushy eyebrows at me, making me wonder how long he spent at the mirror each morning plucking the strays off the bridge of his nose.

"That's why we want, no, strike that, that's why we *need* your help."

"My help for what, Phil? Nobody's contacted me since I gave the statement to the cops at the church. I don't even know who the IO is now that Kelsey's off the case. Your call is the first official piece of business I've received. Assuming you didn't bring me here to debate the inevitable march of history. Or something else."

"Naturally," he said, flustered, splaying his hands in front of him as though to fan away the smell of guilt.

"But we have a slight problem with your story," he added.

"What's the problem? He killed Shana and he tried to kill me. End of story. What else is there to talk about?"

"Let me give you the lay of the land. We can't find any corroborating evidence that any of the parties you said were with you in fact were there that night."

"What?"

Fuentes got up, made a halfhearted attempt to sort through the files in his roll cart.

"It's somewhere in here. I'll get it to you later. The long and the short of it is, the police went over the place with a fine-tooth comb. They couldn't find a thing of what you told them. No body. No knife. No blood. No gun. The officer who interviewed you thought you were delusional. He recommended you be committed forty-eight hours for observation. Fortunately he checked with the watch commander first, who knew me and gave me a call that night."

He stopped, grinned sardonically.

"Now, I know better. I believe you. I believe something happened out there. But we don't have the evidence. And I don't know how to take this either, *carnal*."

A beating of drums, a cry in swirling mist, a chilling realization slowly creeping up my consciousness.

"I am invincible!" he hollers.

"Yo, wait up. You can't tell me that, I was there! With my own two eyes I saw Díaz cut Shana open and tear her heart out on the . . . of course, the rain. It must have washed away the blood. That's why you couldn't find any traces. But the knife . . . bullet casings . . . Look, I am not insane! She was there!"

"What part of no don't you understand? No knife, no bullet casings, no sperm anywhere. *Nada.* You're right about one thing. If she was killed where you said, the storm could have washed away most of the blood and what was left would be degraded. We did pick up a couple of drops from an overhang and from a ledge. The blood on the ledge turned out to be Díaz's. The one in the overhang, preliminary police analysis says it's of animal origin, most likely avian. You know, like in dead chickens."

"I know what avian means."

"Good, because we can't find even those remains, my fine-feathered friend. I'm as big an animal rights activist as the next guy, but slaughtering chickens on your rooftop hardly amounts to murder in the first degree."

"Your rooftop, you said?"

"Yeah. His rooftop. Díaz bought the church months ago. His plans for a condo conversion were being held up in City Planning."

The laughter, the drumming, the emptiness of failure.
   Will he win again?

"Look, what about Shana's home? Did you check that out?"

"Believe me, we did our due diligence. Turns out the land you thought she owned still belonged to Customs. She was a squatter. We did find the remains of her cabin, though, right where you said. It had been burned down. Investigators say it was arson, they think some punk kids from the fancy development up the hill did it."

Fuentes watched me, silently waiting, as the room began to spin.

The laughter again, the maniacal cackle.
   I am invincible!

"Okay, fine," I said, recovering my voice and my reason, barely. "But he attacked me. I can always testify to that."

"We're not sure about that either. Turns out when you walked in, a cross beam from the ceiling fell down. Cops found it on the floor, with your blood on it. In the darkness, that might have been what hit you. We figure somehow you made it up to the roof and that's where you had your confrontation, Díaz thinking you were an intruder. Because he didn't invite you in and you certainly didn't have a search warrant."

"I was making a citizen's arrest!"

"Well, that's more like it. You knew he was a suspect in other crimes so that justifies your breaking in. We can finesse that."

"But what about the shooting? 'Cause he was shot. Or are you saying Díaz just decided to leap off the roof from fear?"

"No, no, that's a given. He was shot all right. Left shoulder, knicked his lung. Díaz is not claiming you did it so we assume your story is correct, that some gangbanger saw you two struggling and decided to give you a hand. Or a bullet, as it were."

I stared down at the floor. A tiny cockroach scuttled across the linoleum and hid under the filing cabinet.

"So what do you need me for? You don't sound like you're going to press charges."

"Wrong again, boobie. We need you bad. But not the way you think."

"How's that?"

"We're pretty sure we can tie him to the murder of your *santería* priest friend and to the guard. We found his prints at Armando's. Plus, some fabric on the guard's head has been traced to Díaz's car."

"Like I said, what do you need me for?"

Fuentes leaned over, his face wrapped in blood lust and ambition.

"We want you to prosecute. We want you to nail him bad. Just like he fucking deserves."

CHAPTER

"CALL for you, Mr. Morell."

The waiter procured a cellular phone from his apron pocket, placed it on the snowy white napped table, in between the Clos du Val Merlot and the small container of extra virgin Napa olive oil. The party at the booth behind us was bragging about his daughter bagging the quarterback from Arizona State and maybe even getting a diamond ring out of it. I turned away into the upholstered booth to muffle the sounds of misplaced pride.

"Morell speaking."

"Mr. Morell?" came Tina's eager-to-please voice. "I finally located your son, like you asked me to. I have him on the line. Please hold."

I smiled at the picture of the turn-of-the-century fireman on the wall, stern mien, dark red shirt, walrus mustache and weak chin.

"Hello?" drawled Julian. I felt proud of myself for once, thinking maybe things could be repaired between the two of us, that for once I would have some semblance of normalcy and a measure of forgiveness.

"Hey, big guy, you're hard to find. I'm not calling at a bad time, am I?"

Across the table Lisa smiled graciously, brushed her bob cut off her forehead, took another sip of her San Pellegrino.

This is what I wanted to hear: "Dad, I'm so glad you called! I read about you in the newspaper, I'm so sorry I was such a jerk the last time we spoke."

This is what I heard instead: "Dad, stop bugging us. Let me make it perfectly clear. I don't want to talk to you. Mom doesn't want to talk to you. Even Gladys doesn't want to hear from you. Just leave us alone, all right? Pretend we don't know you. Forget you ever had a son."

Storm clouds gathered outside the converted firehouse, shadows falling on Figueroa, a smell of moisture gathered in the man-made canyon. A wine cork popped at the table behind us.

"Why are you acting like this? Why do you hate me so much? Tell me what I've done to you," I whispered still.

"Why are you still alive?" came his reply, then the horrifying emptiness of a dead line. I set down the phone, dizzy and weary, the taste of ashes in my mouth.

"Anything wrong?" asked Lisa, taking a bite of the frico-laden focaccia.

"Wrong?" I repeated. I emptied my glass of Merlot, poured another, bolted that one down too, then sank into my seat. I could only take so much defeat.

"You mean aside from the fact that my son wishes I was dead, that my girlfriend forsakes me and my partner breaks up with me, that I've been punched, kicked, shot at and hospitalized and that I don't know why I bother to get up every day? Other than that everything's just hunky-dory, peachy keen, top o' the world, riding on a star, coming up roses. I feel like ten thousand 1986 Michael Milkens rolled into one."

"Stop feeling sorry for yourself, Charlie."

"Sorry? Sorry doesn't begin to encompass what I feel. More like absolute, total, unmitigated misery. Let me put it this way. If I weren't me, I'd hate to shake hands with myself, I'd be afraid my bad luck might rub off. In fact, if I weren't me, I don't think I'd want to be in the same room as me. The same city. The same universe as me."

She draped her slender jeweled hand over mine. "Don't take it so hard."

"Hard? Rigid, isn't that how you like it? So stiff you can pound nails with it? Isn't that what Phil is giving you?"

"Stop it! This is unbecoming of you! You are much too intelligent a man to indulge in this kind of childish tantrum. Grow up, Charlie. We all get left behind sometimes. It's your turn now. Put that aside and concentrate on what you do best."

"What's that, whine?"

"No, the law. You're a great lawyer, Charlie, but you have to bring back your own soul. This is your redemption, baby. Don't walk away from it."

"I see. You are getting a promotion to be lead attorney prosecuting Díaz and you want me to play second banana because that way I can free my soul."

"What do you want me to say? You can make this happen. If you don't help us out, this case is as dead as Armando. You know the office doesn't have anybody with your kind of depth in the field. There's only a handful of *santería* experts in the country and you're the only one who's also an experienced attorney."

"So the real reason you're buying this lunch is so I can rescue you from your own ineptness."

"I really wish you would stop all this. You're also the only lawyer in the world that has successfully mounted a *santería*-based defense in a murder trial. You know intimately all the weak points of that kind of defense and how it can be defeated. And we must defeat it, Charlie. You can't hold yourself above the fray. The dead are calling for justice."

Ghostly bodies appear before my eyes: my waxen mother in her black dress, white-robed Shana with a gaping wound in her chest, Armando's disembodied head, impatient harpies gathering improbably about me.

I am, I realize, slowly losing my mind.

"That's not true," I muttered, putting my napkin back on the table.

"What's not true??"

"All of it. The dead don't ask for justice. The dead are beyond caring. It's we the living who build shrines to them and use them for our own purposes. None of this will help the dead any. They're already gone, Shana. And so am I."

I stood up, dropped a ten on the table as a tip. Our neighbors, quiet for once, looked up from their plates, tiny quail feet sticking out of their mouths.

"Charlie."

"What?"

"My name is Lisa. And I'm still here. If we fail, it'll be on your conscience."

"That's fine. It'll have plenty of company. My failings are legion."

A crisp wind blew off the Harbor Freeway on-ramp, bringing the first hint of autumn. Construction on Figueroa had squeezed all traffic into two lanes and the ensuing jam stretched down to the Coliseum.

I walked down past the rocket-shaped Bonaventure and the glistening Sheraton Grande and up the slope past Cesar Chavez and through Chinatown and found myself at the edge of Elysian Park, staring at the swiftly moving cars on the I-5 and the outline of the squat tenements in Frogtown a short distance way.

The air was clear and the snowy peaks of the San Gabriel Mountains loomed in the distance like an ineffectual bulwark against the madness infecting our whole country, a useless Maginot Line breached time and again by heartless criminals who thought only of money and power and couldn't care less for a single soul in this polluted vale.

I sat on a graffiti-covered rock and watched a falcon slowly wheel around in the thermals off Chavez Ravine, then dive in for its prey somewhere in the bushes behind the cinder block ticket house near the Fire Department. Phil Fuentes's voice somehow came back to me, mocking, cynical, but truthful all the same: 'Twas ever thus, Charlie. 'Twas ever thus.

I shouldn't do it, I thought.

It's a blatant conflict of interest in a situation where even the appearance of conflict can cause the case to take a dive.

I shouldn't do it because I will be just propping up their mistakes, covering up their complicity.

I shouldn't do it, yet . . .

It's true what Lisa said. There are very few people with my expertise. Of all the attorneys in this country probably I'm the only one who has handled this kind of situation with any kind of success.

Like it or not, I'm the only who can put Díaz away. I can make sure that beast never walks the streets again.

I have no choice.

Yes, you do. You can always walk away. Like you've done all your life. What's to stop you now?

●

After a while I retraced my steps back to my car at the garage on Fourth, headed home on the 110 and placed the call from my den after the courts had closed but before everybody went home.

"Phil? It's Charlie. I've been thinking about it. Yeah, I'm on the case."

CHAPTER

JUDGE Abrams, still perspiring from his morning game of racquetball, rushed up to the bench in Division 80 of the Criminal Courts Building. He flashed an outsized grin at seeing the full house, then glanced down the well to make sure his favorite court reporter, Ivy of the frosted shag, was ready for his pronouncements.

Normally confined to the wooden world of preliminary hearings, stuck in the mire of nickel-and-dime drug deals, wife beatings and petty thefts, this was Abrams's time to shine as substitute presiding magistrate in the largest arraignment court in all of Southern California. He intended to make every minute count.

Three buffed deputy sheriffs bunched around the judge like a pack of Mae West's bodyguards, scowling at the wall of noise in the courtroom. A sea of hundreds of brown and black faces, sprinkled occasionally with the pasty-white complexions of the newly arrived East Coast poor, were engaged in a tumult of conversation. Dozens of languages—Tamil, Tagalog, Thai, Chinese, Korean, the ever-present sibilant Spanish—all were heard arguing, whispering, weighing and bewailing the offers prosecutors made to settle cases. A dozen public defenders and paralegals toiled mightily through growing mounds of papers at a table to the right, in front of a glass partition behind which the detainees would soon parade. On the other side of the vast hall, a handful of city and district attorneys went through their paces at a slower rate, confident of their inbuilt advantage. Behind them, stacked against the wall, a panoply of TV cameras were trained on a glass cage.

I sat on the front bench next to Lisa and Phil, thinking that my place was with the brown faces behind us or with the overburdened public defenders trying to wrest some measure of justice from the system.

"Quiet in the court!" shouted one of the deputies, glaring at the crowd as though if it were up to him he'd throw the whole lot into lockup, the vast holding pen three walls behind the bench reeking of urine, feces and sweat.

"Quiet in the courtroom now!" he bellowed once again, this time finally getting everyone's attention.

Behind us, a little Mexican girl, round face ringed with curls, tiny ears pierced with tiny gold earrings, gave a piercing scream and tried to wiggle out of her loaded diaper.

"Ma'am, you're going to have to take the child out of the courtroom," ordered one of the deputies. The mother, dusky and overweight, looked around befuddled, getting no help from the African-Americans on the bench who stared blankly back at her.

I interpreted over the cries of the girl, who, ignoring all courtroom rules of decorum, kept on wailing her little heart out.

Phil stood, addressed the court.

"Your Honor, Deputy District Attorney Philip Fuentes. We're ready on number 256 on calendar, the Díaz case. Defense counsel phoned. He told the clerk he'll be here in ten minutes."

Abrams's swarthy visage darkened even further at the delay. Everybody knew Division 30 was an early court and he had no time to waste—not if he wanted to make it to the driving range by two.

"Counsel, why don't you and Miss Churchill approach? Mr. Morell too, if he can extricate himself from charity work."

The woman wheeled her child out of the courtroom in a Kmart special baby stroller. I picked up my briefcase and walked the forty feet to the thronelike judge's bench.

Phil and Lisa were already in a huddle with the diminutive judge, who towered above us. Thin, dark and sarcastic, Abrams suffered from the compensating viciousness of short men who have been fighting aggressors for so long they have become snapping human terriers.

"Judge, sometimes charity is law," I said at sidebar.

"Not in my courtroom," he snarled. "I leave compassion to the United Way. What are we doing with this case, folks?"

"Your Honor," warbled Phil, ever so sweetly, "we just wanted to let you know that District Attorney Antonetti has made Charlie a special. We're going straight upstairs."

Abrams raised his bushy eyebrows, then signaled at his reporter to come to her second steno machine by the bench.

"We better put this on the record. Ready, Ivy?"

She nodded and her fingers started to dance over the keyboards.

"Well then, Mr. Fuentes. You have just informed this court that Mr. Charles Morell has been appointed special prosecutor by District Attorney Benjamin Antonetti to handle the Ricardo M. Díaz case and that there will be a waiver of preliminary hearing in said case. There is also an agreement that the aforesaid case will be sent directly to Superior Court after arraignment in this courtroom. The district attorney's office does not foresee any situation of fact that would otherwise necessitate a grand jury indictment either and therefore will not seek one. Am I correct so far in my recitation of the facts as you understand them, counsel?"

"Couldn't have put it more succinctly myself, Your Honor," said Phil. Abrams ignored the sarcasm, he had a lecture to deliver.

"Now, Mr. Fuentes, who Mr. Antonetti appoints to prosecute his cases on his behalf is none of my concern, although I must say I do think it's highly unusual for a private counsel who has always, I emphasize, *always* dedicated himself to the defense side to all of a sudden become a spear carrier for the district attorney of the County of Los Angeles in the great State of California."

"Your Honor, I can explain," said Phil but Abrams would not brook any interruption.

"You don't have to explain to me, sir. What you are doing is perfectly legitimate, on the surface. I can offer no legal objection so I will not stand in your way. I am merely advising you that this appointment looks highly suspect and that somewhere down the line the specter of prosecutorial misconduct may rear its ugly head if motives other than an impartial search for justice are discovered to be behind this appointment. I refer specifically to the possibility of financial gain, given that Mr. Morell is a published, one might even say a noted, author.

"This is merely a warning. As I said there is nothing improper in the appointment of Mr. Morell, at this point. But I do feel I would be remiss in my duties as a bench officer were I not to point out the reefs on which your ship of justice may flounder."

I couldn't resist. "Founder, judge," I said. "Flounder is a fish that's all wet, just like your warning, with all due respect, sir."

"Charlie!" warned Phil. Lisa rolled her eyes, incredulous.

"Young man, are you being insolent?"

"Not at all, sir. It's not my intention to belittle the dignity of your robe. However, sir, I will not be the lead attorney. Miss Churchill will. I will be second seat, advisor on certain technical aspects dealing with the rituals of *santería,* which we anticipate will have an important bearing on the case. I may not even get to question a single witness. Most likely I will be the inspiration, the soul, if you wish, but not the arms of the prosecution. So for all we know your reservations may turn out in the end to be baseless, or if you prefer, moot."

Abrams huffed, checked for the time being.

"Fine, then. Let's proceed with this . . . off the record . . . travesty. Don't say you were not warned at an early stage. Back on the record. Now, as regards the waiver, don't you think we should have opposing counsel here? There has to be an express waiver from the defendant. Who is counsel, anyhow?"

The judge rifled through his case file, scanning the pink arraignment sheet.

"He was originally interviewed by the office of the alternate public defender, a conflict having been declared by the PD. Then he gave notice he was going to hire private counsel . . . off the record . . . who I presume is going along with your cockamamie scheme although for the life of me I can't see why. Yes, Patrick?"

The latest tall, blond, boyish waif Abrams had hired as his clerk—the previous one having lasted all of two months—floated next to the diminutive judge. He whispered in Abrams's ear, handed him a card, then pointed at the audience. Abrams looked up.

"Well, folks, I think the show's about to begin. Mr. Díaz's counsel has arrived."

He read from the card.

"On the record. He's Jacobo Bloomberg, from the law firm of Bloomberg, Morales and Watson, out of Miami and San Francisco. Off the record. Know him, Charlie?"

I turned to the clerk's desk where a gray-haired gentleman in a pin-striped suit, large leather satchel in hand, smiled agreeably as he awaited his turn. I shook my head no.

The judge called him over. The moment he came near, even before the telltale accent, he was betrayed by the sweet scent of Florida water.

"We're on the record with all counsel on the Díaz matter," said the judge.

"Good morning, Your Honor," he said with the soft consonants of most Miami Cubans, "Jacobo Bloomberg. You can call me Jake. I will be representing Mr. Díaz."

He shook hands all around, giving me a special nod.

"I informed Mr. Fuentes over the telephone that we would be waiving prelim so we can proceed directly to arraignment in Superior Court."

"Fine, fine," said the judge, surreptitiously wiping his hand on his robe. "Let us proceed then. One thing, Mr. Fuentes. Are you making any offers on this case?"

"No offers, Your Honor. We will be seeking the death penalty."

"Really?" said Bloomberg, as surprised as if he'd been told he'd won the Super Lotto Fantasy Five. "Well, never say never. I'll be in touch, Mr. Fuentes."

"I will not be handling this case; Miss Churchill here will. Mr. Morell will be second chair. You better contact them from now on."

Bloomberg turned appreciative liquid brown eyes on Lisa.

"It will be my pleasure."

●

"Ecch! What a slime doggie!" whispered Lisa as we walked away from the bench. "From what rock did he crawl out under?"

"I don't know, but I have a feeling we better find out real soon," I said. "Let me call Miami."

"Stand back! Stand back!"

As if on cue, the six cameramen lined up against the wall swiveled, following with their lenses the slow, almost triumphal arrival of Ricardo Díaz. Pushed down the courtroom aisle by a fullback-sized deputy sheriff, Díaz nodded amiably from his wheelchair at the audience in the benches. Six deputies, side-arms strapped on, safeties unlatched, posted themselves in different angles of the courtroom. The black deputy selected as Díaz's aide-de-camp gestured violently at a stoop-shouldered Mexican woman at the bar attempting to find her elusive public defender. The moment she noticed the full panoply of security and the lanky, grinning prisoner in yellow jailhouse uniform heading her way, the woman sat down and made the sign of the cross.

The deputy pushed Díaz into the well. Díaz glanced all around, his wide hazel eyes registering every nook and cranny of the courtroom, as though inspecting it for possible future use. He had lost weight during the weeks of confinement, his long tapered nose becoming sharper and more beaklike, his sharp cheekbones cutting into the air around him with every careful, considered move.

Even with his most ingratiating smile, his left arm in a cast and shackles on his legs, Díaz still seemed danger personified, dormant, perhaps, but never dead. His gaze rested on me. He raised his thin eyebrows in mock surprise, lifting his right hand to point an accusatory index finger, which he wagged as though saying, you bad boy what have you done this time?

Bloomberg engaged him in a brief conversation, diverting his attention.

"He gives me the creeps," whispered Lisa. "He's just like in my dreams."

"You mean your nightmares," I countered.

Abrams shifted in his seat, turned his profile to the cameras.

"In the Díaz case, counsel, your appearances, please."

"Lisa Churchill for the people."

A moment of silence as Bloomberg continued to urgently confer with Díaz. I overheard him whisper in Spanish, "Don't do it, it's too dangerous!"

"Counsel for the defense?" prodded Abrams.

"Yes, Your Honor," finally answered Bloomberg. "Jacobo Esterhazy Bloomberg, for Mr. Díaz."

"Fine. Proceed with arraignment, Miss Churchill."

Lisa walked over to the prosecutor's table, her hands barely shaking as she read from the complaint in a loud, clear voice.

"Ricardo Díaz, is that your true and correct name?"

Díaz took notice of Lisa for the first time, his thin lips smiling in appreciation of her long legs, her shiny brown hair, her deep blue eyes.

He nodded.

"You'll have to answer out loud so the reporter can take down your answer, sir," she said.

"Yes, that is my name," came Díaz's voice. A natural tenor, I thought.

"In complaint number BA7289786, you are charged on count one with violation of section 187a of the Penal Code, murder in the first degree, in that you willfully and intentionally and with malice aforethought took the life of—"

"Your Honor, the defendant is ready to enter his plea," interrupted Bloomberg, who again had been whispering to Díaz while crouching next to the wheelchair.

Abrams fixed them with his most supercilious look. Díaz may have killed, skinned and decapitated as many people as he wanted outside, but in Abrams's courtroom he was as inconsequential as the many roaches that ran underfoot in chambers when he turned the lights on in the morning.

"Doesn't your client want to hear the rest of the charges?"

"He's ready to plead right now, Your Honor. He would like to place a statement into the record afterward."

Abrams arched his eyebrows, granted himself the luxury of a smirk. Anything Díaz said would be used against him. He certainly wasn't about to stop a murderer from digging his own grave.

"I will be most happy to allow your client to put his statement on the record. But he *will* wait. We follow procedure in this courtroom, sir. Miss Churchill, please continue to advise the defendant of the charges."

Lisa continued intoning the main charges in the information: murder, mayhem, assault, rape and sodomy on the persons of Armando Ponce and of William James Chase, the hapless guard killed in my backyard.

Not a word on Shana's death.

I had had to give up trying to find traces of Shana. She had been with me, I had seen her cruelly slaughtered before my eyes, but without the corpus, the actual body, Phil felt there was no way we could reasonably support a murder charge. Adding her death to the complaint would have meant eliminating me from the prosecution team, for I would be a witness in the case. In fact, my testimony would be practically the only evidence a crime had been committed. I'd argued for including her all the same but with all traces of Shana's existence having vanished after her shack burned down, I'd had to give up on it for the time being.

There was de Palma, it was true, but in spite of my best efforts, I'd been unable to reach her. She had vanished, as though I'd imagined her visit, as though she had never been alongside me on that fateful drive to Frogtown. I had called Miami, even sent an investigator to locate her. She had moved out of her house. My PI told us she had quit her job at the college after an argument with the head of the department over her political views—apparently too liberal for her fellow exiles. I knew I should have pressed the issue, but that way lay the scent of madness and tropical magic and I didn't know if I was up to it. Like the stubborn monks of old, I saw the horizon curve but still I swore the world was flat, even though I knew better.

"How do you plea to these charges, Mr. Díaz?"

"Not guilty," said Díaz.

"Do you admit or deny the special allegations?" finished Lisa.

"Deny, of course. May I speak now?"

"Just a moment," said Abrams. "Do you know what a preliminary hearing is and do you waive it?"

"Yes, just let me talk."

"Counsel concur and join in the waiver?"

"I do, Your Honor," resounded Bloomberg's measured voice.

"Now may I talk?" whined Díaz again.

"Be my guest," said the judge, taking off his reading glasses and placing them on his desk blotter. "You have my undivided attention."

"With all due respect and consideration, Your Highness, I would like to say that this case is one of malicious prosecution."

Abrams shot a look our way as though saying, I told you so. But Díaz quickly reversed field, flushed, almost as if the words had unwittingly escaped from his mouth.

"Excuse me, I meant to say religious persecution."

Abrams shifted his gaze back to Díaz. This was something new.

"I am a practitioner of *santería,* a legitimate form of worship, as ruled by the U.S. Supreme Court in the case of *Church of the Lukumí Balalú Ayé* v. *City of Hialeah.* We honor the ancient gods and we make sacrifice to them. For this only have I been accused of murder. We do not slaughter humans, for we hold the human soul to be the highest expression of life on this earth. But unfortunately certain people . . ."

He turned to me, knowingly glowering.

"Certain people have profited from the misconception, the big lie that the enemies of our church have propagated. In order to obtain their profit, they make us out to be unnatural monsters who feed on the blood of the innocent. We are not monsters, Your Highness, natural or unnatural. We are only people. We respect the sanctity of human life and we uphold all the laws of this and all other countries under the watchful eye of Ollodu-mare, the father of us all."

Abrams put his bifocals back on, his gesture as languid as that of a plantation belle fanning herself in the Mississippi heat.

"That's all very interesting, Mr. Díaz. But it's you who are charged with murder, not this, what do you call it? Your religion."

"I disagree, Your Highness. *Santería* is on trial here."

"Reasonable men have a right to differ, I suppose. But do me a favor, don't call me Highness. I'm not the pope, I'm Jewish."

Laughter in the courtroom. For the first time in all my years in so many courtrooms, I actually saw something I'd seen previously only in cheap movies and bad TV series: the judge gaveled the place into silence.

"Order!" he said, using a round steel puck instead of the usual wooden mallet. "Order here!"

The laughter died down. Abrams returned to Díaz.

"Mr. Díaz, you strike me as a very intelligent young man. Let's see if your reasoned arguments will convince the ultimate trier of fact, the jury. Your case will be heard in Department 224 of the Superior Court on October 17, at 8:30 A.M. for arraignment. Have a good day, sir."

Abrams shook his head twice as though to dismiss the

annoying arrogance he had just witnessed. In seconds Díaz and Bloomberg were ushered into the lockup behind the bench and onto the back elevators. Other attorneys stepped forward with their cases, the camera people stopped rolling tape. Phil Fuentes came up to us, face crimson with embarrassment.

"Upstairs. My office."

CHAPTER

"'THE last thing we need is to make this a religion case."

We were in the district attorney's lunchroom, available since Antonetti was off to San Francisco on a fund-raiser for his exploratory run for the attorney general's office. Phil toyed with his empty Crystal Geyser bottle, while Lisa licked the foam off the cappuccino she'd brought in from Pasqua's. I took a sip of the coffee I'd poured out of the lunchroom thermos and quickly put down the cup, the bitter brew tasting like the dregs of a bad dream.

"Especially since he has AIDS. That could be a sympathy factor."

"He does?" I was stunned. Lisa looked in her file, checking the County Jail's clinic's records.

"So they say in County. That's why he was wearing hospital

yellow. But you know how it is with HIV, it can bloom in a month or stay inactive for years. I would expect them to try to milk that for all it's worth."

"I don't see how," I replied, laying aside the implications of his disease that came to my mind. "He's making unsubstantiated allegations about *santería* which are totally irrelevant to the charges."

"I don't know about that, Charlie," countered Phil, almost but not quite regretfully.

"What, did we pick up on him because he's a *santero?* You know that's not true."

"Charlie's right," piped in Lisa. "It's Díaz's prints at the scene. He can't deny those."

"A palm print, folks, let's not forget," said Phil. "A partial palm print, at that."

"That's enough," I said.

"Barely. And only if we can bring in the whole power thing over *quién es más macho* and how Díaz wanted to enslave the old man's soul and all that. In essence, we are putting *santería* on trial, since we'll be arguing it fosters that kind of thinking."

"We don't have to bring that in," I argued. "We have enough circumstantial evidence. There's the fibers and the drop of blood."

"All of which were gathered by someone the defense will make out to be unreliable," countered Phil again, spinning the empty bottle on the tabletop. It pointed at me when it stopped.

"Kelsey? You mean to say that the defense will bring in the fact that the accused had a relationship with the investigator as a means of discrediting the evidence? Shades of Mark Fuhrman."

"Hey, O.J. rewrote all the rules in this department. Nobody wants to make the same mistake twice. Besides, it's a perfectly legitimate defense," said Phil. "What do they care about Kelsey's ass? Speaking of which, Lisa, what's the latest word from Internal Affairs?"

Lisa wiped her lips carefully on the scratchy blue napkin, gathering her thoughts.

"You both know Kelsey's been suspended with pay while the investigation on his role proceeds. Here's the thing. He claims he didn't put two and two together, that when he went to the church he thought he was talking to one Rocky Chevarría, a drug dealer he thought might have info about a drive-by out in Rampart."

"Wait a minute," I said. "You mean to tell me he's claiming he never got a picture or a composite of Díaz?"

"Right. He says he put in a request but that the computer at JDIC crashed. When it went back up, it turned out the prints and photo were not in the system but down somewhere in San Diego County. So he tried hitting S.D. but it didn't show. Then he found out Díaz had originally been picked up by Chula Vista PD, which still had the info he needed."

"What a frigging mess," I said. Lisa shrugged.

"Typical. Anyhow, he put in the request to Chula Vista, which as you know is a really small department. They had to look for it, fax it, blah blah, so by the time he actually got the mug shot and a copy of the six-pack, the whole thing had blown up in our face. You never did give him a photo of Díaz, did you?"

I shook my head no, embarrassed by my own screwup.

"Well, there you go," said Lisa. "Kelsey's excuse is, how was he supposed to know that this guy involved in all those murders in Baja was the same guy who did these two guys here in L.A. Unfortunately, he's got a point."

"No, he doesn't," I said, beginning to think that Lisa and Phil were going beyond playing devil's advocate, they were actually really dubious we could successfully prosecute.

"I told Kelsey I was certain it had been Díaz when he was at my house. He can't possibly deny that," I said, angrily hitting the table.

Lisa looked at me balefully. Once again I was losing control.

I took a deep breath. It's a game, I told myself. It's the law, blind and impersonal. You're just its tool.

No, you're not, insists another voice.
This is your soul you are trafficking with.

"Well," drawled Lisa, raising her pretty plucked eyebrows, "he could deny it. Which then would put us in a pickle, don't you think? We'd have to have a 402 hearing and you'd be called in to testify as to what you told him and what Kelsey knew and when he knew it. Luckily he's not making that claim so far. He hasn't said either way."

She took another sip of her cappuccino. "Are you following me so far?"

"Perfectly," I added. "So what can the defense do with that?"

Danielle, Antonetti's personal secretary, walked into the lunchroom, a self-possessed image of middle-aged Teutonic efficiency in a bright blue silk tunic that ended well above her perfectly preserved knees.

"There's a gentleman to see you, Philip," she said, with just the slightest trace of a Bavarian accent. "A Mr. Bloomberg. Says he's on the Díaz case."

"Speak of the devil," said Lisa.

"Show him into the conference room. Lisa and Mr. Morell will be with him in a moment."

Danielle nodded, softly padded out of the room in her Maud Frizon flats. Phil wheeled his chair around.

"Conference room is wired for sound. It automatically voice-activates anytime you close the door, so you don't have to worry about notes."

"That is illegal!" I blustered. Phil shrugged.

"Welcome to the real world, Charlie. I'm going to leave it to you two to decide what to say to the devil's advocate. Don't sell the ranch, okay? We gotta win this one."

Jake Bloomberg was doing something totally out of character for a Cuban when I walked into the conference room—he was sitting patiently at the table. His Mark Cross portfolio was by his side, yellow-lined legal-size notepad set precisely at a ninety degree angle in front of him. I sneaked a look at the tablet as we shook hands but couldn't decipher his scribbling.

"Don't bother, it's Hebrew steno," he said in Spanish, noticing my downward glance.

His large brown eyes lifted at the corners in amusement, his deeply tanned face in smiling repose. I tried to place where I had last seen his type, then it came to me.

"You know, Jake, you look like an entertainment lawyer," I said with the utmost insincerity. He lifted his hands partially in the air, flattered by the comparison.

"What are you doing in Miami," I added, pronouncing it the way old time Dade County natives do, MEE-*AH*-ME, "when you could be out here eating with the stars? Eating out the starlets?"

He put his palms outward, shooing this rich dish away. A single, flawless aqua sparkled on his right ring finger; on his left, a diamond-studded wedding band.

"*Qué va*, I leave that to my cousin, he's VP Legal over at Columbia Tri-Star. I prefer the quiet rewards of a local clientele. The Myerses, the Maases, the Hazlits. Besides, the stars are moving to South Florida. Cher just bought this great house down the road from Madonna and Rambo and all the others are coming our way too. I figure they'll be knocking at my door when they need me. Eventually everybody does. I'm in no hurry."

He grinned again, the pleasant habit of the appliance salesman who lets his products do the talking.

"But you're obviously Cuban. Where did you learn Hebrew?"

"*Coño, chico,* papa was *polaco,*" he said, using the Cuban term for any Eastern European Jew, "so after the revolution he took us to Tel Aviv. Hell, I was even in the '67 war, only nineteen at the time and fighting the poor Arabs. But when I grew up I decided to be with my people. Because, I may be a Jew but I'm a Cuban first and foremost."

"A Jewban," I said.

"That's right. I always say all good Cubans should be in Miami, where they belong. We've taken over the place since you left, you're aware."

"So I've been told. If that's the case, how can you defend this guy? He's a shame to our people."

"Hey, business is business," he said in English, dispensing with the Cuban niceties. "I was hired to do the job the best I can. You can understand that. You were defense counsel up till yesterday."

"Who's paying you? It sure isn't Díaz because he's flat broke."

"C'mon, Charlie, you know I can't tell you that. Disclosing that information would be unethical. Besides, what does it matter? The point is, I'm here, you gotta deal with me as long as Ricardo wants me. By the way, where is Miss Churchill? Is she coming?"

I shook my head no. "She felt we should meet first, *hermano a hermano,* brother to brother, and try to get this settled. You know your boy's gonna fry."

"Fry, schfry. You've got the flimsiest case against him. The physical evidence will not hold water. Not after our experts go through it. Contamination, timeline, handling, chain of custody. Very, very dubious. The whole world knows how sloppy the LAPD Scientific Investigation Unit is, especially jurors here in L.A. And with a downtown jury pool, well, need I say more? Half of the jurors are probably clutching some kind of *prenda.*

The blacks clutch their rabbit feet and gold chains, the Chinese and the Vietnamese have little altars to their ancestors back home and in the restaurants. And the Mexicans with their *lim-pias* and *curanderas*. I don't think you're going to find a sympathetic jury that's going to believe Ricardo is guilty of murder because he practices a different religion. Because that's what we're talking about, freedom of religion."

He paused, making sure the words sank in, then adjusted the sleeves of his charcoal gray Brioni suit. I shrugged, unwilling to show my concern.

"All we have to do is draw a distinction between what the Supreme Court ruled on, *santería,* and what Díaz practices, which is black magic of the worst sort," I replied.

"That's BS and you know it," snapped Bloomberg. "That's the kind of thing people used to say against Jews and Catholics, that one kind of worship is better than another. Look, who in their right mind is going to believe all that stuff about killing people to enslave their souls? Who? Because that's going to be your argument, your motive for the murders, right?"

I said nothing, letting Bloomberg's sudden ire boil over and spread its foul fumes in the room.

"Jews too were once accused of killing babies for their ceremonies, Christian babies slaughtered on the altar of Moses. That was the reason for the pogroms, the original rationale for Hitler's slaughter of millions of innocent souls."

"What's your point, Jake?"

He suddenly settled down, modulated his voice to his most charming Southern tone.

"My point is, you're barking up the wrong tree, son."

"We've got the bodies."

"Very unfortunate. My heart goes out to the victims and their families. But more innocent blood spilled will not wipe away this tragedy."

I was stunned by his brazenness. "You're telling me to my face that your client is innocent?"

He nodded his head, gripped my hand with fierce intensity.

"He's as pure as the driven snow."

I took my hand away, a feeling of physical revulsion sweeping over me.

"Right. Like the snow on a New York sidewalk, black and full of shit. Listen, Jake, *mi hermano,* your client killed—"

I stopped, fortunately right before blurting out that he had killed Shana and tried to kill me as well. If I let on that I had been one of his intended victims, Bloomberg would file for vindictive prosecution faster than you could say *hasta la vista.*

"Yes?" drawled Bloomberg, a half smile on his lips.

"He's killed a lot of people. We've got Decker's confession. We've got him in possession of Armando's things in Mexico."

Bloomberg moved his head sideways, sighed, as though disappointed by what he interpreted as my misguided earnestness.

"Carlitos, who the fuck is going to believe any kind of evidence obtained in that outhouse south of the border? People get beaten and tortured into confessing. It's wetback justice. That's why nobody believes it. Which is why we're going to beat the extradition charges. Besides which, even if you brought her here and somehow you convinced her to give a statement against Díaz—which God knows would be hard to do given her daddy's influence in California and the district attorney's office . . ."

He wiggled his eyebrows to let me know he too was aware of Senator Decker's relationship to Fuentes.

"Even then her statement cannot come in. Of course, I don't have to tell you why."

"Go ahead, enlighten me."

"Charlie, you know better than that. C'mon, second-year law school. It's a self-serving exculpatory statement given by a codefendant in the case. It's not valid, cannot be used. I know I don't have to explain this. Like the man said, I ain't got to show you no stinking badges. Speaking of which."

Suddenly he sat up, looked around the discreet wood-paneled room, where many a failed conference—like mine—had been held in the past.

"Is it on?"

"Is what on?"

"The tape recorder. I've been told this room is wired and I want to make sure you got everything I'm going to tell you next."

"I don't know anything about that," I lied, equally brazen. "I just work here. Besides, California law precludes the use of tape-recorded statements unless the person being recorded gives informed consent."

Bloomberg looked hard at me, shook his head in disbelief.

"*Coño*, you are full of beans, aren't you? All right, fine. Be that way. Here's what. We have evidence of the most exculpatory kind for our client. Normally I wouldn't disclose it unless there was a discovery motion pending before the court but . . ."

He resorted to the best jivey Cuban Spanish, the kind heard most often on sultry nights at José Martí Park on SW Eighth Street. "For a Cuban buddy in a jam, I'll make an exception."

"Don't jerk me off, just tell me what's the cunt shit you got," I replied in kind.

"*Chévere, 'mano,*" he said, still teasing. Then: "I got an undercover videotape recording of my client discussing a drug shipment with your investigator, Sergeant Kelsey, and guess what? It puts him ten miles away, with witnesses, at the time Armando Ponce was killed."

He leaned back, slouched confidently in his chair, hands entwined behind his head.

"How do you like them guavas?"

• • •

Once I got my hands on the surveillance tape, I played it at home dozens of times, observing time and again the site of the meeting, the players, the swagger with which Díaz walked in camera range, the way he made a show of checking his hair at the two-way mirror. Throughout, the fateful time code rolling out the date and time, marking down to the last fraction of a second the time when Armando had been so brutally murdered.

If it wasn't Díaz, then who had done it? And if not he, who else would have the motive to slaughter him so hideously?

It took me three days to locate Phil and Lisa, finally making contact with them on Columbus Day, the *Día de la Raza,* commemorating the date when an Italian Jew working for the Spanish crown had sailed into a sand spit, called it land and bragged he had reached India. American history as a comedy of errors from the start.

In a way it was all too fitting that our rendezvous was at the hilltop mansion of Danny Griswald. A onetime talent agent, he'd built the largest independent music and entertainment outfit in Hollywood, only to sell out later to a friendly Japanese multinational for a cozy couple of billion. Like all arrivistes, Griswald was obsessed with the past. For his Los Angeles residence—he enjoyed others in Fire Island, San Francisco, Paris, Positano and Belize—he had bought the old Antonio Navarro estate, built by the architect to the stars, Wallace Neff, on a hilltop in Beverly Hills.

The occasion was a black tie affair and, like the old publicist hacks used to say, there were more stars in the Spanish Revival manse than there were in the sky on that foggy night. Modeled after the castle of La Guiralda, the estate took up thirty acres of prime land; the mansion's quarter-mile-long forecourt, graced with a fountain ripped out of a thirteenth-century monastery in

Navarre, was packed with luxury cars. A small squad of red-vested Mexican valets stood ready to take your wheels at the gate, sending you skyward up a garden path lined with exotic flowers flown in from Hawaii and Indonesia for the occasion. When the party budget was half a million dollars, what was a mere fifty thousand spent on sweetly scented flora? Chump change.

A chump was what I felt like, waltzing among the glitterati in my cheap cotton suit, swept forward by wave after wave of implausibly fit men and dazzlingly gorgeous women poured into Valentinos, Azaias, Donna Karans, Calvin Kleins and all the other couturiers whose careers are a testament to moneyed beauty.

And those were just the assistants. The stars—Jack, Michelle, Barbra, Tom and Nicole—they were in another universe altogether, animated by the force of their personalities, with the brittle nerves of those who know their careers, glorious as they might be right now, are always just a couple of box office flops away from extinction. Only the managers and attorneys seemed immune, gobbling up hors d'oeuvres and quaffing champagne like there was no tomorrow.

Phil and Lisa were in the vast groin-vaulted ballroom, doing a sedate fox trot to "Blue Moon" sung by a blond chanteuse in a red satin gown who thought she was back in some old TV series spoofing the noir 1940s. Only to Lisa and Phil, the music and the world it came from were real. By dint of dogged pursuit, they had made the magical leap to an era both of them had only dreamed of.

Looking at them it was hard for me to stay sore at Lisa for leaving me; she was Phil's perfect fit. I thought I was going to be their reality check, their nagging buzzer, but a little man in a black velvet tux, long red hair gathered in a ponytail, cut ahead of me. He pulled them off the dance floor and was making emphatic gestures, gesturing at another man across the hall. By the French doors, tall, silver-haired Senator Tom Decker stood waiting, sipping what looked to be a club soda. Phil and Lisa shook their head no and were about to walk away when I made my move, hoping to save them the embarrassment of a conscience.

"Fancy meeting you here," I said, walking up behind them. They did a double take.

"Charlie?" said Phil first, smoothly recovering. "I didn't take you for a Save the Kids contributor."

"I've been known to give my share every so often," I said, shaking his hand, kissing Lisa on the cheek.

"Better not get near Decker," I whispered in Lisa's ear.

"That's what I've been telling him," she whispered back, nibbling on my earlobe.

"Mr. Griswald, this is our special counsel on the Díaz case, Charlie Morell," said Phil.

"Yeah, yeah, Charlie, I know you. Your partner Farris froze me out of the Coolio deal a few years ago," said Griswald. He sniffed, then wiped his dripping nose on a handkerchief produced by one of several muscular goons standing next to him.

"I had nothing to do with that. I handle criminal in the office."

Griswald shrugged. "Hey, that was a crime! I could have made a cool twenty mil out of Coolio the first couple of years. He could have been the next Tupac and lived to enjoy it. Don't you think, guys?"

He turned to his muscular companions, who nodded in agreement to such sagaciousness.

"What the fuck," he said, shaking his head. "I'm supposed to be retired till next year when the no-competition clause ends. But you tell Farris next time I'm going to make him my girlfriend, you know what I'm talking about?"

"I'll be sure to give him the message," I said, thinking their love match would be something to watch.

"Enjoy yourself. Have some more Cristal on me."

He adjusted his flowing ponytail, then strutted away on his four-inch-high sneakers. "That thing is a hairpiece," said Lisa, to no one in particular. Three waiters suddenly surrounded us, as if by magic, offering trays of champagne and canapés. We all declined.

I took out the video Bloomberg had given me.

"You guys think Mr. Big will lend us his VCR for a couple of minutes?"

Phil popped the tape out of the hundred-thousand-dollar state-of-the-art VCR in the audio-video room somewhere in the basement of the mansion. He came back and sat next to us on the Mario Buatta chintz sofa. Lisa shifted in her seat, the rustling of her taffeta a promise heartlessly broken, then lit a cigarette, tilting her head as though seeking to see more clearly.

"Put out that thing, will you? It's going to screw up the machine," said Phil. Lisa stuck out her tongue, blew a great big mouthful of smoke our way.

"How solid is this?" he asked me.

"Solid enough. The camera was inspected regularly, the date was on automatic. There's no sign the tape was altered. He might have some problem with the chain of custody but it is pretty convincing."

"This could destroy our case. How did Bloomberg get it?"

"He's not saying. Claims a friend in the department slipped it to him. It must be O'Haran, the guy Kelsey walked up to the church with."

"So it's not official, then," said Lisa.

"Well, no, but as you can see, we can't deny its existence."

"We'll have to attack the credibility of the technician," said Phil. "Maybe there was a blackout that affected the machine, maybe someone tampered with it. We don't know how it came to be."

"Bloomberg's going to bring it up. It's exculpatory. How do you want us to handle it?"

Phil glared at Lisa, who blew another cloud of smoke our way. Now you know what we went through, I thought. Phil took a deep breath, forced himself to concentrate.

"Hold off on that for a moment. What have you found out about Bloomberg?"

"I made a couple of calls. The guy seems to be what he promises."

"Meaning?"

"He's connected all right. In his last big case he got Miami councilman Jimmy Bernardes off on a bribery charge, even though they found a satchel of greenbacks in his house, as well as stolen files from the Public Works Department with altered bid docs."

"Capital cases?"

"He was past president of the Dade County Bar, has handled over fifty death penalties. Bloomberg has never lost a single one that went to trial. That's about half. The others he dispo'd down to manslaughter or even time served. Man is charmed."

"Or in league with the devil, if you ask me," said Lisa, throwing yet another cloud of smoke.

"Nobody asked you," snapped Phil. He snatched Lisa's cigarette out of her mouth, threw it on the floor, then stepped on it to put it out. To my surprise, I saw Lisa actually enjoyed this little exercise in machismo. Live and learn.

"Let's go upstairs. I'm sure the band's playing again," he said, taking her by the hand.

"What are we going to do about this tape?" I insisted.

Phil paused by a minor Fragonard on the wall.

"He can't use it. He's bluffing. He wants to force our hand."

"And if he does bring it up?"

Fuentes grinned, the player who knows his hand has been called, the sharecropper who hears the *patrón* demanding his half of the crop.

"Like Doris Day said in *The Man Who Knew Too Much*, *qué será, será*. C'mon Lisa, I got dancing feet."

She sighed and the two swept away. I sat in the media room for a moment, then followed them upstairs. It was time for me to go too.

Phil could be right and the tape could prove to be inadmissible in court. But even so, like I had told them, that didn't change the fact that it existed.

So if Díaz wasn't the murderer, who was? And if he was the killer, after all, how could he be in two places at the same time?

CHAPTER

20

THE crowds on Ocean Drive surged down the broad sun-kissed sidewalk as though hurrying to a bikini contest—bronzed, ripped and bursting with the sweetness of the flesh, revealing as much of their bodies as they thought they could get away with before getting busted by the bicycle cops.

Across the street, past the swaying palms and over the gleaming dunes of imported sand, European models went topless in the closest equivalent to the Riviera that Florida had ever known. But I didn't have the heart to budge from my barside table to take a peek. Instead I stared at the dregs of my fourth *mojito*, feeling old and wrung out by the last four days, beached on a shore without shelter.

A school of shirtless, long-haired strapping hulks in Harleys revved their throaty engines as they swarmed around a stopped

Ferrari Testarossa, broke ranks and regrouped on the far side of the muscle car. I asked the waiter for another double, my eyes drifting to a framed cover of an old *Bohemia* magazine, the pre-Castro *Life* magazine of Cuba, showing a pastel drawing of a tall mulatto dancer wearing a tight spangled costume with a long feathered train.

Carnaval en La Habana, 1957.

Carnaval in Miami, 1997.

Plus ça change.

Remarkably, I had come to South Florida with high hopes.

I'd finally made contact with de Palma, laying aside the gnawing fear that her visit had been a hallucination. With the timeline on Díaz's link to Armando's murder now in doubt because of the revelation of the surveillance tape, de Palma's testimony was more important than ever, in case everything else went wrong. She confirmed over the phone that Shana had indeed been with us and had never come out of the church. De Palma herself had called the police from a phone booth on hearing the first shot. She had hung around town for two days, waiting for me to come out of the hospital, but ultimately continued on to Oregon and British Columbia on a speaking tour after she was told my prognosis was uncertain. I made arrangements then to fly out right away and take her sworn videotaped statement.

Once in Miami I drove up to her house on Coconut Grove, a Spanish concoction of pink plaster and gray coral surrounded by flanks of royal palms and overgrown trees, sheltering the house from the blazing sun with a canopy of dark green.

I knocked at the old wooden door. A pleasant-looking matron with a mop of champagne curls opened the door dressed in a pale green housecoat.

"You must be *Señor* Morell," she said in Spanish, still pleasantly, as she led me into a foyer scented with basil and gardenia, replete with long-legged statues from Nigeria and Benin. I saw my questioning reflection in a seashell-encrusted mirror perched on the plaster wall. A glass vase full of copper coins in clear water rested on a fruitwood console.

"I'm Marta Habib, Graciela's friend. Please, make yourself comfortable," she said, gesturing at a down-filled sofa. "Let me tell Berta to make you a *cafecito*."

A spray of African textiles covered the floor; one living room wall was lined with African masks, the other with a stylized altar to some *santería* god. In silver frames scattered throughout, on the low coffee table and the bookcases, photo after photo of de Palma and Habib, laughing, embracing, cutting flowers. Picture-perfect lesbian bliss.

Habib returned with a tray bearing two thimble-sized cups of Cuban coffee.

"I hope you like it sweet," she said, passing the cup. I tasted the bitter brew and wondered what she meant. "Graciela unfortunately had to leave but she said to tell you that she will be in touch with you soon."

I put down the cup, stunned. "Excuse me, but did she say how soon exactly? I came all the way from Los Angeles to interview her."

"I know, it's so sad. I told her to call you but you know how she is, she's so forgetful, she remembered this morning when I took her to the airport, would you believe it? She said to give you her fullest apologies."

"Apologies are not going to do. I will have to subpoena her if she won't cooperate."

"I'm sorry. I had no idea this was so serious."

"Extremely serious. She could be charged with obstruction of justice and hauled off to jail if she doesn't show up to testify."

Habib put down her cup, not at all offended that I would have the insolence to make such threats in her own house.

"Well, *Señor* Morell," she said sweetly, "if you can get her back, I'm sure she will cooperate."

"Believe me, we will try our best. Where is she right now?"

"*Ay, Dios mío,* you mean she didn't say? She went to Nigeria on a Rockefeller fellowship to study the Ekué Yamba O cult and its links to *santería.* She said she might be back for Christmas, if that's any help. Tell me, what is this all about?"

What is this all about. I laughed into my drink, remembering. That's a fine question, I decided. A fine fine question. Almost as good as what is the truth. But which side am I on, the judge's or the judged?

Unwilling to totally write off the trip, even if for once my personal life would prevail over my professional life, I drove up the bay to the Spanish mansion I'd worked so hard to acquire and given up so easily for a cheating passion. This time I saw Livvie, lovely and bitter as ever.

"He really doesn't want to see you, you know," she said at the door, dressed in crisp tennis whites, like an image from some dated Palm Beach magazine. Her equally pristine partner —raven-haired, square-jawed, a 1920s Arrow collar ad come to life—sat patiently on my beige Longhia chaise.

Her beige Longhia chaise now.

For the briefest moment it occurred to me that the secret to a happy life in South Florida is a willing disbelief in the present. Like boats beating against the current, Floridians are always trying desperately to recapture their past—be it the Anglo dream of Mizner and Flagler or the Latin vision of Arnaz and Batista. How different from Los Angeles, where the future stares down at you every time you open your front door, its fatal modernity grabbing you at the throat, daring you to ignore it.

"I think Julian should be the one to decide," I told Livvie, still standing in the cool, umber-tiled foyer.

"As you wish. But make it quick, I have a set of doubles in ten minutes at the club. You know the way."

She skulked silently back to the living room, sat next to her partner, making a show of placing his hand on her lap.

"Who's that?" I overheard the man say as I walked up the stairs to my son's bedroom.

"Someone that I used to know," she said, in chilling echo of an old cheap song. Not that well, I wanted to rejoin, but I kept silent and trudged on.

At the landing I ran into Gladys, coming down with a folded comforter. She looked startled for a moment, then she understood.

"You never give up, do you, Mr. Charlie?"

"If I lose, it won't be for lack of trying. Where is he now?"

"He's in his room. I don't believe he's expecting you," she said, cautiously.

"Let's see if we have better luck this time, then," I said, winking at her.

"I sure hope so, sir," she replied, brightly.

Julian had moved into what used to be my study, a forty-by-twenty-foot room looking out on the Italian cypress enclosed courtyard, with the gurgling fountain Livvie and I had bought after a visit to Rome. Now, like a latter-day Fornese, Julian was practicing his karate on a mat by the window. His black fighter's gi exploded with sound as the canvas uniform flapped in the air during the Seize the Lion kata, the most complicated of all the brown belt forms. He noticed me while spinning around and deftly disabling three imaginary opponents but still finished the kata perfectly. He had come a long way from the awkward five-year-old I'd taken to East West Kenpo Karate on Red Road.

I clapped. "Very good, son. You should get the black tip no problem."

"We'll see," he said, adjusting his belt, refusing to acknowledge my presence as anything out of the ordinary. "Sensei is a slave driver." Then: "What do you want, dad. I'm busy."

He stood, powerful arms crossed, not moving a muscle, waiting for . . . what? An explanation? An apology? A reason for being?

"I was in town on business and I thought maybe we could spend some time together. Go to the movies, grab something to eat. Whatever you want to do."

"No, thanks. Like I said, I'm busy right now, so, if you don't mind."

He walked to the counter, picked up a bottle of water, guzzled greedily from the sports cap, his back turned to me. I spoke to him all the same.

"Look, Julian, I don't know what your mother has told you about us but whatever happened, it happened a long time ago and it was just between her and me. It had nothing to do with you. I have never stopped loving you."

Julian put down his water, turned and looked at me. He sat on a stool, crossed his arms again. I stood before him and unburdened myself, once and for all.

"You see, the funny thing is, I was never physically unfaithful to your mother. But that wasn't necessary, the deed had already been done. In my heart. That probably made it worse. That and the fact that I was willing to lay it all on the line, gamble everything away, my family, my career, my money. All for the promises of someone who used me and abandoned me. Maybe I was just looking to be punished for something I did a long time ago. Maybe not. But whatever my subconscious reason, I think I've done enough penance. I'm tired of being outside. I want you to let me in.

"What I mean is this. I can't help being who I am. I'm older now and I'm way past the time for tricks and subterfuge, especially with my family. Especially with you. You can love me or not, but you'll have to recognize me for what I am. A man who's a little wiser. A father who only wishes for his son to acknowledge him."

I stopped, uncertain of what I should do next, as surprised by my outpouring as Julian must have been to hear it. His eyes glazed for a moment but then a sneer came over his Renaissance features.

"Nice speech, dad. Maybe you can put that in your next book. Little late to be sorry, don't you think? I mean I waited for something like this a long time. You could have been here, dad, but you ran away, feeling sorry for yourself. You're a dollar short and about ten years too late. Now, I would really appreciate if you would just get the hell out of here."

"Okay. Whatever you say. But let me give you a word of advice. Don't be too hard on others. The measure you use on others is the one that will be used on you."

"Save it for court, counsel."

"Goodbye, son."

I walked out, he slammed the door behind me.

"What did he say?" asked Livvie, waiting at the foot of the stairs.

"Nothing you should worry about. Aren't you late to your game?"

I let myself out the front door. At the car I glanced back at his window and thought I saw him looking down at me, arms by his side, hands clenched into fists, as though waiting for my next move. I waved, opened the door to my rented Chrysler and drove on out of my past.

I looked at my watch, enjoying the notion of being thoroughly smashed at twelve something in the afternoon, then perversely pushed the button to light the fluorescent nighttime dial. A slight flicker and it died. I put three tens under the last *mojito* glass and I stumbled out to the street.

The Testarossa had barely managed to crawl another hundred yards down Ocean, its progress impeded by a restaurant valet and a van of tourists fighting over a curbside parking space. My polo shirt clung to me like a damp towel, the unaccustomed white sunlight dazzling in its intensity.

A long-legged woman in an acid green Gucci revival outfit stepped out of the Cardoza down the block, signaled at the Ferrari to hurry up. The driver shook his hands, hit the steering wheel, then stuck his head out the tiny window, spewing a string of South American obscenities at the idiotic monkeys blocking his path.

I was flabbergasted, stuck to my spot on the sidewalk like a piece of gum, staring open-mouthed at the woman. For a moment I was a child again at the New York World's Fair, my baby sister still in diapers, strolling with my parents away from the Belgian Pavilion while eating a giant strawberry and cream waffle, when my father became flustered and ran up to a couple down the way.

"Antonio!" he cried.

He hugged the man, his long-lost cousin, whom he believed still in one of Castro's prisons, headed with his wife to the General Motors exhibit on the future of the American city.

I forced myself to take a second and then a third look at the woman, but there really was no need. Twenty years of life together had etched her face and figure in my memory for all time.

"Hey, peanut!" I shouted, hurrying down the sidewalk before the Ferrari reached her.

She turned, lowered her Armani wraparounds.

"Hey, knucklehead," she answered, deep dimples on either side of her face.

I stood in front of her, both of us grinning wildly at each other. The Ferrari cruised to a halt. She told the driver in Spanish to go around the block a couple of times, she had some catching up to do. Again the driver let out a string of Colombian curses but it was no matter, my sister, Celia, had already put him out of her mind as she hugged me on that crowded dizzying sidewalk.

"I'm taking a flight out in a couple of hours, I have to get back to my business," were practically the first words out of her mouth when we walked across the street to hear ourselves talk.

We sat on a bench by the playground, where a blond tourist chased after her manic little girl while the proud dark-haired papa took pictures with his pocket Canon.

"That's fine," I told Celia, not knowing where to begin, sipping the *café americano* I'd picked up at the News Café. "I'm here on business too, only a few hours and I . . . excuse me."

I walked to the men's room and vomited the six *mojitos* I'd drunk on an empty stomach. I exited quickly, fearing Celia would be gone but she was still at the bench, smiling sweetly at the little girl hanging upside down from the monkey bars.

"You still can't hold your liquor," said Celia, shaking her head, amused still by the big brother who never quite matched her in dissoluteness.

"I guess I never learn," I said.

I had last seen her years before, around the time of the Valdéz case. Thin, haggard, her thick brown hair butchered by a jailhouse cut, she was being herded out of lockup at the L.A. Criminal Courts Building after her Superior Court arraignment. Held on a quarter million dollars' bail for house-sitting a load of Colombian cocaine, she had walked when the leader of the group cut a deal with the prosecutor.

I'd offered to help her out, two siblings lost in the winding path of crime and politics. She had turned me down, rushing down the stairwell to the women's holding tank on the fourteenth floor rather than put up with her moralizing older brother. Either time had taught her more tolerance or my halo had tarnished enough to make me human again.

"I missed you at mom's funeral," I said, looking at her profile and seeing my father's slender nose and round green eyes, our mother's fleshy lips and dimpled chin.

"I know, I was so upset. Mercedes sent me the telegram to my old address in Bogotá. I'd told her I'd moved to Antioquia to be near the flowers, to make sure I'm not getting ripped off, but the *viejita* just forgot. It really hurt me. Mom and I hadn't been close lately but still . . ."

"Flowers? I thought you were still in the—"

"Drug business? *Por favor,* Charlie, that is so passé! Anyhow, after a certain age a girl has to stop fooling around and get down to serious stuff. We grossed five million last year, all legit, I'm happy to say."

"Life goes on," I said, unthinkingly.

The little girl across the way ran from the monster face her dad made, hid behind the cross beams of the dome-shaped monkey bars.

"It sure does. Either you get on board or you get left behind." Celia put her glasses back on.

"Did you ever remarry?" I asked, remembering her brief adventure in marital discord with her South American lothario.

"*Ay, chico, no.* I learned my lesson. I'd only get married again to have children and then I'm not so sure I want to have any. I mean, look at us. I don't think the folks did such a great job, do you?"

A breeze picked up offshore, the brown fronds of the palm tree stirred overhead, a hand waving goodbye.

"I don't know. I think they did the best they knew how. It was hard for them."

She removed her glasses, fixed her knowing eyes on me, shook her head in dismay.

"You haven't changed. You're still asking the world to forgive you for something it doesn't remember. It's all over, Charlie, it's just you and me who count. The others are not like us."

"I'm not following you."

She put her glasses back on, checked the time in her platinum Patek Philippe, glanced impatiently around.

"I really ought to get going. I hope Oscar didn't get upset and leave me stranded. He did that once, you know. These Colombians are super macho shitheads."

"Will you please stop trying to avoid the subject. What is it?"

She looked me up and down, sisterly compassion commingled with the contempt of the scarred survivor.

"I read about your case," she said at last.

"You mean Díaz?"

She nodded.

"That's why I'm here," I went on. "I was hoping to interview a witness but she skipped town. But that's really local news. I'm surprised you heard about it in Medellín."

"Antioquia. And it was pretty big news down there too. You know Díaz at one point was very popular in Colombia. Lots of big-time cokeheads put out a lot of money for his protection."

"Did you ever meet him?"

"No. Well, yes, I did. But it was a long time ago, when we were still living here in Miami."

"How could that be? He was only a kid then."

Celia took her glasses off one last time, extracted a lime green chiffon scarf from her quilted bag, cleaned the lenses.

"*Coño*, I should have kept my big mouth shut," she said, muttering to herself.

"What do you mean?"

Celia looked almost sorry for the blow she was about to impart.

"I mean that you've had your eyes closed. Your case is much more personal than you think. You see, Ricardo Díaz . . ."

"Is our brother," I said, finishing the sentence for her.

CHAPTER

"How long have you known?" asked Celia.

It was my turn to look away, to lower my eyes and wish I hadn't disclosed my thoughts. But it was too late for that. I was past pretending.

"I suspected almost from the beginning."

"How come?"

"He looks just like dad did when he was in his twenties, only with dark hair. And his last name. He used to be called Morell, Ricardo Morell Díaz, the surnames arranged Spanish style, father's first, mother's second. That's how they got him in the earliest rap sheets. But then he dropped the Morell. It was Ricardo M., then after a while just Ricardo Díaz. The coincidence was too much. But I didn't know who to turn to for the information. I certainly wasn't going to ask him."

"I'm so happy I live so far from you. He won't stop until we're all dead."

"Why? What did we do to him?"

Celia looked away, at the cavalcade of fancy vehicles on Ocean and seeing, I am sure, the paint-worn, tattered Jewish ghetto that was the Miami Beach of our childhood.

"You probably don't remember Monica. She was this little bleached blond girl from Cienfuegos that worked as a cashier at dad's last service station. She was married to Raúl Díaz, one of the people in Omega 69. You know the group."

I nodded. How could I forget? Two hundred men, either fat from their success in Miami or rail-thin from being recently released from Castro's gulag, slogging through the Everglades, M-1s held overhead, retraining for yet another Bay of Pigs fiasco. Water moccasins, fist-sized mosquitoes, unrelenting heat and humidity. That and army surplus rations designed to toughen me up into the fearless guerrilla that would depose the hated dictator.

I bowed out of the war games at age thirteen but dad never outgrew playing soldier. Every other weekend he'd put on his fatigues, his cracked army boots, strap on his commando knife and battered backpack and head out for the swamps. To him I was an ungrateful turncoat, a bad son who denied the pride of country to lust after the charms of the Anglo Gomorrah. To me he was a deranged old man who lived in a make-believe world where all opposition was heroic even if, or perhaps because, it served no purpose.

"Well, during one of their expeditions to Cuba Raúl got killed," continued Celia. "I don't know if papá was on that trip or not but he felt personally responsible. There was talk at the time that they'd had to leave the body behind when they burned down a sugar mill in Santa Clara, I don't know. What I do know is that dad took a very personal interest in Monica after the death of her husband. He got her set up in a place at Hialeah, an efficiency over somebody's garage. He bought her a bed, kitchenette set, even an old Buick to get around in."

"David and Bathsheba," I said.

"What's that?"

"Famous story in the Bible. King David lusted after Bathsheba, so he sent her husband to war. He put him in the front lines so he would get killed. When he died, she became his mistress. David repented eventually, but not before he'd had his fill of her."

Celia looked me up and down again, shook her head.

"I never knew you paid such close attention to Sister Mary John. Well, I don't know if that was the story with dad or not. At first everybody thought he felt sorry for Monica. I mean, she was —is, I suppose, if she's still alive—the meekest little thing. Big green eyes, little upturned nose, little hands and feet, a little thing. But that little thing had a lot of pull and I don't know how or when but pretty soon they started doing it."

"Now, hold on. When did all this happen? I don't remember any of it."

"Oh, Charlie, you've always been off in your own little world. Even when you were fourteen you lived inside your head more than you did in Miami. You were never really there with us, know what I mean? You were always listening to the Beatles and the Stones, you used to walk out of the house when *tía* Mercedes would come visit."

"All right, then, how did you find out these things?"

She folded her scarf again into squares, stuffed it into her bag. The little girl scampered away with her family, happy dad pushing the brightly colored Prego stroller stuffed with purse, camcorder, water bottle, backpack.

"I'm waiting."

"*Coño*, I'm trying to remember, all right? I think it was cousin Raquel who told mamá."

Celia was momentarily distracted by a muscular Roller Blading male model cruising by in a suede loincloth and a coat of suntan oil. She blinked repeatedly, then continued her tale of familial woe.

"Let me tell you, mamá was mad with grief. She said she'd had a feeling, papá hadn't been loving to her for months and you and I both know what that means, we've both been there, haven't we? The worst part is that when she confronted papá, he didn't deny it or say he was sorry or anything like that. On the contrary, he got very Spanish, just like grandpa José Julián used to get, all huffy macho shithead. He said, 'I'm very happy that you have brought this out in the open because I have been meaning to tell you. I'm divorcing you.'

"Just like that, out of nowhere, poom! Your life down the drain, out in the street on your ear. Mom couldn't believe it but the old man went on, saying he wanted out, he couldn't take all of mamá's religious nonsense, that she was old and had gotten ugly and that he was still too healthy and too good-looking to be tied down to an old witch like her. I wasn't supposed to hear all this but you know how kids are. Once mamá realized I knew, I became her confidante. Sick, isn't it? A grown woman confiding in an eight-year-old.

"Like I said, poor mamá was devastated. It's true she was prematurely gray but she wasn't all that old or wrinkled, dad was just looking for the exit. Mamá begged him not to leave her but he said it was too late, he had already filed the papers and as soon as they were final he would be moving in with Monica. He said he wouldn't do it before because he didn't want to spoil her reputation. Like anybody gave a shit about that!

"So mamá and I went out to see this Monica. She had stopped working at the garage a few months before and when we got off the bus and walked up to her house, we saw the other side of that argument.

"Monica was pregnant, very noticeably so, about six months along, probably. Mom begged her to leave, said she'd give her

money to go to an abortionist that would take care of the problem, even offered her all the money she had saved up, five
thousand dollars, a big deal back then. But this meek little
thing, this *mosquita muerta*, she turned into a lioness. Monica
said no way she was going to give dad up, that theirs was a love
that would last for all time and that the belly she had was its
proof. She said dad no longer loved mom, that he loved her. I'll
never forget how she said, it was eternal love, *"es un amor
eterno, va más allá de la tumba,"* an eternal love beyond the
grave, her exact words. I got chills when I heard that. She was
like a witch, commanding us to leave her house and never to
enter it again.

"Mamá was beside herself. She didn't know what to do."

Celia stopped, as though to catch her breath or perhaps only
to weigh what next to tell me. The cars on Ocean Drive honked
on, a light airplane buzzed overhead, trailing in its wake a sign
for Cuervo Gold.

"What did she do?" I asked. Celia wrung her long, tapered
hands.

"Nothing. Papá had his stroke a few weeks later. It was almost
like the answer to her prayers. Maybe that was why she always
felt so guilty about his condition. She probably thought it was
all her fault."

"What about Monica?" I asked.

Celia again looked at her watch, but with distaste this time,
as though she were reaching a justifiably unpleasant end.

"The divorce was never finalized and she had no money. She
had to go on welfare. *El refugio* was giving her a shopping bag
of food every week and some money a month, I don't know how
much. She had a boy. Monica named him, as we know now,
Ricardo.

"One time, when you were away in college, Monica brought
him over to see papá. Ricardo must have been around six then.
He was the spitting image of the old man, his hair sandy brown

244

like dad's. Monica was really apologetic, said she didn't want to bother us but that the boy was constantly asking for his father. She thought he should see him at least once.

"Ricardo was all wide-eyed, pale as a ghost when he saw the old man in his wheelchair. Papá just blinked a lot, two big fat tears came out. Then he shit all over himself. When mamá and I came out from changing him, we found Ricardo in your room, just as wide-eyed. He was looking at all your things, touching your school banners and books. 'I want to go to the university too someday, *mami,*' he told Monica but she whispered back, 'You can't, these people took all your daddy's money.' She thought no one had heard her but I did and I told mamá. She escorted them out of the apartment on the double.

"The next time, which was the last time I saw Ricardo, he was in Colombia. This was about four years ago. Ricardo had become a *santero,* he was into *palo mayombé* and all these Medellín types were taking care of him in exchange for his spiritual protection. Somehow he found me, I was working in a boutique I owned back then. I didn't recognize him at first, his hair was dark and I thought he looked more like his mom than dad. He was very nice, very polite and all. But what he said chilled me. He said, 'Get your *traje de muerta,* your dead woman's robe, ready, because you're going to hell soon.'

"I totally freaked out, so much so that I sold the store right away and moved back to the States for a while. Later I found out he had left Colombia and that's when I moved back. Well, there's Oscar, I really have to go."

Celia stood, kissed me on the cheek, slipped a business card into my hands.

"If you're ever in Antioquia, do give a call. How do you people out on the Coast say it? Let's do lunch sometime."

She turned, ready to dash back to the pollinated valleys of brave Bolívar's homeland. I grabbed her arm.

"Why didn't you ever tell me any of this before?"

"*Qué tú quieres, Carlitos?* I haven't seen you in years. Look, there's a lot of things you don't know. This is only one of them. Mamá swore me to secrecy as long as she was alive and now she's gone. I gotta go."

She dashed to the Testarossa, clambered in. From the bench I could hear the string of obscenities Oscar was spewing. Celia slapped him. That seemed to quiet him down, then the car roared out of Ocean like a beast wounded in its self-esteem.

I felt the world spin, closing in on me, and I heard, from somewhere, a high tenor voice taunting me:

"*Ya tú vé, mi hermano? De tal palo, tal astilla.* Right, bro'? Chips off the old fucking block."

CHAPTER

22

THE woods are lovely, dark and deep.

I have just come back from a long run, my shirt dripping with sweat, my quadriceps burning from the uphill battle. It's that time right before dawn or right after sunset when shadows and light become one and what you see is right next to what you imagine. There is no past or future, only a present where everything is suspended as in a dense liquid.

The hum of the freeway is a bass note, a continuum against which the crickets play their chirrupy cellos and the cicadas their throbbing organ. I'm breathing hard, the smell of jasmine, oleanders and magnolias mingling with the stewy richness of wet loam. I lean on a light pole, admiring the graceful lines of the Arroyo Bridge, its light globes arrayed like a string of glowing pearls.

Something draws my eye to a culvert down the narrow street. I walk some steps, find myself on a stone bridge over a wash, the branches of the tree forming a lovely bower before my eyes. A rustle in the leaves. A squirrel, I think.

I step back. Then, from the dried-out wash comes a flash of white. I glance up. Floating, almost stately flying, is Shana, staring at me with eyes full of love, her outstretched hand pointing at me. She is dressed in white robes, a clump of weeds crowning her bloody forehead, at her throat a gash through which the light shines.

Shana says something but I can't hear her, the noise of traffic grows unbearably loud. I want to run but I am fixed to my spot, the thumping of my heart a drumroll to my fears.

A car drives by, stops. The door opens and slams closed in the darkness. I see the shadow of my father before me. He carries a small bundle in his arms.

"This is my son in whom I am truly pleased," he says, then he shows me the babe in his arms. A yellow-eyed monkey child with horns bares his yellow teeth, then it jumps on me and sinks two long fangs into my neck while my father laughs.

I woke up with a start, shirt soaked in sweat, a fragrant mist creeping through the open window from the arroyo.

Six fifteen on an autumn morning. A child's cry somewhere in the foggy distance, the hum of the refrigerator down the hall. I get up from the couch where I had fallen asleep, going over the Díaz case file, reviewing the dates and places and names. I shake, trembling, as though ill with malaria or some other dreadful tropical disease and wonder how long it will take before I go as mad as my brother.

· · ·

For once the Pasadena Freeway flowed the way its planners must have intended, smoothly and well mannered, a genteel drive down a garden parkway. I marveled at the absence of traffic until the KFWB announcer read a news item about renewed fighting between Palestinians and Jewish settlers in Hebron on this, the high holy day of atonement, Yom Kippur. I glanced to my left at the salvage yard where the notorious derby rooftop of the old Hollywood Brown Derby restaurant had come to keep company with Joe Camel figures, Red Rooster papier-mâché cockerels and a host of other unwanted symbols of our wasteful era, the walls of the yard covered with the cartoon-shaped graffiti of local gangs. Symbols all, competing for the soul of modern man.

He's no different, I thought. It's a matter of degree.

And no one ever feels remorse.

God help us all.

At the district attorney's conference room, Lisa and Phil stared balefully at me when I gave them the news. Either the shock was too great or in some way I couldn't discern it liberated them from action.

Lisa, ever the woman, was the first to address the paternity angle. "But how do you know for certain that he was your father's child? You can't draw a blood sample of your dad and just because he claims that name doesn't mean it's true—or even, if the name is true, that he is any relation."

"I already thought of that. Unfortunately a friend of mine in Miami did me the favor and pulled the birth certificate at the Dade County Registrar. There's an entry there for a white male child, illegitimate, born of one Monica Díaz and Juan Pablo Morell. My dad. He sent me a copy FedEx. Here it is."

I pushed forward the doleful paper confirming my brother-hood to the very beast I sought to put away. Phil picked it up, shook his head slowly, in admiration.

"Certified and everything. I've been meaning to ask you, who is your friend down there?"

"Deputy city manager. We went to Brown together."

"Uhm. Well, Charlie, I don't have to tell you that this is definitely a major conflict of interest. Now you really can't be seen prosecuting this one."

"Excuse me, but I don't see this as a problem, Phil," insisted Lisa, her dark brown Prada dress giving her the vague air of a minor military attaché.

"There is nothing in the books that specifically prohibits him from prosecuting his brother. If anything, that would add to our case, were he to come out during arguments and tell the jury he is prosecuting his own flesh and blood for the heinous crimes he's committed."

Phil looked aghast at her, then twirled his gold Cross pen, looking for a reply that would not give offense.

"I don't think that's such a hot idea, Lisa. First off, I don't think any judge would allow that kind of argument. Too inflammatory, more prejudicial than probative, sets up the whole thing for appeal. It also deprives the prosecution of the appearance of fairness and impartiality. We are supposed to be doing justice here, believe it or not. Pass."

"Okay, then, suppose we weren't to tell them," insisted Lisa, still unwilling to let me go. "Suppose . . . well, now, mind you, this is just a hypothetical situation, of course, because as we all know it would be wrong because we are supposed to be doing justice here. But let's say we weren't to bring this up. It's not part of the case in chief. If Bloomberg does bring it up, we could argue it's not germane. Even if the trial judge were to agree with Bloomberg, we could still take a writ, which I'm sure we could win without sweating it."

Much to my distaste, I felt compelled to intervene.

"I'm not so sure about that, Lisa."

"About what?" she said, almost barking. Why is she so insistent, I wondered.

"They could decide to bring it up on appeal," I said. "You know, set us up so that even if we win the case, they could claim this was all a personal vendetta."

"Prosecutorial misconduct," piped in Phil.

"That's right," I concurred.

Phil now felt compelled to intervene, swinging his large broad shoulders toward Lisa, who sat ramrod straight, unwilling to bend.

"Then, since the defense would be able to allege that we the people already had had constructive notice of the fact that we are related, via the filing documents, the felony records, etc.," said Phil, not even bothering to stop for a breath but rushing it all out like a father blowing out the napkin on fire before the entire piñata goes up in flames, "even if we were to lie, that is, and claim that we never knew about it, which of course like you said we could never do because that would be an obstruction of justice and that would be plain wrong, even then the burden would still be on us to prove that this was not prosecutorial misconduct. I'm afraid in that case we wouldn't be able to clear that hurdle."

"Which would mean we would have to start all over again. I see," said Lisa, crestfallen.

"No, no, more than that," I said, continuing the painful lesson. "It could mean the game is over. *Finito*. Done. Díaz gets a get-out-of-jail-free pass."

"How's that?" she asked, truly perplexed. I looked at Phil, who blinked his thick eyelashes, perhaps asking himself if Lisa was truly up to the par he had hoped.

"Double jeopardy," he said finally, a long almost hurtful sigh flowing out of him.

"Double jeopardy?" repeated Lisa, stunned that he could have come up with such an obviously arcane concept. "No way!"

"Way," croaked Phil. "If after conviction, hell, if after we picked a jury and jeopardy attaches, the defense could prove we had constructive notice and should have known or even actually knew Díaz was Charlie's brother, that it was our knowing, willful and deliberate decision to hide that material fact, it would not be harmless error. They would have no trouble convincing the Court of Appeal this was a deliberate case of misconduct. The case could be thrown out and we'd be enjoined from trying him again and Díaz would walk. You know that. Nobody gets tried twice for the same crime, we only get one bite of the apple. You fuck it up, you lose."

"I see your point. But, we could also lose if we didn't fuck it up," countered Lisa with her own tart logic.

Phil glanced at his watch. "Well, I think maybe we should brainstorm a little more about this. Maybe a conflict will come up, right, Charlie?"

"What kind of conflict?" I asked, disingenuously.

"Oh, I don't know. Maybe you have a trial in San Francisco that suddenly is requiring your full and immediate attention. If you're out of town we'd have to handle it ourselves. Very unfortunate at this late a stage in the game but these things happen. All too often. You know what I mean. Because if Díaz were to find out that we know he knows, he could set off the whole thing ahead of time."

"You think this is a time bomb, deliberately set?" I asked.

"Absolutely. If you two are related, that's why he was after you. Perfect setup. I just wish we hadn't pressed you so hard to do this. What a waste."

He got up, pocketed his Cross pen, slapped shut his Coach portfolio.

"C'mon, Lisa, let's go to my office and go down the list. We got to see who else in the office can handle this case."

"Where does that leave me, Phil?"

"You, buddy? You're on standby until we decide how to proceed. We'll get back to you."

Lisa got up, smoothed the wrinkles out of her dress, took a last swig of her latte.

"Sorry, Charlie, maybe some other time," she said, then opened and closed her hand goodbye. I sat in my chair, feeling the emptiness of the room surround me and invade me, the echo of nothingness in my brain until the silence became overbearing and I got up and walked out, whistling, for reasons I still can't fathom, "Mack the Knife" and headed to my office.

Of course I'd been had and there was no way I could prove it. But my sixth legal sense was ringing off the chart, telling me that Phil, aware of my relationship to Díaz, had planned the entire thing, insisting I come on board so as to discredit the prosecution's case.

Even that didn't make sense unless one supposed that Senator Decker, pulling his long pliant strings, had convinced Phil to hire me. This trial then was to be a political chit to be cashed in by Phil when he ran for DA in a couple of years. After all, who cares about the gruesome murder of an old Latino and a black security guard? Their families. And maybe other minorities. And as everyone knows, in California, minorities don't count for much.

Of course I could be wrong. And there is no racism in L.A. And the sun rises out of the Pacific.

The question then became, what was I going to do about it? This was not a time for anger. It was a time for cold cunning, inspired but not distorted by the horror and the suffering I'd witnessed. I was trying to come up with an answer but it's hard to think of trial strategies when you have to deal with a grown woman crying her heart out in front of you.

I tried to console Tina, telling her that I'd find her work with some of my attorney friends, that this was no reflection on her or her skills but only one of those sad facts of life we all have to bear occasionally. I guess she sensed I lacked the killer instinct.

"Uh-huh. But Mr. Morell, Spiro just got laid off at the printer's and he's already on unemployment and he's not feeling well and he has to go to the doctor's for analysis and we just bought our condo in Van Nuys and we don't want to lose it!"

I stood there, marveling at her wondrous display of emotion, feeling it move me in spite of myself, when she argued the ultimate undefeatable plea.

"Besides, I think I'm pregnant and you tell me, who's going to hire someone who's pregnant? All I'm asking is another six months and then I'll be on maternity leave and you won't have to worry about me anymore, please!"

"I don't know, Tina. I really can't afford you."

"Please! Pretty please!"

I stopped her before she could say with a cherry on top and agreed to keep her another three months. All at once her tears dried up, she wiped her nose on her sleeve and handed me the partnership dissolution papers to sign.

"*Gracias,* Señor Morell. *Efaristo, efaristo para poli!*" she repeated in Greek.

I shrugged, smiled. I was always a sucker for a good rug trader. I needed someone to look after my mail, anyhow.

I had just finished my conversation with Farris when the phone rang again.

"My most esteemed colleague, Mr. Morell," came the malignantly mellifluous voice of Jacobo Bloomberg in perfectly modulated theatrical Spanish, the kind you hear in *telenovelas* and radio soap operas. "And how did Miami treat you?"

"Like I'm the prodigal son who should stay a swineherd," I replied. "You have sharp ears."

He chuckled, pleased with himself. "That's what *he* pays me for," he retorted in English. "Are you going to be out on the West Side today?"

"Matter of fact, I'll be in Century City this afternoon."

"Excellent. Why don't you drop by Coletta's on Rodeo around three, let's say. There's something I want to talk to you about. In private."

"Coletta's? What's that?"

"You'll see. You could use what they're giving. I'll be waiting."

He hung up, certain that I would keep my appointment. Unfortunately, he was right.

Farris was ecstatic when we signed the papers dissolving our partnership. He hadn't been half that happy when we became partners.

"Look, kiddo, why the long face? It's time to start a new life, be a new man, all that jazz. You've always been the lone-wolf type. You know what they say, he who travels alone travels fastest. I was just extra weight."

His pleased, pudgy features shined with pleasure behind his gleaming Biedermeier desk. I took in his office, with the Ruscha, the Jasper Johns, the Diebenkorn, the swiftly growing collection of abstract art and I saw I had become an object as well, an unwanted piece that was being traded for something newer, hipper, sexier. Criminal law was nowhere, it was time to concentrate on the real moneymaker, Hollywood and its acolytes.

"So have you given any thought to what I told you about the movie rights? People at Fox are starting to cool off. They haven't seen your name in the headlines lately and now's a good time to close this deal before they go away. It's two hundred grand, remember. That's a whole bunch of pro bono work, the kind you like to do."

"Farris, you are a pig."

"Why? Because I want to make an honest buck? Okay, a buck? That's the name of the game, Charlie. A free market economy. Let the market speak. Water rises to its own level. To the victors belong the spoils, all that crap. You know how it is in L.A. If you're not busy eating, you're busy being lunch."

"You are also the most winded bag of clichés I've ever had the misfortune of hearing. If you weren't such a good negotiator, I think most people would shoot you."

"But that's part of the secret of being a good negotiator! That's why I'm on top."

"Maybe. For now. But your attitude is all wrong, *amigo*. There's more to life and the law than winning no matter what."

Farris looked truly puzzled, the possibility of another way of living never having seriously crossed his mind.

"We can't all be saints in training, like you, Charlie. Personally I've always felt the command to grow and multiply also applies to bank accounts. So what's it going to be? You're going to be saintly and poor? Or human and comfortable?"

"What about evil? What about Díaz?"

"He's not on my radar screen, bubbe. I do divorces, torts and tarts, no dark-night-of-the-soul stuff. I leave Díaz to guys like you. You can do it for all of us."

"And in the meantime I can get rich by exploiting it."

"Hey, if you see a diamond ring in the middle of the street, are you going to stop everybody walking around and ask them if it belongs to them, knowing they're most likely going to lie and take it from you? Or are you going to put it in your pocket and thank the Lord for sending it your way? I went to yeshiva, Charlie. You're dealing in false pride. Be humble, brother. Recognize who you are and where you came from and give thanks to the Lord for what you've got. Who are you to question His ways?"

"Who am I to question anybody. That's a good point. Who the hell am I?"

Farris nodded, adjusted the knot of his Jhane Barnes tie.

"Is that a yes, Charlie?"

Jake Bloomberg leaned back in his chair, eyes closed in near ecstasy, while the white-uniformed attendant hacked with a clipper at the gnarly toenails of his right foot. His left foot was propped on a padded stool, pointed toes spread out with little wads of cotton, the clear varnish on the toenails almost dry.

It figured that the only straight man at a hair salon would have a woman at his feet, cloven though they might be.

I knocked on the accordion door to the cubicle. He opened his eyes.

"Sal por un ratico, Liliana. Tengo que hablar con el señor," he told the pedicurist. She nodded, put his right foot in a soapy solution in a gleaming steel bowl. I pulled up a stool, sat across from my brother's advocate.

"Come here often?" I asked. He chuckled, happy at being found out.

"Whenever I'm in town. My toes are very strange. Minor little defect. All the bones were fused together when I was born. As I'm sure you're aware, plastic surgery wasn't exactly the forte of Havana surgeons back in the 1950s, especially for poor *polacos* like ourselves. They did the best they could but as you can see, the nails grow at all kinds of weird angles."

"That's nice, Jacobo."

"Jake, please. Call me Jake."

"All right then, Jake. I'm touched. I'm always touched by human imperfection. Did the surgeons also remove a little pigtail while they were at it?"

"Now that you mention it," said Bloomberg, shifting in his chair, grabbing at his robe as though to look at his behind.

"No. Still there." He smiled.

"That's good. I was wondering if I was going to need a padre or a rabbi to cut through all the bullshit."

"I don't know, Charlie. I've been told you know from bullshit."

"I've heard it ladled in my time."

"And you have done your fair share of ladling yourself."

He moved to a crocodile skin briefcase, extracted a sheaf of documents, which he tossed at me.

"Don't tell me I'm being served."

"A civil suit? Let's not get paranoid. Bullshitting is not an indictable offense. But drug dealing certainly is."

I glanced at the papers. Metro Dade police reports, a grand jury indictment.

"Old news, Jake. I was cleared years ago. Besides which, I put it in my book. Everybody knows."

"Naturally. But it's not you we're interested in, it's your sister, Celia. If you would take a minute to read the papers you'll see she's named as an unindicted co-conspirator in a little smuggling ring headed by someone near and dear to both of us."

I was chilled, my heart skipped to a tattered turn. I read on, trying to keep my hand from shaking.

"Nice going, Jake. I don't see any disposition in this."

"Of course not. But you must have noticed the party indicted in these papers is a certain Ricardo M. Díaz. Funny, don't you think, that the prosecutor in my client's case also turns out to have a sister whose reputation was besmirched—at best— because of his association with my client?"

I dropped the papers in the bowl of soapy water where Bloomberg was soaking his right hoof.

"Piece of shit, Jake. So you got a private dick to go through my family history."

"Do you always have to be an asshole?" asked Bloomberg, fishing out the papers.

"Takes one to know one."

"Oh, that's funny, Charlie. What, fourth grade or fifth? Okay, Mr. Letterman, here's what," said Bloomberg, drying the copies with a hand towel. "Either you cut my client a sweet deal or I see the *Times* moves your story back to page one, left column, above the fold."

"They'll spell my name right so go ahead. I could use the business. She was an unindicted co-conspirator. It means absolutely nothing."

"Except for the fact that the prosecutor might be seen to be carrying out a personal vendetta."

"I am not my sister's keeper. I don't make deals."

"One month in the office and you already sound like Eliot Ness. I hope you will inform your superiors about this."

"I am not your message boy either. What I tell them is my business. Their business is making sure I put away that slime you call your client." I turned, ready to walk out of the cubicle.

"Why don't you tell him that yourself?"

"I will, in court."

"I mean in County Jail."

I stopped in the hallway, almost bumping into the pedicurist, who came bearing a fresh load of towels and cotton balls.

"*Ya acabó?*" she asked.

I stuck my head back inside the cubicle.

Jake scratched the corner of his eye, right where a telltale discoloration signaled the removal of a nasty wart.

"My client wants to talk to you tonight. Alone."

CHAPTER

23

THE entry to the salliport clanged open, the deputy sheriff in the glass booth motioning at me to pass through. I walked into the enclosure, waited for the next set of barred doors to slide and jolt away.

Before me sprawled the gray-green interview room of the Los Angeles County Central Men's Jail, reeking of Pine Sol and nervous sweat. Two long tables with a glass divider took up the center of the room. Seated on one side, shackled to their low metal stools, the defendants in their blue, white or yellow uniforms, telling tales of woe and perdition. On the other side, their lawyers and probation officers, listening with bored concentration to the barrage of lies and subterfuges custodies offer as the excuse for their existence.

"Your party's at the far glass booth, counsel," came the female deputy's voice, distorted by the squeaky intercom. But there was no need for her to tell me that, I'd already spotted my dark brother in his wheelchair, gesturing at me like the farmer showing off his prize steer to the judges at the county fair.

He had lost even more weight in the last few days. He was now hermit spare and jailhouse pale, our father's nose cutting the air around him like a scimitar the neck of the infidel. He'd shaved off his hair and his scalp was stubby like a death camp prisoner's. Great hazel eyes shone with controlled madness below spare eyebrows, a band of freckles spreading over his nose and cheeks like the flag of a foreign country. He extended his sinewy arm to offer his hand, a long vein popping out over the biceps, ending in the hollow of an elbow only now healing from the scabs of so many puncture wounds.

"*Coño, tú*, long time no see! How you been?"

I didn't, I couldn't, shake his hand. I sat down, took out a pocket tape recorder, set it on the metal table between us. The voice activator kicked on when I spoke.

"This is a conversation between the defendant, Ricardo Díaz, and the special prosecutor assigned to his case, Carlos Morell, case number BA7289786. These are the ground rules, Mr. Díaz. Our entire conversation will be tape-recorded. Nothing you say will be off the record. Everything will be official. Anything you say can and will be used against you in a court of law. No deals have been offered, no promises have been made. I am here at your request, which was conveyed to me by your attorney of record, Mr. Jake Bloomberg. As per your request, I have come here alone. I assume you wish to waive your right to remain silent—is that correct?"

Díaz leaned back, a dancing yellow light flaring in the back of his eyes. He nodded.

"You will have to speak aloud, Mr. Díaz."

"Yes."

"So then do you also wish to give up your right to have

an attorney—your own or a court-appointed attorney—present during this interview?"

Díaz waved his hand, carving a hollow in the air.

"Yes, I do. This is being done per my specific request, like you say. In fact, it's against the express advice of my attorney. But I call the shots and I'll deal with the consequences."

"Finally, you are aware that everything you say can and will be used against you in a court of law?"

"Yes. And you can also use it in a divine court, if you wish," he taunted. "It's all the same to me."

"All right. Let's proceed then. What did you want to talk to me about?"

Díaz stared back silently, the irises in his hazel eyes growing wider by the minute. My lips suddenly felt dry and hot, my mouth parched.

"You can smoke, if you like," he said. "It doesn't bother me, I'm used to smoke." He paused. "And flames."

He chuckled at his own jest, supremely amused.

"Even if I wanted, I couldn't. It's against county ordinance. The jail is a no-smoking area."

He tsk-tsked, the soul of sad sophistication.

"That's a stupid rule. Men should be allowed to have little vices, otherwise they'll indulge in bigger ones."

"Mr. Díaz, I know you didn't call me here to talk about venial sin. Suppose you tell me what you want to talk about. Otherwise I will conclude this meeting and leave the interview room."

"What do I want to talk about?"

"Yes."

"Things."

"Things. What kind of things?"

"Things in general. Like the Dodgers losing to the Braves, what an asshole Governor Wilson is, how the three-strikes law is cruel and unusual punishment and doesn't work. You know, things."

I looked at my runner's Seiko, which in the morning rush I'd neglected to switch for my usual Timex. This interview was going to be shorter than I expected, though longer than I wanted.

"That's a nice watch you got there, Charlie. Is that one of those things with microchips that tells your heart rate and body temperature?"

"No, I can't afford those. This is a cheap twenty-dollar runner's watch."

"That's too bad. Those microchips are something else, you know. Tiny computers on your wrist. Courtesy of Bill Gates and Microsoft."

I didn't bother to tell him Bill Gates just makes software, not microchips. I wanted to see where the conversation was going and I didn't feel like playing Techie Tutor. But Díaz had thought this through already.

"Bill Gates, man, now there's someone who has his finger in everything. *Coño*, that skinny son of a bitch *se lo sabe todo*, he knows all the tricks. He's out to take over the world, you know. Did you hear about that big castle he's building up in the Cascades?"

"Seattle."

"Whatever. He's taking the soul of everything and putting it inside his electronic cauldron, you know—he buys all these artworks and captures their image and then plays it back in these giant state-of-the-art VCRs so that he's got Velázquez's *Las Meniñas* or *Guernica* or the *Winged Victory* or whatever forever and ever, better than life-size, all the masterpieces of the world, they're his.

"*Coño*, man, that's what I do with my *nganga*, you know—only he does it high-tech. Bill Gates is tearing out the heart of Western civilization and enjoying every minute of it. Now there's somebody I could learn from. It's not too late. Once I get over this hump we'll trade professional secrets. I mean, once upon a time computers used to be as esoteric as *santería* is now. Let me tell you, Bill Gates is the number one *babalawo* in the whole fucking world. I know he could teach me a lot but you can bet I can teach him a couple of tricks too. Nothing like a little blood to seal a business, *mi hermano.* By the way, did you know that the *ifá* books operate on a binary system?"

"You mean the *santería* divination books?"

"*Coño, sí,* you didn't know that? We're like a computer already, everything is on a yes, no system, plus or minus, positive, negative. Same thing, *mi hermano.*

"I think about these things, you see. I'm not the crazy ignorant shit you think I am. I know my stuff. And you, Carlitos, are dead meat."

I stood, pushed the chair back. The deputy at the far end of the room looked up at me, wondering if there was any trouble.

"All right, this meeting is over."

"Your problem is you have a guilty conscience because of what you and your family have done to me."

I looked at the deputy in the elevated desk, about to rush down to our glass cubicle. I gave him the thumbs-up, sat back down.

"Okay, let's take this from the top," I said, putting the recorder back on the table. "I want to hear what you claim my family did to you."

"Oh, man, where do I begin?" He moved back in his wheelchair, contorted his face into the grimace of a smile.

"You sold out, Carlos. You bought into the whole Anglo trip, down to your name, your watch, your pin-striped suit. As if having white skin and green eyes is going to make the Anglo forget what you are—another highfalutin uppity spick who doesn't know his place, thinking he's the equal of Gates, Reagan or Wilson. That's why I'm glad they came after you 'cause you sold us down the river, you fucking Judas. Only in your case you don't even get thirty pieces of silver, just a pat on your back from your Anglo masters."

I sat silently, watching the tape roll. I wanted him to feel comfortable and keep the conversation going. Besides, he wasn't all wrong, either.

"In this society, *mi hermano*, all we ever amount to is trash. Cuban, Puerto Rican, Mexican, Argentinian, we're all spick shit to the guys who run this country. Loud guys with greasy hair and bad tempers good for doing dishes, picking grapes and dancing salsa. Oh yeah and selling dope, that's about it. 'Course you don't want to acknowledge it. You're in denial, *mi hermano*, total fuckin' denial. Maybe you should get into some Latino twelve-step program to wake up your consciousness, *asere*. That's why I understand what we've done in Miami. I'm proud of the way we took over. Why just the other day those shit-eating asshole Anglos wanted to bust up the city but the Cuban vote held them back, saying, no way, Mister Cracker. Cubita calls the shots here.

"My only regret is that I left Dade before we took over completely. I thought to be successful I had to make it away from Florida. I was a fool. I thought I could have a future away from our people.

"But you know what? You can't. In the end you have to return to your roots and that's what I'm doing. And in the process pull out the bad weeds like you, Carlitos, the mutants that stink up our garden. People like you shouldn't exist, *cabrón*. You're shit, bro', you're *pura mierda, coño*, you're nothing and all of us and all Cubans and the whole wide fucking world would be better off without the likes of you. Too bad Fidel is not here to crack your nuts and send you to *el paredón*, to the firing wall, which is what you deserve."

Then, fury spent for the time being, he shrugged, leaned back smiling, bad teeth showing, like he had finished telling a story out of *A Thousand and One Nights* and he could now expect to save his neck the next twenty-four hours.

"So, other than that, how have you been?"

"I still haven't heard anything about my family."

"C'mon, Charlie, don't fuck with me. You know who I am."

"Yes. I know you're Ricardo Díaz, charged with carrying out two heinous murders and rapes in Los Angeles County."

"Yes and I'm also your brother, the one your family chose to forget about when the old man had his stroke. I'm the runt of the litter, the kitten you drown in the toilet before you wrap it in newspaper and put it out with the trash. But you know what? This cat has nine lives. This little kitty will not die. This little kitty is going to scratch your eyes out and then he's going to slash your throat."

"That's enough," I said, again standing up. He grabbed me by the arm. His hand felt smooth, his grip strong, his skin ice cold.

"Don't you want to hear my confession? That's what you're here for, right? You want me to dig my own grave with my own words. Well, maybe I'll let you bury me. Maybe I will confess. Sit down. Please. I have a secret to tell you."

He held me down with the same hypnotic force he'd used at the chapel. I looked at the tape, making sure every word was recorded.

"Even if you kill me, I'll be back again. You may destroy this temple but I shall rebuild it. I will live again. That's part of the deal I made with my master."

"Who is your master?"

His smile dropped from his wan, feverish face.

"He has many names. I call him Kadiempembé, Tata Nkisi. But you Christians call him the Prince of Darkness, the fallen angel, God's first beloved."

"You worship Satan."

"Satan, Lucifer, Beelzebub, Mephistopheles, Set, Loki, Prince of Power, Old Horny, Old Poker, the Tempter, the Fiend, the Evil One, His Satanic Majesty, of thee I sing."

He laughed, tilting his head backward, chilling me to the

bone. I looked away at the interview room outside and a cloud came over it, then lifted in an instant. I wished I'd had a cross but I knew it was there in that room with me.

"All right, then, tell the devil to get you out. Better yet, tell your story to the devil."

"Don't you want to know how he died?"

"Who died?"

"Armando, of course. Armando Ponce, your *padrino*. He screamed a lot. Of course his tongue had already been cut out so he wasn't really screaming all that loud. It wasn't easy to skin him either. I mean he was still alive. I think. Maybe he went into shock by then. What do you think?"

My heart raced, I felt a sweat breaking out down my back and with every fiber of my body I wanted to get up and beat Ricardo to a pulp, grab him and throw him through the plate glass so that the shards would slice him into tiny little bloody bits. Instead: "I don't know. You were there, I wasn't."

"I was? Funny, I don't remember. I guess I was possessed. If I was there, I mean. But of course if I was possessed, then I wasn't really there because I wasn't cognizant of my actions so therefore I'm not really guilty of anything I may have done while in a trance, right, counsel? I mean, I believe you've had some success with that line of defense before. The Valdéz case, if I'm not mistaken."

"Tell me something new."

"Okay, I will."

He leaned forward, exhaling through his mouth, his rank breath a foul mix of rotting teeth and cigarettes.

"Armando's in hell. With our old man. They're both boiling in oil, Carlitos, in a big vat of burning oil, for all eternity. And they only get out when I tell them. And you know what else?"

"What?"

"Your mother sucks cocks in hell!"

I couldn't help laughing.

"I'm so glad you said that. It just proves what a joke you are, Díaz. The best thing you can do is quote from a cheesy movie."

He looked stunned, shaking his head as though he found it impossible to understand my reaction.

"What movie? It's true! She takes it up the ass every day while she sucks the devil's dick!"

"Yeah, right."

"It's true!" he roared, slamming his fist on the table. "It's all true! You're always laughing at me, just like your whole fucking family! Poor Ricardito, he doesn't know how to shit. Poor Rickie, his mom is such a slut. Well, fuck you! Fuck you, you hear me!"

The booth's door slammed open. Dirk, the deputy, appeared with his backup, both of them wielding nightsticks, ready for action.

"Do we have a situation here, Charlie?"

"We're cool. Mr. Díaz just got a little emotional."

Dirk stood at the threshold, undecided for a moment, then he bent down and whispered in Díaz's ear.

"One more little scene like that and it's the hole and jewball for you, *comprende, pendejo?*"

Díaz looked down at the table.

"I understand."

Dirk nodded, jerked his head at his backup and both men eased out, softly closing the door behind them.

"What's jewball?"

"Vomit. A slop they make out of dog food and chili peppers for troublemakers in solitary. But you know what? When I was a kid there were times when even jewball would have tasted good. But you guys had the money, we had nothing. Until I found out I had someone who gave me power. Tata Nkisi. He's a demanding master, he wants a lot of sacrifices and *ebbós*. But he doesn't let me down. Just like you won't."

"What makes you say that?"

"Because I know how much you love Julian. I know he really can't stand you but you'd give your life for him, wouldn't you? Even if he'd rather work on his karate than listen to you."

I was chilled. There was no way he could have known that, other than having been there or having talked to Julian, which was impossible. My God, I thought, if he knows that, what else does he know? My astonishment must have shown, for now he sat back in his wheelchair, confident that he finally had me where he wanted me.

"You've never believed, have you?"

"In what?"

"In the saints, *mi hermano*. In powers that you can't even imagine. But that's all right, it'll be our secret. I'll tell you what I'm going to do. Here's my offer. I won't mention our family to anybody if you drop the murder case on Armando and you get me a manslaughter for the guard. You've got that and you got a plea. Even though that was a copycat. I didn't kill the guard but I know you have to have something to take back to your masters, Mr. Fuentes and Mr. Antonetti. So what do you say, *hermanito*, lil' brother, we got a deal or what?"

I got up, turned off the machine, showing more confidence than I felt. "You know it gives me a great deal of satisfaction to tell you this."

"Tell me what?"

"Go fuck yourself. I'm not making any deals with you. We're going to nail you nice and solid. We got the evidence, *you're* the one who's dead meat, Díaz. This interview is over."

I walked out, but not before Díaz hurled the worst insult he could have come up with: "You'll be sorry!"

The sound ended, the hiss of blank tape filling Lisa's office. Looking out the window down the street, a great big plume of white smoke issued from the chimney of the foundry, like the College of Cardinals announcing to the world, *papam habemus.*

I stopped the recorder.

"Well, he doesn't really admit to anything," said Phil, lying propped up on an elbow on the cowhide-covered Wassily chair. "All the stuff he mentions he could have picked up off the paper."

"That's just what I was thinking," chimed in Lisa. "It's all mumbo jumbo."

"Yeah, Charlie, and you fell for it. You should have pressed him on the Ponce case, gotten him to talk about how he knew the old man suffered so much, give you some details only the perp could have known. Like, what did the note say, or what did he do with the old man's skin. I mean, this is all pretty useless."

I shook my head. "You're both wrong," I said. "Any jury that listens to that tape will know just what kind of man Díaz is, the state of mind he was in when he committed the murders as charged. True, he doesn't quite come out and say, I butchered them myself but he comes close. This is how I would handle it.

" 'Here we are, ladies and gentlemen. The accused, knowing that the people have the evidence of his terrible crimes, tries to come up with a deal, any kind of deal that will save his skin. But think about it, why would someone agree to plead guilty to manslaughter unless he knew he had committed the murder? What kind of monster would call in his own prosecutor, laugh at him and then offer to plead guilty?

" 'It's all of a piece, ladies and gentlemen. This meek-looking man who now sits before you in his wheelchair is really a devil in disguise, who literally feeds on the life of his victims. He tears out their hearts, drinks their blood and devours their liver. This man is a beast, as dark and foul as the devil himself and he should be sent to join his brothers in the flames of hell itself!' "

I realized at some point I had stood up, and was now gesturing before Phil and Lisa, as though they were the imaginary jury in my mind's eye. I stopped, dropped my arms. Phil clapped, slowly, for sarcastic effect.

"Nice rhetoric but you're forgetting that in California discussions regarding plea bargaining are inadmissible in court. That's, let's see, Evidence Code sections 1153 to 1153.5 and Penal Code section 1192.4. Jake would object if you even allude to the plea bargaining in argument and the judge would sustain the objection. Hell, he might even grant a mistrial and we'd be back to square one."

"Not to mention that calling him a beast would probably also raise another objection, as inflammatory and prejudicial," chimed in Lisa.

Phil continued with their tandem team of criticism, as though they had heard the tape before and already knew its weaknesses.

"You want this guy to fry, Charlie, and it shows. The jury would pick up on it. But this is not the South. Jurors here are not used to the fire and brimstone you guys like in the Bible Belt. Californians want to do in the bad guys just as much as anybody else but they'd rather do it in private, with a nice overdose of their favorite chemical. They're not into burning at the stake."

"What is that supposed to mean?" I snapped. "I've been practicing law in this state for years, I know a thing or two about juries myself."

"I'm telling you it won't work. He's got us by the short hairs. We're going to cut him a deal."

"You can't do that!"

"Watch me. This case has been compromised from the beginning. With the kind of evidence we got I doubt we'd find a jury willing to convict on a 187a. And we don't want to risk throwing it away. Antonetti is not into losing the big ones. If we can get a voluntary manslaughter, he'll be in for twenty, do sixteen and who the fuck is going to remember any of this by the year 2013? If AIDS doesn't kill him before. And if it doesn't, then we'll be able to deport him to Mexico to face charges there, so fuck it."

"It's not right," was all I could say. Phil shrugged. He stood up, put down the cup of Kenyan decaf Lisa had brewed that morning.

"What is right? What is wrong? We have to deal with what's legal and what's possible. Work with what we've got. Destiny handed us lemons so we, my friend, are making *agua de limón.* Tough tamales."

He tried to walk out of the office but I grabbed him, spun him around.

"This was all a setup, wasn't it? You wanted an easy way out and you got me to play doormat."

Phil shoved me back, allowing a sneer of satisfaction to cross his fleshy lips. He jerked his hand up and lifted a shock of black hair, revealing the pale washed-out scar of plastic surgery behind his ear.

"Don't start playing Torquemada. We wanted this case as bad as anybody, that's why we hired you. If anything, you're the one that's under suspicion for not having revealed your whole relationship until this late in the game. We are choosing not to believe you were in with him, so let's call it quits and go home, okay? You want perfect justice, wait till you're dead."

He walked past me out the door to the green-tiled corridor. I stared at Lisa wordlessly for a moment. Then Phil stuck his head back inside the office.

"By the way, you're fired. The check is in the mail."

"You can take your blood money and stuff it!"

He smiled, relishing every small degree of indignation he could squeeze out of me.

"Okay, just sign it over when you get it. I know what to do with my money, right, honey?"

He winked at Lisa, then walked out. I looked back at Lisa, her expression as beguiling as a serpent's tooth.

I picked up my briefcase and headed out to breathe the polluted air of Temple Street. It smelled a thousand times sweeter than the flatus of corruption in that room.

CHAPTER

24

THERE is something I should mention before this whole story ends: when all was said and done, I felt sorry for my brother. What if my dad had acknowledged him? What if mamá had supported him? What if he had not turned to the darkness for solace?

Of course, I have no answers to any of those questions, for murder and speculation are as troubled a match as honesty and politics. I believe nothing is predestined, that everything in human affairs is subject to our will and our intervention. However, it is healthy to remember that ignorance, though not a legal excuse, is often the only palliative for our own tragic failures of understanding.

In other words, I felt sorry not so much for the Ricardo I knew but for that other, possible Ricardo he could have been, had not man and circumstance taken a hand in a boy's destiny. Would I have spared his life, commuted his sentence or asked for anything less than the maximum allowed by law for his crimes if I could?

No. I would have sent him to death row all the same. But I would have done it with the heavy heart of wasted possibilities. Hypocritical? I don't think so. Just human.

In the event, all my caterwauling was an exercise in futility. Ricardo quickly grabbed at the deal that Phil made him, knowing the offer would only go up after the first appearance in Superior Court.

I sat in the courtroom watching Díaz, still wheelchair-bound, give up all his constitutional rights and plead no contest to the manslaughter charge. Judge Powell's warning that a nolo contendere was the equivalent of a guilty plea fell on coarsened ears. Díaz jeered, winked and nodded all through the proceeding, prompting the judge to call for a sidebar to ascertain for herself that the defendant was competent enough to enter his plea.

Less than a week after the plea, even before he was transported to Chino to serve out his sentence, the *Los Angeles Times* ran the story about his family relationships: a half-sister who initiated him into the Colombian drug-dealing world, a half-brother working for the prosecution to extract his last ounce of revenge against him for blighting the family name.

The *Times* reporter called me for an interview the day before the piece came out; I refused, however, to comment on any of Díaz's allegations. I immediately tried to warn Phil but was unable to reach him. When the ten-thousand-word smear was published, I saw why Phil was incommunicado—he and Lisa had made me out to be the true culprit, the instigator who had weaseled his way into the innocent bosom of the prosecution and screwed up a case that otherwise would have been a slam dunk.

In record time Jake filed a writ and in equally record time the Court of Appeal heard it, threw out the no contest plea and ordered the case be handled by the state attorney general due to the district attorney's conflict of interest. I knew then for certain that it had all been an elaborate charade, a farce worthy of Feydeau, meant to deliver us step by careful step to this foregone conclusion, our exhausted justice system unable to press charges because all the players had been morally compromised.

I was more than off the case, twice I was removed from the courtroom where the preliminary hearing was being held on the objection of the defense, who alleged I was intimidating poor Ricardo with my somber stare. Ultimately, after an in camera hearing, Judge Stromwall let me stay and watch the proceedings, as long as I did not make any gestures or faces. So I sat in the back row, along with the assorted media who had given up trying to interview me when they realized I would not say one word until the case was concluded.

It was a painful experience. A tow-haired, fair-weather attorney from the AG's office, who could not have been more than two years out of law school, handled the prosecution. Or rather, mishandled it. Four days it took him, four days of incomplete sentences, rambling arguments, leaden cross examination, all conducted with the stern self-assurance of the truly blind, of the man polishing the handrails while the ship founders on the heartless reef.

Díaz was the picture of meekness throughout, bent over, feeble and withdrawn, wrapping himself in the cloak of disability in his attempt to deceive even the magistrate herself.

I must admit, Bloomberg was brilliant. He sat back, letting the AG entwine himself further and further in his own ineptness, raising just the minimum number of objections needed to destroy the foundation of the prosecution's case.

The half palm print found in Armando's house? Both a statistical fluke—it could not be stated with any degree of certainty that it was Díaz's—and a random act of chance—if it was Díaz's after all, there were many other prints in the house as well and a half print does not a killer make.

The fibers found in his car matching those of the guard? Millions of GM car carpets were made with the same kind of fibers. Who was to say which car it came from?

The hairs? Obviously Caucasian. Here Jake turned the whole identification argument on its head, counting on the not so well disguised racism of Southern Californians. He pointed at Díaz and claimed that he was a Latino and therefore he could not possibly be the source, even though Díaz's skin was whiter than anyone else's in the courtroom, the judge included.

As regards the writing on my house walls, Jake was quick to note that the exemplars given by his client were not a perfect match with what was found. The graphologist could only say that there was a fifty-fifty chance Díaz was the author.

Every day Bloomberg hammered away at the prosecution in the media, giving interviews before his court appearance, the boarded-up Hall of Justice building looming behind him in the camera shot like a symbol of the treatment Díaz and other ethnic minorities could expect to get in Los Angeles. He was available for quickie interviews in the hall, during coffee breaks, even while peeing in the men's room.

I, of course, was made out to be the ogre who manipulated the disaster, the Mark Fuhrman whose bloody fingerprints were all over the case in a warped attempt to doom my half-brother to his death.

Three days into the hearing the AG finally opened his eyes and ears and tried to get a gag order but Stromwall, her red cheeks flushed with even more booze than normal, denied the motion as an infringement on the First Amendment. She claimed that as the sole examiner of fact she would not be swayed by mere public sentiment. Anyhow, the whole thing was almost over and it was time for the AG to either put up or shut up.

No one called me, no one asked me to testify about any of the things I had seen or experienced. I was damaged goods. Anything I said, no matter how truthful, simply would not be believed.

In his closing arguments Bloomberg reminded Judge Stromwall that mere suspicion is not enough to bind a case over to the Superior Court. Although the burden of proof is much lower than at a trial, since a mere reasonable suspicion that the defendant may have committed the crime is ordinarily enough to kick the case upstairs, a decent concern for our constitutional rights compels a dismissal when the entire case of action is predicated on mere conjecture, which is what a fifty-fifty chance was.

So it was no surprise that at the conclusion of the hearing, on a Friday at five-thirty, when the rest of the CCB was long emptied out, its terrazzo hallways as desolate as a killer's heart, Judge Stromwall dismissed the entire case with prejudice, meaning the prosecution would never again be allowed to present the same evidence against Díaz in California.

She allowed herself the luxury of a few comments at the end: "Counsel, this has been a strange and confusing presentation," she said, brushing the bangs of her white hair behind her ears. "I hope that in the future the state attorney general's office will take greater care in the prosecution of its cases. I realize we are very close to elections but certain things are untenable in a court of law.

"This case has smelled of a witch hunt. Literally. The defendant seems to stand before the court solely because of his religion. I must remind you that his is a religion, not a cult, and that religious rites vary from culture to culture. Just as to a Muslim or an observant Jew the eating of pork is repugnant and the Christian consecration of bread and wine incomprehensible, so to us modern Westerners it is repulsive, offensive even, that a religion may countenance the slaughter of animals. But I remind you that is exactly what the Hebrews did in the Old Testament. As the Psalms say, 'Offer the sacrifices of righteousness and put your trust in the Lord.'

"You have taken a great leap in logic, saying that because *santería* believes in animal sacrifice that it also encourages human sacrifice. That is not a step that this court is prepared to take. And, failing any convincing evidence to the contrary, I see no reason why this man cannot be discharged in this instance. I do not take kindly to travesties of justice. As I said before, case dismissed. With prejudice."

Díaz turned to me on hearing the ruling and smiled, wagging his index finger at me, as though reminding a naughty boy of the warning he'd given him. The media surrounded me but I refused to comment. Evil had triumphed under the guise of good. Righteousness would have to wait its day.

That night on the news I saw Ricardo miraculously walking out of County Jail, one hand on Bloomberg's shoulder, the other on a cane. Dozens of followers had come out of hiding, dressed in white, with the black and yellow beads of Oyá, chanting welcome to their leader, who now raised his proud head.

"Praise be to Ollodumare," he said in Spanish.

"Praise to the Lord of all Creation," he said in English.

Those were his last words as a free man. Two burly U.S. marshals stepped up to Díaz and snapped handcuffs on him, telling him he was being extradited to Mexico.

Bloomberg raised his voice, the followers caused a ruckus, the camera jerked around as it quickly followed Díaz down to the unmarked federal van that would take him to Terminal Island for detention.

Over the next few days Bloomberg attempted to spring him, although how hard he really tried was open to question. Now that he was out of state custody, Díaz had become a political football, tossed from place to place because nobody wanted to be responsible for him. A week later, he was ordered extradited to Mexico to face multiple murder charges there.

Díaz was removed in the middle of the night to avoid attention but somewhere between San Diego and Imperial Beach, his van was rear-ended by a semi headed to a *maquiladora* across the border. The van flipped, its back doors burst open and Díaz, who perhaps had planned the entire caper with the aid of the shadowy political figures he once served, took off for the chaparral and escaped once more.

One reporter who had hounded me from the beginning of the case later told me that Díaz had thrown it all away with his escape. A Hollywood producer had optioned his life story after his discharge from the murders, while a book publisher stood ready to give him a six-figure advance for his autobiography. Now it was all gone, all his profits evaporated after his flight.

"He wouldn't have known how to spend it, Amy," I said. "That's not what he's after."

"What is he after?" she asked with all the dewiness of her twenty-two years.

"The life everlasting. I hope somebody gives it to him."

CHAPTER

ENDINGS often come your way when you least expect them.
So my closure in the Díaz case came about a month
later on a Saturday afternoon, while I wondered whether to
paint my umber dining room walls white or to tear them down
and open up the hall to make the house seem larger to pro-
spective buyers. A realtor friend had already offered to put
the house on the MLS and the Internet *and* give me a break
on the six percent commission. All I had to do was give her
the word and it would be on the market within the hour. She
didn't anticipate too much trouble selling, not with the market
full of yuppie couples with kids moving from the crowded West
Side to the woody glens of Pasadena. I might even come out
ahead a few thousand dollars, in spite of the price drop of the
last few years. The only question then would be, what would

I do with the rest of my life? That, of course, she couldn't answer.

I'd stopped handling cases. Tina had mercifully found another job sooner than anyone expected so I closed my downtown office. I'd also turned down Farris's offer to sell my book to the movies. If I was going to sell out it would be to Lucifer himself and not some minor djinn in Culver City. I wrote an outline for my next novel and I waited, pondering how to end it, until the answer came with the hurried ringing of my mail carrier.

"Mr. Morell?" said the small, wiry Filipina, a tangle of charcoal hair tumbling over her bushy eyebrows.

"Yes?"

She took an envelope out of her satchel, handed it over.

"Postal service had a little problem. Mail truck gang steal the truck, your letter get lost in shuffle. Cops now find, your letter too. Here you go. Better late never!"

She giggled, then walked across my front yard to the house next door, bounding over the bed of red vinca.

The letter was postmarked from Miami, months before, at the time of Ricardo's arrest. The sender was Graciela de Palma. My hand shook as I tore open the envelope.

"Dear Charlie,

"By the time you read this I will most likely be somewhere up the river Niger, trying my best to find the secret relationship between the sacred and the profane in the daily life of the Yoruba, the other half of the spiritual mix of all Cubans. I should add that I'm assuming there is such a relationship. If not, well, at least I will have suckered the Ford Foundation into underwriting my belated rite of passage.

"I am not writing to bore you with my professional aspirations. Far from it. This is sort of a coward's goodbye. This way I can say farewell without having to make in person the painful admission I owe you. Then again, that's what the written word is for, isn't it? Invention and dissimulation.

"I hope you will forgive me for what I did: I surreptitiously took out two pages from the letter your mother left you. Why am I telling you this now? Because now that you have brought Ricardo Díaz to justice I feel I can reveal this secret, which your mother's handwriting bears out. I did not . . ."

I stopped reading de Palma's apology, anxiously took out the two handwritten notes from my mother.

"You have a brother whom you never met," she wrote in Spanish. "His name is Ricardo Díaz. He is the offspring of your father's weakness with the widow of a friend. Please try to forgive me for never having mentioned this to you but I carry such a heavy burden that I did not know if you would find it in your heart to forgive me had I told you this while I was still alive. Now that I am in the other world, your disappointment will be easier to bear.

"Know this then: I was the one responsible for your father's condition. Fearing I was losing his affection, I gave him a magic potion to keep him by my side. Instead the potion turned him into the poor soul you saw for the last years of his life."

I stopped reading, stunned by her disclosure. This was the part that Celia didn't know, this was the reason that explained mamá's slavish devotion to that living carcass, her refusal to put him in a facility, her resigned acceptance that the man she had married was a gray-haired infant.

She was doing penance and we were all doing it with her.

I read on.

"To my unending shame, I neglected his son, who grew up I don't know how or when. Carlos, you should know that this Ricardo has come to extract his revenge for my abandonment. I do not fear what he will do to me but I fear for you and your family, that is why I write this.

"Ricardo is a *santero,* an evil one. He came to see me several months ago. He cursed me and told me I would pay for the suffering I put him and his mother through. He foretold the disease that consumes me and he said he would steal my soul from my grave and that I, your father and you would be his slaves for all eternity.

"I do not know if there is such a thing as witchcraft. Certainly the Church teaches us that evil will not triumph, that Our Lord Jesus Christ will come again in glory to judge the living and the dead and His kingdom will have no end. Yet there is also a Devil, a Tempter—and Our Lord did drive those demons from the possessed and cast them into swine.

"In my hour of need, then, I turned to a good friend, Graciela de Palma, who I met at the Chapel of Our Lady of El Cobre and who knows greatly about these things. I hope that she will teach me what I need to do to combat this evil I have unwittingly brought into this world.

"In the meantime, my son, be good, protect yourself and your loved ones from the evil incarnate that is Ricardo and please, please try to rescue your poor sister Celia from her wasted life."

I searched through my drawers, found the letter I already had and put the pages together. A scent of violets came into the room and I felt my mother's touch in the sultry breeze.

After I wiped my tears I returned to de Palma's letter. She explained she had swiped the pages so I would not scoff at the whole notion and think that my mother had lost her mind. That was why she had asked me to find Ricardo, exposing me to the evil, true, but confident that my powers would defeat him in the end.

As far as the bullet I had found in the envelope, she had put it there. It was a memento of a stay in Croatia, a charm to spur me into fighting Díaz.

"Please forgive me but try to understand. I can only tell you this now that Ricardo is crippled and in jail, his powers taken from him. There is nothing left to fear.

"Your friend and sister in the saints,

"Graciela de Palma."

I put down the letter and laughed until the tears came out again and the certainty of imminent madness invaded my mind again.

I made a long and deliberate work of my cache of vodka bottles and afterward crawled on my knees through the house, digging in drawers and cupboards, consuming every drop of alcohol in my possession, down to a bottle of ten-year-old soured sherry I'd packed with my papers from Los Feliz down in the basement.

I fell asleep sometime in the early morning, the spectral chords of Rachmaninoff's Second Piano Concerto on the radio echoing in my mind and it all became perfectly clear.

I was back in the church again, entering for my final confrontation with Díaz, only this time the door opened to a vast white alabaster hall and a long curved staircase that seeemed to reach to the open sky. Shana climbed down the staircase, again dressed in dripping white robes, a clump of seaweed as her crown. She smiled and spread out her fingers, showing her long, blood red fingernails.

I woke up covered in sweat on the damask sofa in my den, shivering but warmed by the thought burning brightly in my brain, like the stamp on the forehead of the damned.

I picked up the phone, dialed Tijuana.

"*Bueno?*" snapped the voice at the other end of the line.

"*Teniente, es Morell.*"

"I was wondering when the hell you were going to call," said Ortega in his best border growl.

CHAPTER

26

WE parked under the freeway overpass. I had sold the Saab and now drove a used Kia, a fate almost worse than death in Los Angeles but perfect for someone discarding everything superfluous. Ortega looked in his canvas bag one last time, touching the burglar's tools for quick reassurance before our mission started.

Two days had passed since we'd spoken that early morning. In the meantime I had driven down to Mexico and smuggled him back into the States in my car trunk, like a peon out to do field work in *el norte.* Which of course, in a way, he was.

"What happened to you that you can't come legally into the country?" I asked him once I'd eased him out of the trunk in a park off Del Mar Heights.

Ortega stretched out, yawned, lit a cigarette, then just like a scruffy mutt went and peed against a tree.

"I killed a man in Fresno about twenty years ago. I was a kid, picking grapes, my first time here," he said, his cigarette bobbing in his mouth as he talked while relieving himelf. "He was a *gabacho*, the son of one of the growers, wanted to rape my girl and I stopped him in time. Had to get out of Dodge in a hurry. Murder raps are good for a lifetime. Now with the car I borrowed to follow you, I got enough to last me two lifetimes."

He zipped, strutted back to the car, all 138 pounds, five foot five of him, counting the three-inch stacked Cuban heels of his cowboy boots.

"That's okay, I don't really like this country anyhow. It's pretty but it's no place for a Mexican. It's like that *corrido* says, everybody here thinks God is white when he's more brown than I am. What's funny is that the gringos always think the *mejicanos* are itching to invade the Southwest but you know what? I don't think we'd take it back even if you paid us. Too much time has gone by. Besides, what would we do with all you Anglos?"

We got back in the car, drove up the I-5 and made it past the Border Patrol checkpoint at San Onofre without a hitch, Ortega calmly looking around the slowed-down traffic, waving at the immigration Brown Shirts. At San Clemente I finally turned to him.

"I really appreciate what you're doing."

"*Bueno*, the way I see it, your police is even more crooked than ours. We may not be able to arrest the criminal but we always know who he is. Your cops don't even want to find out who did the crime. Professional pride, *entiendes?*"

"Is that why you saved my neck?"

"I am a man of my word. I said I'd get that *pinche* sumbitch. Anyhow, I think it was your ass I saved, not so much your neck, *amigo.*"

I brought him home, ordered some Pollo Loco but he insisted

on Spago Pizza, which fortunately I was able to find at Bristol Farms. After the last slice of duck sausage and the last swig of Hess Cabernet, we went over our plan. We then took a nap and woke up at three in the morning, soldiers in the fight against the darkness.

He took out his Glock, checked it, loaded it, put two spare clips in his back pocket and went out to the car to wait while I washed my face and brushed my teeth.

Now, in the harbor of the shadowy overpass, I asked him, my hand on the door lever: "Ready?"

"*Orale,*" he rejoined, dropping onto the foggy sidewalk.

The church still was festooned with bright yellow police tape but otherwise gave no sign of life. The small stucco and wood bungalows of the neighborhood were all dark—four o'clock Sunday morning, too late for the gangbangers, too early for the weekend workers.

Ortega stood on the opposite sidewalk, examining the building with the concentration of the artist eyeing his canvas, then stole across the street, his cowboy boots barely grazing the pavement. He raced up the steps, extracted a slim jim from his bag and in the time it took me to cross the street he had opened the door and slipped inside. I followed.

I stood in the darkness of the empty hall for a moment that seemed to last years, the fears of the past attacking me, icy-cold hands of fate entwining around me, fixing me to my spot.

"Hey!"

A hand on my shoulder. Intinctively I turned, swung a right. Ortega, with the practiced ease of the prizefighter, ducked and rolled under the blow.

"*Cálmate!*" settle down, he said, turning on his flashlight, which flooded the cavernous room.

We spent the next half hour inspecting the building, from the basement to the belfry to the terrace where I had almost become a sacrifice to my brother's thirst for revenge. Rats scurried down the stairs, assorted bugs and creepers darting away from the invading light we shined on abandoned offices and broken-down bathrooms smeared with shit and gang graffiti. On the wall of the kitchen someone had drawn a frieze of three dancing swastikas and below them a giant cross with the caption, *Dios murió aquí,* God died here. But we did not find a trace of anything remotely connected to Shana.

We returned to the main hall, both of us staring dumbfoundedly at the transept, with its raised stone altar, illuminated by our flashlights.

"Are you sure you didn't dream this whole thing?" he asked.

"I am not *that* crazy, my friend."

All at once we heard a rushing sound, the sloshing of water somewhere near. Ortega looked around him, surprised.

"It must be the river," I said.

"Excuse me?"

I went to the window, looked out at the sewer drains emptying a cascade of greenish water into the basin. I pointed out the gushers to Ortega.

"That's the Los Angeles River. Or what remains of it. It was the reason why L.A. was founded here instead of out by the coast. The *fundadores* wanted a source of drinking water. Nowadays all this polluted water flows out to the river and nobody's been able to trace it. Some people think it's from some kind of factory north of here. EPA would love to find it."

But Ortega could not have been less interested at the sight of the mysterious pollution of the *zanjas* that once watered the *pueblo* of Nuestra Señora de los Angeles de Porciuncula. He was much more interested in the altar, which stood forlorn in the middle of the transept. He put his ear to the altar, knocked on it.

"Just as I thought."

"What are you looking at?"

"This wasn't always a, what you call it, a cryptic church, was it?" he asked, bringing his flashlight closer to the altar.

"Coptic, you mean. I don't know, why does it matter?"

"It matters, my friend, because history matters. We are what we are because of what was before us. We must understand the past if we hope to understand the present."

"Cut the riddles. What do you mean?"

He gestured at the building. "I thought there was something funny about the building when I first saw it. Now I realize what it is. It looks like another kind of temple, the kind the Protestants built when they first came to Mexico. Church steeple and everything. There's one like this near Querétaro, where my mother's family is from."

"I don't get it," I said. "Let's say you're right. Let's say this was built by another congregation and the Copts took it over. So what?"

"Well, Charlie, you're an educated man. You take a look at this writing and you tell me what language this is."

He pointed at the Gothic lettering stretching like a ribbon on the edge of the altar.

"I used to be an altar boy," he continued, "and I can tell you that is not Latin. And that's not a Coptic cross either."

I crouched by the altar. The lettering, fluid and formal, was either German or Swedish. I recognized the word *vasser*, water, and a frieze of a light and a dove above a river.

"I will bet you this says, in whatever language that is, 'Except a man be born of water of the Spirit, he cannot enter into the Kingdom of God.' "

"A baptismal font!" I said, stunned by the simplicity of it all. "A full-bodied font, like the Baptists use."

"That's right. Give me a hand with this slab."

We got ahold of the thick marble and slowly lifted it. After a few inches we could see an opening beneath the stone. Encouraged by our find, we heaved the slab aside, laid it on the floor. We shone the flashlight inside the font but it was hardly necessary.

Even in the foggy half light from the street lamp outside the window we could see water rising almost to the top of the font. Floating in the water, her skin bleached of all color, her slit throat like a second mouth, lay Shana, her body swollen yet perfectly preserved.

She wore the same white robes of my dreams and her head was wrapped in some plant that somehow had found its way to the font. She lay flat in the font, her arms stiff and her hands raised, as though she had tried and failed to lift the gigantic slab that enclosed her in a watery death.

"This must connect directly to the river," I said, unable to take my eyes off Shana. "The river used to rise much higher years ago before it was paved upstream so the churchgoers could be baptized in the river's water, just like Jesus in the Jordan. My God, look at her hands!"

Ortega took out a penknife, scraped under her short nails, then crouched under my flashlight. He looked up at me, enormous satisfaction creeping into his swarthy face.

"It's human flesh. And a hair torn out with its root. We got the *pinche cabrón* this time."

He stood up, nodded to himself. "I think I can go back to Mexico now."

A comparison of the DNA in the skin scrapings and hair found under Shana's fingernails to a sample of blood that had been drawn from Díaz while he was at County Jail proved a genetic match. The coroner said we were lucky the water in the limestone and the cooler weather we'd been having the last few weeks had lowered the temperature in the font enough to halt the degradation of the genetic material in her hands. Shana's actions, leaving her hands above the water in her last attempt to get out, had preserved the sample, telling us who was responsible as clearly as if she had sat up in that font and proclaimed in a loud voice, Ricardo Díaz killed me.

So once again Ricardo was charged with murder, but this time not even Saint Peter himself could get him off.

This time I told my entire story to the media. I was walking out of the *L.A. Times* building on First after my interview when I ran into Bloomberg, hustling up the hill to the Criminal Courts Building. He saw me, crossed back across the street to talk.

"I heard about the poor woman," he said. "I'm terribly sorry. Believe it or not, I really thought Díaz was not guilty."

"Jake, don't you always think your clients are not guilty?"

He gave me a guilty smile, fingered his gold and red rep tie.

"Let's say that I always try to suspend my disbelief for the duration of my services. Like Stendhal says, there is no better mask than sincerity. But seriously, I mean what I said about Díaz. I just hope I don't run into him in Miami."

"Why do you say that?"

He coughed, stole a glance at his Cartier tank watch.

"Well, I don't want to be known as telling tales out of school but . . ." He looked around him again, making sure none of the office workers out for their lunch break or the homeless beggars shuffling by were really undercover officers or, worse yet, disbarred attorneys out to turn in one of their own. He whispered in my ear, his words barely audible above the backfiring of an RTD bus.

"He said he was going to get in touch with your father before he left the country."

I was chilled by his words, in spite of the blustery Santa Ana and the blazing sunshine that November day.

"My father, you said?"

"No, his father. Of course, I meant your father as well. I forget."

I shook my head. "It doesn't matter, Jake. Same difference. He's still dead."

"So then, how do you figure?"

"How do you think?"

CHAPTER

27

A cold moon rose over Miami, a giant white disc propped against a funereal black marble sky. I leaned on my father's tombstone and again tried to finish counting all the winking stars above. I was up to three hundred forty-five, somewhere around Perseus, the hunter, when I gave up and stared morosely at the fog creeping out of the swamp at the far side of the cemetery.

It was the anniversary of my father's death—or perhaps I should say, of his mercy killing at my hands. This was the secret the two of us would carry for all time, the weakling son, who always ran in time of trouble, finally finding the courage to grant his father the final mercy of a decent death. I had no idea where my father's soul was but of one thing I was certain—he not only forgave me, he thanked me for what I did for him.

But I was not there that night to render homage to the man who had brought me into this world forty years ago in Cuba. I was there to capture the bizarre half-brother I'd never known, who, I was convinced, would come dig up my father's remains in a crazed attempt to capture his soul.

By the entrance to the cemetery, in a van parked with its lights off but with a night scope focused on my sorry person, two Miami Dade police waited for their trap to be sprung.

When I approached Dade PD and the FBI with my idea they had been reluctant to go along, finding it hard to believe anyone would risk his life and liberty for a handful of dirt and broken bones. It wasn't until an expert on cults intervened on my behalf with the police chief at his shack in Islamorada Key that I was finally assigned the couple of agents keeping me company. The FBI had turned me down, claiming they did not have enough manpower to track down every nutcase on every half-assed lead.

I dozed off into a dreamless sleep and woke up again shortly before midnight to what I thought was the rattle of two rolls of thunder. A few, scattered drops of rain left their viscous sheen on my clothes. Then, out of the swamp, my brother slogged through, prodding someone before him.

I spoke into my wireless microphone.

"Don't shoot, he's got a hostage!" No response.

"Do you copy? Don't shoot!" I hollered, desperately.

Even as the words came out of my mouth, drops gathered in black curtains and gushed down from skies that moments before had been clear and for a moment I asked myself how can a heart harbor so much hate for so long when I saw that the prisoner was my son, Julian.

Later I would find out that Díaz had silently slit the throat of the PI I'd posted to keep guard over Julian. Later I would find out that Livvie had run out of the house screaming, after cutting with her shaving razor the duct tape binding her hands and feet, her nightgown torn, her rectum bleeding. But all I knew at that moment was that evil had returned to carry out its eternal travesty and that Julian was the intended sacrifice.

"Let him go, Ricardo! *Suéltalo!*"

My cry was drowned out by the thunder of a lightning bolt that surged out of the sky which erupted in a storm lifted from some print by Hieronymus Bosch, howling wind and rain in vertical sheets as though the end of the world were near, which it was for one of us but for which one it was still too early to tell.

A bolt of lightning struck by the van bearing the agents, who had parked under a towering ceiba tree. The flash lit, with chilling clarity, the carnage Díaz had strewn in the open van, the bodies of the surprised officers sprawled in the bloody rictus of death by gunshot at close quarters.

I stood in the rainstorm, waving my hands so Ricardo could see I was not armed.

"I'm here, Ricardo! My life for his! Let Julian go!"

Ricardo sees me, his sawed-off shotgun still to Julian's head, the two of them marching down the soggy yard while the kettle drum of thunder echoes across Miami and a host of tridents light up the sky.

"Kill me! I'll be your sacrifice! I'll be your slave!" I shout.

Ricardo grimaces for a smile. He's nothing but skin and bones, the AIDS that infected his body coursing through him like the curse he wanted to hurl at us.

I am his ticket to life everlasting.

"I'm here! Come and get me, Ricardo! I'm the one you really want!"

As he nears, just like the other two brothers who fought in that other garden aeons ago, I scream again, through the cracking of

thunder: "Un cambio de cabeza, *a change of fate! My soul for
yours! I will be your puppet and you will be me! Take me, leave
him go!*"

*Ricardo's eyes shine bright with temptation, he's only about
twenty feet away. He stops and hesitates. Julian, trained in the
art of self-defense, sees his chance and throws an elbow that jams
Ricardo's weapon arm sky high. The gun goes off. Julian races,
zigzagging across the lawn, to the safety of a grove of palm trees
nearby. Ricardo lowers his gun, about to fire again. I run to him,
grab his gun, struggling to save the only life that really matters
to me now.*

*He turns, a raven in the night, knocks me to the ground
with a blow from his rifle butt. I fall, then he grabs me by
my hair, orders me to kneel. I see my son safely away, running past the palm trees, clambering over the fence and on to
life.*

*God bless you I think and I try to pray but my thoughts are
just one: Let him live!*

"Get ready to die, Charlie! Beg for forgiveness! Beg! Beg!"

I say nothing, I can say nothing. I am resigned to my death.

*The blows come again, the edge of the gun barrel tearing
bloody gashes on my cheeks, my forehead, my mouth.*

*I know his game. He wants me frightened, begging, so the
dark forces will keep me in thrall to him forever. But I will never
plead. I will never give in. I will die with my dignity.*

*"Beg!" he screams again. He kicks me down, I fall face for-
ward. He stomps my head into the lawn, I smell the dirt that will
soon cover me in sleep everlasting.*

*He jams his gun into the back of my neck, the rain still pelting
us with the force of an unexpected hurricane. Then, out of nowhere, a light surges into the field, like dawn rising from the
swamp.*

I feel the pressure of his gun ease. I turn around, glance up at

his panic-stricken face, pale with the knowledge of impending
doom.

From all the graves in the cemetery rise bubbles of light, balls
of lightning, a mass of luminous energy floating over the ground,
lighting up the field not like the will-o'-the-wisps that they are
but like the souls of the dead of night, rising up to claim the
one who had sent them forward, demanding their justice, their
revenge.

The spheres of energy all coalesce, blend into one mass, one
giant wave that with an eerie high-pitched sound, like the breath
of rage escaping through a tear in the invisible tissue separating
this life from the next, like luminous protoplasm joining up in
one body, hurls itself at Ricardo, who screams in terror, firing his
gun at the metamorphosed souls of all those he killed coming to
the aid of this sinner.

"Away! Away! Váyanse! Solavaya!" he hollers. "He's mine!
Mine!"

In his terror and confusion, I manage to break his grip and
roll away. I get up on one knee. Realizing I'm about to flee, he
pulls the trigger and shoots.

The blast scorches my shoulder, rams me back to the ground.
I'm wounded but the shot has merely grazed me and he finally
takes his eyes off me and then he goes wild with fear when the
swirling blanket of energy falls on him, covering him like Medu-
sae on the hapless prey, the orbs of static electricity piercing him
through his heart.

"Go away! he screams again. "GO AWAY!"

I reach for my ankle holster, slip out my Beretta and fire the
silver bullet de Palma has left me. The bullet hits him in the
chest at fifteen feet distance, the tip opening up like a falcon's
talon.

He touches his wound, then stares open-mouthed at me,
stunned that even now I can still triumph, that his victory is

denied in spite of his power and his loathsome plans, then he falls face down, dead, on the puddle that is my father's grave.

All at once the rain stops and the will-o'-the-wisps vanish and everything is quiet and fresh, like a new night, like a new life.

In the mist that now engulfs the yard a shaft of eerie moonlight falls and I see my father and my mother arm in arm smiling and a voice clearly says, "Agape" and I know then for certain that God is eternal love for all and I black out.

I came to in an ambulance, the driver racing at top speed down the rain-slick streets of South West Miami. Julian hovered next to me in the crowded van. All I could manage was a wan smile, a nod of thanks that he too had made it through the awful devil's night. He smiled back, stroked my forehead with a love he'd never dared show before.

"Dad," he whispered, "is the invite to L.A. still open?"

"Have to check my calendar," I mumbled through thick lips, "but you can bank on it."

Julian hugged me and I knew then that I was forgiven and I knew then that I would be better than my father, that I would be better than I ever was and that for once and forever I had finally connected.

ABOUT THE AUTHOR

Alex Abella is the author of *The Killing of the Saints,* a *New York Times* Notable Book, and *The Great American,* a novel of the Cuban Revolution. He lives, writes, and dreams in Los Angeles, with his wife and children.